DISTANT EARLY

WARNING

ELIZABETH HIRST

Renaissance.
Diverse Canadian Voices

Cover art and interior design by Nathan Fréchette.
Interior art by Robin McLean.
Edited by Meaghan Côté, Vicki Martin and Evan McKinley.

Legal deposit, Library and Archives Canada, October 2020.

Paperback ISBN 978-1-987963-93-9
Ebook ISBN 978-1-987963-94-6

Renaissance Press
http://pressesrenaissancepress.ca
pressesrenaissancepress@gmail.com

For Poe,

Because dogs are the bearers of forgiveness, healing, loyalty, and simple joy, for the price of a pat on the head and a bowl of food and water.

And for My Parents,

Who never trained out of me the belief that animals can be siblings, too.

THE SQUATTERS FROM UP NORTH

Felicia Dennigan, "Denny" to her friends, pulled her book bag onto her lap so that a man in a well-worn plaid shirt could squeeze in beside her. She breathed in, tentatively, through her nose. This one smelled of fry grease. There were much worse smells on the bus—just this morning, for example, she'd come across a hybrid of cheese, toes and rotten potatoes. She normally left her bag on the seat next to her, to avoid sitting beside people who made a fuss, or smelled like pee, or made inappropriate conversation because their wife had just left them. But, with the bus nearing the station, it had become far too crowded for people to keep a polite distance from one another.

Denny had a book in her bag, several in fact, but she left them there. She had been reading and analyzing books all day. Mentally, it was time to mellow out in front of the TV, but she had to get home for that. Denny leaned against the bus' damp window frame and watched the bright signs of downtown St. Catharines drag by. She also wondered how the bus driver could see out of the side windows when they were covered with an inch of road grime. There was the student favourite shawarma place, with its bright red-and-yellow sign, and a couple of new nightclubs that Denny wondered if anybody really went to.

Downtown St. Catharines had a lot of nightclubs that flitted in and out of existence in the blink of an eye, tacky places in badly-wired old buildings along the St. Paul strip. A lot of them were flophouses now, but some of them still kept going, changing hands every few months. There was something transient about them, like the people themselves, the ones that came down from the North looking for jobs, shelter, anything they could lay their hands on with their homes and their livings gone.

The bus turned into the station, then came to a stop, accompanied by the squeal of the brakes and the acrid smell of burning rubber. Denny picked up her book bag and squeezed it to her chest, keeping one hand on the zipper pulls and the other on the pockets. She thanked the bus driver, stepped down the stairs, and entered the odoriferous crowd of beggars, peddlers, and thieves surrounding the bus.

Some people at school put padlocks on their bags, but Denny lived cheap, and she liked that the bag hugged to her chest and doubled as a sort of "bag-ering ram" to separate the crowd in front of her without her having to shove. She didn't really like to shove people out of her way, as she suspected some of the others in her class did. Class... A funny word, that...especially when only a lucky few could afford school.

Hands appeared in front of Denny's face—dirty hands, attached to tired-looking people in tired-looking clothes. There were Native people and Asians, but most of them were white, and all of them had faces full of creases, as if fear and hunger, those great feral tigers, had dragged unyielding claws down their faces.

"Money, please," cried a woman with rotting teeth. "A quarter, anything!"

Denny shook her head, and the beggar retracted her hands. She had stopped carrying cash a long time ago, less because of pickpockets and more because her empathy had been costing her upwards of twenty dollars a week.

A skinny teen, in ripped jeans and a t-shirt pulled from the charity bin at one of the downtown churches, bumped into her shoulder. It changed Denny's angle slightly, and as she turned, someone at the edge of the crowd caught her eye. She popped a wide grin, instantly, without realizing that she was showing her crooked front teeth. It couldn't be...but he was due for a visit. Long overdue, in fact, but Denny had had a feeling, from the moment she got up that morning, that she would hear from him. Her father's visits were irregular, rarer than his calls or postcards, but when she got that feeling in her gut, that deep-down excitement, the phone would always ring. If fortune smiled down on her that day, she would hear a knock on the door.

His last visit was just after Christmas. He had apologized for missing the big day, although most years he did, and brought her a tattered copy of Blake's *Songs of Innocence and Experience* he had dug up in a used book store in Waterloo. The feeling in Denny's gut had receded then and not come back until today. Today was June 30, 2050. Even for somebody like Dad, with no permanent address, six months was a long time—too long for Denny.

That man, standing on the edge of the crowd… Denny forgot her normal scruples and shoved people out of the way. Short, heavyset, with dark brown hair like hers and a brown bomber jacket, the man had to be him. Denny shifted her bag to one hand and put the other out like a quarterback, eager to get to him.

The man in the bomber jacket turned around. His face was jowly, covered with stubble. His ears stuck out and so did his nose. In fact, he didn't even have the right skin tone to be Dad…he was definitely Middle-Eastern. Dad was Irish.

Denny stopped cold, as the crowd dispersed around her, the beggars and thieves moving out to catch the number seventeen and the number two buses, which were pulling up to platform A. The man in the bomber jacket shot her a dirty look, and Denny realized with some embarrassment that she had been staring at him. She scurried into the glassed-in waiting area, swiping her pass over the scanner at the door to prove she was a paying customer.

Inside, the waiting area smelled like cooking pizza and tracked-in mud. With no admittance for vagabonds, the rows of metal mesh benches were almost empty, except for a few old ladies in plastic rain bonnets. A young man in a fast-food uniform slouched against the window. It had been almost six straight days of muggy heat in the mornings, breaking into torrential rain in the afternoon and continuing on all night until the cycle began again. Even with the air conditioning on in the waiting area, the Great Lakes humidity hung in the air, making breathing a bit like drinking an insubstantial soup.

Denny felt her heart thumping in her chest as she sat down on one of the many empty benches. Why did she always have to see his face in crowds? Why did so many characters on TV remind her of him? It happened often...too often for a grown woman. Grown women accepted the exigencies of life and moved on. She sighed and placed her head in her hands.

Her wavy, thick, auburn hair spilled into her field of vision, waving gently to and fro, taunting her. People had always known she was Sean Dennigan's girl because of that unruly crop of hair. Wild and curly until she straightened it. She could walk into a shop two hours behind Dad and, if she got the same cashier, she would get picked out as a relative. Denny had found it funny at the time, but when she looked back, she just longed to *belong* like that again, to have someone with whom she could be identified. For those brief times when Dad decided to stay in St. Catharines, for a night, or a week, or—during good times, without any episodes—two weeks, Denny could introduce him to her friends. She could take him out to restaurants and not ask for separate bills. He would talk to her and not try to discuss the intricacies of literature as spouted by Professor So-and-So, or how much he knew about everything (an irritating trait of university men, especially at parties). They could remember things together…things that meant something, like losing her first tooth, or the time that Mom got caught in the sprinklers at Cave Springs golf course.

The ding of a bell cut into Denny's thoughts. She raised her head out of her hands.

The rolling LED sign above the waiting area said: *Bus Number Eighteen is now arriving at Platform F.*

Denny picked up her things and headed for the door. Grown women did not wallow in misery in deserted bus stations. Grown women got themselves home, to a glass of lemonade and the evening news, and attempted to forget the things they could not change.

Denny left the bus at the corner of Welland and George Street and began the short walk home. The neighbourhood was filled with old Victorians and the new housing that had sprung up from their graves, brick structures mostly, with sagging porches and more character than insulation. Denny loved the old growth trees along the walkways and the unruly character of most of the lawns.

She reached the end of the walkway leading up to the house she shared with three other students, lucky number one-thirteen, a small brick house with yellowed siding and a screened-in porch.

Like most of the houses on the street, it boasted a big, gnarled maple with cracks in its bark as deep as fault lines. *The poor old thing has seen thousands of better days,* Denny thought as her shoes crackled over the gravel drive. Like all old trees these days, black patches of rot crawled over its trunk, a nasty side effect of all the extra rain that had swept over the peninsula lately.

Some kids in ill-fitting overalls, Northern squatters' kids from down the street, swarmed across the lawn, brandishing fallen sticks from last night's rainstorm. One of the boys brandished a big, gnarled stick they had picked up in someone's backyard. The long grey toque hanging down his back indicated that he was Gandalf today.

Another little boy, baring his teeth and growling, whacked the old maple on the lawn with an especially big stick. Several others followed suit.

"Oh no, the orcs are trying to cut down Treebeard!" said Gandalf.

"I'm Galadriel and you thall not path!" said a little blonde girl with a gap between her teeth, holding out her hand with a regal swish. The orc kids ignored her and kept on swinging their sticks.

Denny climbed up the sloping lawn to the tree and laid a hand on it. The kids stopped and stared at her. She had become somewhat of a neighbourhood guru after giving Jason Mandrake, the boy whose family squatted in her backyard, an old copy of The Hobbit, which was subsequently passed around to every child on the street.

"Hey, you orcs should be more careful. You know what happened when they attacked the Ents, don't you? The trees got together and made them all disappear," she said, hoping to distract them from knocking off any more bark that the tree couldn't spare. The kids all stared at her, wide-eyed. One of the orcs cast a furtive glance in the direction of the other trees standing along the road. Another looked up into the leafy canopy, so far overhead. Denny wondered if she may have overdone it a little. Time for a re-direct...

"But you know what's down there on the corner?," she said, gesturing toward the red fire hydrant, "A balrog!"

Little Gandalf's eyes widened, solemn and deadly serious.

"Let's get him!" he called to the others, and soon enough the kids had flocked away off of number one-thirteen's lawn, toward the fire hydrant on the corner.

Denny patted the tree like the shoulder of an old friend during a shared joke. She wasn't so sure she and the tree hadn't shared a joke, anyway.

DISTANT EARLY WARNING

The presence of the children had reminded Denny that it was rent collection day. The girls took turns collecting money from the squatters in the backyard, and this month, it was Denny's turn. She made her way down the empty driveway, to the grey garden gate, and knocked. The latch was easy to pick from the other side, but Denny never intruded on the Mandrake's scant privacy.

At the back of the house, she could smell multiple aromas that, because of the damp, stagnant air, had not been apparent at the front. The first was smoke and meat, corresponding with the plume of campfire smoke rising over the privacy fence. The second was laundry soap (Denny wondered where squatters had got real laundry soap, but she applauded the feat), and the third, much less pleasant to the nose, was baby diaper, sour and somehow powdery.

Mrs. Mandrake answered the garden door. She was a thin woman, once genteel, with brassy blonde hair and sharp lines around her mouth. She wore a patched, stained, button-down shirt that was probably a nice pink stripe once, and a picked brown flare skirt. In one arm, she carried a baby girl, and in the other, a knife.

Her dour expression softened when she recognized Denny.

"Oh, Denny, it's you," she said. "I thought it was Yasmeen again to complain about the noise."

Denny stepped into the yard—the Mandrakes' home, for what it was worth. A long stretch of tarp and duct tape covered their living space, a complex of crate pieces nailed together and

9

supported in places with broomsticks. Underneath, plastic Rubbermaid crates doubled as storage space for all their worldly possessions and a means of keeping their sleeping bags off the ground. Jason, their seven-year-old, poked at a glowing fire with a stick. A miserable place to live—but every available room in the house was full, including the living room couch, and most houses nowadays were the same. Hopefully, the government would finish the relief camps soon, so people like the Mandrakes could at least have a state-issued tent to live in.

Mrs. Mandrake had been a secretary, or so she said, for a lumber concern in Thunder Bay. Mr. Mandrake had run a landscaping business. Both of them had lost everything when the Screamers rose. The dead had risen from the ground, at night, and chased families from their homes, and screamed, and screamed, in a strange gibberish language that pierced the ears and warped the senses. People had gone mad in those first three months, unable to sleep and unable to rationalize what was happening to them.

No one in Ontario had believed the refugees at first, because who, in the age of cell phones and the internet and all of the other trappings of modern-day life, would believe that the dead could actually rise? And yet, the North was rapidly emptying itself...and there were the testimonies, thousands upon thousands of them...

Denny had believed the Mandrakes, even before Foster Towers Media Corp. had gone up north and gotten the first national broadcast out. As someone who read made-up stories all day,

Denny could recognize a yarn, and Mrs. Mandrake told stories that no one could or would make up.

For instance, there was Mr. Mandrake's old business partner, the stone wholesaler, who jumped into a river glen after one of the Screamers turned out to be his brother. That one always gave Denny the chills. Ghosts, wraiths, zombies...those were one outlandish things, but having one as part of the family? You'd never escape them, or the memory of what they had become, for as long as you lived.

And Dad was still missing.

Denny shook off her macabre thoughts. People like the Mandrakes didn't need any more negativity flowing their way.

"It's that time again, Mrs. M. It's my turn to collect the rent."

Denny cringed for Mrs. Mandrake's inevitable arguments, the reasons (all true) that she didn't have this month's rent. The rising price of fresh food. Little Jay Jay growing out of his jeans. Needing to go across town to the doctor on the bus. Denny prepared to argue and prepared to feel bad for the rest of the night.

As much as the Mandrakes didn't have money, neither did she. She had covered for them before, to deflect Yasmeen's wrath, but the money had come out of her savings. She'd had to borrow textbooks from a classmate one semester in order to make up the money—and that had been a close call for her grades. No grades, no education. No education, no ticket inland, away from the flooding.

Mrs. Mandrake set her knife down on a bloody piece of newspaper, where she had been cubing some beef. She wiped her hands off on her apron.

"I've got your money, for once. There's something else we need to take care of first, though."

Jason left the fire. He had a lean, freckled face, and wore jeans ripped at the knee.

"I want to keep him! Let me keep him!" he said, dancing around his mother. Mrs. Mandrake stilled him with a firm hand on his shoulder.

"We've got no money, Jay Jay. The only way he stays is if he eats your meals."

"Keep who?" Denny asked. The feeling in her stomach spread out, grew sour.

Mrs. Mandrake did not answer. She led Denny along the board fence, painted an ugly, peeling brown. Jason trailed behind them, sulking. They crossed the yard, to where another alleyway extended down the house between the wall and a chain-link fence. This gap dead-ended at the front of the house and was barely wide enough for a person to squeeze down sideways. For as long as Denny had lived at the house, they had kept old clay pots and faded-out plastic lawn ornaments back there. Denny wasn't sure what they were storing them for—they probably came from previous owners, back in the time when only one family lived here.

A section of white plastic garden trellis tipped upward, then fell over. From underneath it crawled a black and white Border Collie, his shaggy fur tipped with mud. He held his tail down and kept his ears pulled back. Ratty blue collar. Bone-shaped license tag.

Denny's stomach flipped over into full-scale nausea.

"Geoff," she said, kneeling down and putting her arms out, "come here, boy. It's okay."

Geoff wagged his tail, remaining low to the ground. He crept toward Denny and flopped over onto her feet, the tip of his tail still wagging. His eyes were as large and glassy as shooting marbles. Denny scratched his head, ignoring the gross, dander-y substance that collected on her fingers when she did so. Geoff stretched up toward her face and licked her chin.

"This is my dad's dog. Geoff shouldn't be here without Dad," she said.

"Someone kicked him out of a car onto our front lawn this morning, and we let him into the backyard. Ever since, he's been cowering in that pile of junk."

"You never saw a man with him? A man with curly hair and an old bomber jacket?" Denny said, standing up. Geoff migrated over to her right hand, placing his head directly underneath it. Denny petted him absently, lost in a sea of half-formed, fearful thoughts.

Mrs. Mandrake shook her head. "Denny, I've seen your father before. He wasn't here. I'm sorry."

"Right..." Denny said. She headed for the steps to the back porch and the square of cool darkness visible through the screen door. Geoff followed her, not leaving her magical right hand for a moment. Denny wondered how long it had been since someone had petted him.

"Denny!" called Mrs. Mandrake, as she squeezed the screen door handle.

"What?"

"I've still got rent for you."

Denny pulled the door open. She let Geoff slip inside before her. "Could you put it in the mail slot? I have to make a few calls."

She would also have to find a place to hide the dog.

CUT ADRIFT

An hour later, Denny sat sprawled in the old, prickly-upholstered recliner in the living room. She cradled the phone between her head and shoulder, eyes on the driveway. After the fifth cycle of Holst's Mars suite, someone finally picked up on the other end.

"Hello? Have I finally got the right person this time?"

"This is the missing persons unit, ma'am. May I have your name, home address, and the nature of your complaint?"

"My father is missing, and I don't know for how long," she blurted. Great, perfect. Way to convince them that she was in a rational state of mind. She reminded herself to keep her game face on. She pictured herself in the seminar room. A teacher never gave up authority and calm, and neither would she.

"Sorry. Felicia Dennigan, one-thirteen Gregory Avenue."

"Thank you, ma'am. Now, what is your complaint?"

Deep breaths. Denny gulped in air, opened her eyes wide, and then closed them, hard. No crying. Just the facts. He was probably still out there somewhere.

"I haven't seen my father, Sean Dennigan, in six months."

"Is this normal for you? Why didn't you report him missing sooner?"

Oh, dear. Now the questions got harder. Steady breaths.

"He…he's homeless. He has post-traumatic stress disorder, and it's hard for him to stay in one place for long." The statement seemed to hang in the air between Denny and the operator. She could hear what the woman was thinking even now—that she was labelling him. "But he visits on a regular basis. He never misses Christmas. Please understand…he was ill, but he wasn't…*crazy*," she explained. "He visits every few months, and I was waiting to hear from him today. His dog was waiting for me, but not him. I know something is wrong. Dad never went anywhere without Geoff."

"Okay, Miss Dennigan. First of all, you need to tell me the last place your dad contacted you from. Do you remember when that was?"

Denny held up the postcard she had pulled out of the front cover of a hardbound edition of *The Adventures of Sherlock Holmes*— her repository of Dad's postcards. Dad didn't have a lot of money, but he loved postcards, and the older and more dog-eared they were, the better. He would find them in the mission stores, in bundles, or by the check-outs in dollar stores. Denny had a collection of full-cheeked chipmunks, majestic moose, and bears with googly eyes glued to them, proclaiming the wonders of "*Canada!*" The last one had arrived in January, with a faded panorama of the Inco nickel mine, or so the label said, from glorious—

16

"Sudbury," she said. "The last postcard he sent me came from Sudbury."

"Oh dear," said the operator, uttering a sigh that said she'd dealt with this problem twelve times already today.

"What?" Denny gripped the phone with both hands. "What's wrong?"

"Sudbury is above the RCMP perimeter. It's chaos up there, people evacuating, people running to other provinces with no forwarding address, looting, suicide… Local police departments are staying out of it until the Federal troops straighten everything out."

Denny bit her lip, willing herself to stay calm, not to yell. The minute she opened her mouth, her resolve slipped and her voice quavered. The rush of tears that she had been holding back spilled out in hot streams.

"My father is missing! He could be dead! There must be something you can do."

"If he had a fixed address, we could ask the police in his area to investigate his home, ask his neighbours or co-workers. Transients are hard to find in Ottawa or Toronto, but in a state of emergency, in the wilderness? All I can do is add your father to the watch list for the RCMP. Then, if he crosses their perimeter, we can give you a call."

"Please…" Denny said, her chest heaving with the first of what would be many sobs.

"I'm sorry, Miss Dennigan, I really am."

"So am I," Denny said, pushing the phone back into its cradle. She hadn't turned any lights on when she came in, and she didn't stir to turn any on now. She lay, feet out on the rug, hands flopped over the armrests, with her chin on her chest, letting the tears stream more heavily down her cheeks with every blink. Dad deserved better than this. He might have lacked a fixed address, but he was as normal as anyone could be—anyone, at least, who had gone through what he had. He didn't need any more hardship in his life. The way Denny saw it, Dad had experienced more than his due of hardship already. More than five people's due, in a perfect world.

Denny remembered the day of the crash. As the child of her father's second marriage, she was used to Daddy's disappearances every other weekend. Unlike most of the after-school specials and kids' movies she'd ever seen on the subject, Denny liked her step-sisters and brother, and had never really felt jealous of Kendall, Sam, and Mikey's time with her father. Most of the reason for this was that Denny, for most of her young life, had wanted to be like her daddy. And Daddy loved the three of them so much, it was almost impossible not to like them. The youngest, Kendall, was her favourite, an impetuous little twig of a girl with elf-straight brown hair, ears that stuck out, and a freckly nose. Kendall was a little older than Denny, but she never used that as an excuse to exclude her. Once, they had even sat up on a summer night, when

Dad had gotten visitation for a week's vacation at the cottage, listening to the crickets and the loons and braiding each other's hair.

Denny had been thirteen on the day her dad rode out to see her for the last time. There had been an ice warning on the roads, but nothing serious enough to keep Denny's dad from seeing his kids. They had tickets to a hockey game on the other side of town, and Dad had been talking about it all week. He rode out with a smile on his face, waving to Denny from the driveway, the way he always did.

They went to the game. Dad had a single beer. They headed home via that on-ramp Mom always warned them not to take. A truck cut them off. They crashed. Flames sprung up on Kendall's side.

Denny and Mom found Dad in the hospital, barely aware of their presence, waiting for news. When Kendall died, Dad blamed himself. He blamed the single beer he had drunk, and the route he chose, and his inability to jump in and save her. Then the dreams had begun, and the waking flashbacks. Denny would always remember Dad sitting on the lawn at three a.m. on the anniversary of her death, repeating over and over that he had to leave St. Catharines, that he couldn't stay.

Denny sat up quickly in the armchair as Geoff scrambled on the hardwood, trying to skitter behind her. The lights snapped on to reveal a slickly attired Pakistani girl with a knife-straight, indelicate nose and thick-rimmed glasses. Yasmeen shut the door behind her, locking it right away.

"What are you doing in here? It's nearly nine o'clock, and all the lights are off," she said, either pretending not to notice Denny's state of dishevelment or not caring.

Geoff crept out from behind the armchair. Denny had hoped to have him bathed before Yasmeen got home, but the police had kept her on hold for a good hour before she even got to talk to someone. Geoff wagged only the tip of his tail, hoping for another sympathetic pat on the head.

"And what the hell is that?" Yasmeen threw her arms up in the air, causing Geoff to scramble back into his hiding place. "You adopted a filthy dog off the street, without consulting any of us?"

Denny placed two fingers on her forehead. "Jordan and Christina are in London for the summer. There's room for him until the fall at least. This is my father's dog. I don't know how he got here, and I don't know where my father is. I have to keep him until Dad comes to claim him."

Yasmeen shook her head. The look of silent contempt on her face made Denny want to punch her senseless and dump her on the porch of the nearest brothel, rather than live with her one more second. "Maybe the dog was just one more responsibility he wanted to be rid of."

Denny stood up, every muscle in her body tense and trembling. "Geoff is staying, and if you make even one ounce of trouble about it, I'll tell your parents that you've been dating."

Yasmeen's mouth dropped open. She came from a fairly traditional family who believed in arranged marriages. Yasmeen had been using her time away at university to explore more...Western models of courtship. Any hint that she was breaking with tradition would result in an immediate return home and more than a little family turmoil.

"You bitch," Yasmeen said, scowling. "Fine, keep him. But if I find one scratch on this hardwood or any sign that he's been in my room, I'm calling the humane society!"

Denny went to the stairs, and Geoff followed. Time for that long-overdue bath.

"Don't worry," she said, "I'll be sure to let him sleep on your bed."

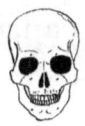

Geoff was surprisingly good about getting into the bath, although he required a rather awkward lift to avoid getting his back feet caught over the lip of the tub. Dad had enjoyed taking him to the beach down at Lakeside Park, once upon a time, throwing sticks for him and watching him run through the breaking waves, then buying him ice cream (vanilla, not chocolate) at the snack bar up the hill.

When Denny turned on the tap, Geoff shifted his weight a bit and panted, but he didn't make a break for it like other dogs might. In the absence of dog soap, Denny just filled up the tub with lukewarm water and used an old movie theatre cup to douse him. When she began massaging the dirt and dander out of his fur, Geoff turned around so that his rear end was facing her. She spent a little extra time scratching the sweet spot on Geoff's back, and he shot her a goofy, open-mouthed dog smile, tongue lolling out.

"I wish you could tell me what happened," Denny said to him, bone-tired and spent of tears. "I know *you'd* help me find Dad, if you could."

Geoff stood up and shook himself, sending murky water and hair flying all over the walls. Another mess to clean up before Yasmeen got there in the morning. Denny had no idea what she would do about the smell, but she hoped they still had a few extra air fresheners kicking around in the linen closet. She pulled the plug, letting the water drain out before she picked Geoff up and helped him out of the tub onto some carefully placed towels. She grabbed another towel off the rack by the toilet and descended on the dog, arms spread. She wrapped the towel around Geoff's neck, rubbing his fur. When she got to his back, she realized that her arms were all the way around his neck. Geoff nuzzled her, licking her ear. Denny stayed holding on to him, there, on her knees on the wet bathroom tiles, for a very long time, as a fresh bout of tears rose, even after she thought she had cried her fill.

When a clogged nose was all that was left of her latest outburst, Denny got up and shuffled down the upstairs hallway to bed. She had red splotches on her knees, and her throat felt thick and hoarse. Without calling Geoff, she heard his toenails clicking on the hardwood behind her. She let him into her room, then locked the door. She climbed into bed. Geoff turned around a few times, sighed, then settled on the rag rug near the door.

Later on, at around three or so, Denny awoke to him crawling up onto the foot of her bed. He was still wet—so much so that she could feel the moisture on his fur soaking through her sheets, but she left him there. After all that the two of them had been through that day, Denny supposed they could both use some companionship, soggy though it was.

Art by Robin McLean

THE CREEPING TIDE

The posters sprang up around campus about a month after Geoff appeared on Denny's doorstep.

Denny got off the bus, her bag hugged to her chest, as always, and her eyes downcast, as of late. She hustled down through Thistle wing, toward the Popular Culture department. Lately, walking through these halls had felt like walking through blurry, inter-dimensional tunnels, like the light-speed blur in *Star Wars*, with no distinguishing features on any side of her. She ignored the milling crowds of freshmen, shoving through them when they spread across the hall in long, slow-moving packs.

She would not have seen the posters either, so consumed was she by her own concerns, had someone not decided to shove a political pamphlet into her hands as she passed the library. She looked up momentarily, at the thin, young woman in a "Think Ink, Not Mink" t-shirt, and saw, behind the woman's bright red bob, the largest poster she had ever seen plastered to the concrete divider between two windows. There, in greyed-out Photoshop filters, was a picture of one of the refugee camps just below the northern border. Army tents, snotty-nosed children clinging to their parents' pant legs, and sober-faced, dirty people crowded in on the camera. Superimposed over this, in a stunning display of graphic composition, was a shot of the high street of some pee-hole little northern town at sunset. Amid the broken windows and detritus, silhouetted against the sunset, a knock-kneed, skeletal figure stood surrounded by a halo of its own darkness. Although the poster contained only this one, subtle reminder of the real reason for the refugee camps and the destruction, Denny's eyes went there instantly.

Text ran across the top and bottom of the poster, as plain and sober as the pictures themselves:

THE NORTH IS IN DANGER. HUNDREDS OF
THOUSANDS ARE HOMELESS.

CAN YOU HELP US?

CALL LOCAL MP MIKE BOONSTRA AT
#SCRMRSICANHELP IF YOU HAVE A STUDY, THEORY,
OR STRATEGY TO HELP GET RID OF THE SCREAMERS.

THE CREATOR (OR CREATORS) OF A SUCCESSFUL
MEANS OF ELIMINATION IS ELIGIBLE FOR UP TO
$1,000,000 REWARD FROM THE FEDERAL
GOVERNMENT.

Denny stared at the poster for a moment—it was the first time in weeks that she'd actually stopped on her way to, well, anywhere. Once she'd read the message there, she turned abruptly toward the Popular Culture wing and departed, her steps more fervent than before. She kept her head down as her eyes welled up, hoping that she wouldn't run into any of her students. She hated forcing polite chit-chat while trying to fend off the whiny five-year-old sound that people's voices get when they are just about to break down.

Denny turned right at the Computer Commons and rushed into the elevator, pressing the button over and over to prevent someone else from getting in with her. The Popular Culture department was on the second floor, shoved into a wing that nobody knew about, above the Computer Commons, which everybody knew about. The result, when Denny had steadied her breathing and the elevator doors popped open again, was rather calming. A gust of cool, filtered air hit her when the door opened, and silence...blissful silence. No freshmen, no club booths, no coffee lines, just clean carpeting, well-padded lounge chairs, and the distant sound of ringing office phones.

Denny made her way down a hallway lined with office doors and politely framed posters for foreign movies. At the end, past a corkboard advertising St. Catharines' small student film festival, was a door wallpapered with political comics. A small, gold sign with interchangeable inserts declared:

Part-time Faculty

J. Carapelli

M. Brown

Denny knocked on the door. No one answered, and for a moment she worried that Jordan had forgotten their lunch date. She had left home early just to get to school on time for this, and Geoff would be none too pleased after ten hours of waiting to go for a walk.

"Looking for someone?" said a familiar voice from down the hall. Jordan, a skinny young man with a dark goatee and a big smile, poked his head out of the photocopy room door. "I'm just putting together some readings. I'll be with you shortly."

Denny wandered down to the photocopy room and peered in. Jordan leaned on the photocopier with one elbow, as sheet after sheet poured out of the top. A stack of two hundred or more pages had already accumulated on the tray and more were stacking up all the time.

"For a minute there, I thought I'd finally found a time when you weren't at school," Denny said.

Jordan snorted. "You've got an MA. You should know better."

"Well, I've been going home more, since…the dog. You know. He can't cross his legs forever, and Yasmeen sure isn't going to take care of things. It's been kind of nice, actually. That is, it would be nice, if circumstances were different. But what I mean is, I enjoy the company."

"Speaking of which, have you got any answers yet? How's the telephone campaign going?"

Denny shook her head. Jordan pressed the stop button on the copier, gathered up his stack of papers, and swung past her heading for his office.

"Come on," he said. "Let's get that lunch. Dessert's on me."

On the way to the caf, they passed more of the same, giant government posters. One was plastered over the glass wall of the Welch Hall convenience store, and another was wrapped around a cement pillar as they descended the set of steps into the caf.

"Where the hell did all those posters come from?" Denny said.

Jordan bugged out an eye at her. "They've got the phone number right on them, Dens. I think it's pretty obvious."

"You know what I mean," she said, flapping out a hand in the direction of the nearest poster. "When did they go up? What's the deal?"

"They've been up for about a week. I'm surprised you didn't notice them."

"These days, I'm lucky if I get to class without dirty socks stuck to the hem of my pants. The other day, when I was teaching, I confused George Eliot with T.S. Eliot."

Jordan raised a bushy eyebrow. They pushed through a turnstile into the grill area and picked up a pair of plastic trays. "Heaven forbid you should forget an important fact like that."

Denny picked up a slice of pizza and said nothing. When they had passed through the checkouts and seated themselves at a table on the second floor, she said, "Look, it's like you confusing George Romero and Wes Craven, OK? It's a key part of the history of English literature. I'm...slipping. I've been calling the police station every day, and they're starting to get sick of me. I think pretty soon they're going to tell me to stop calling."

Jordan washed his bite of sandwich down with a good, long swig of coffee. "That doesn't mean you have to."

Denny rested her cheek on her hand for a moment, then shifted her weight back, slapping the table. She pressed her lips together. "Harassing the people responsible for helping my father isn't going to improve the situation. I just don't know what to do... He could be anywhere, and nobody seems to care but me."

"What about your mom?"

Denny picked at a pepperoni, with no real intention of eating it. "Mom has Mario. She's made it very clear that's all she needs."

"But...you've called her and told her?"

"Yeah, for what it was worth. She changes the subject every time I bring it up. If I bring Dad up too many times, she just makes up some excuse and hangs up on me."

"That sucks."

30

"Tell me about it. And then I come here and see the government offering buckets of money to people totally unaffected by the disaster…it makes me want to walk up to Parliament Hill and start shaking people."

"Now there's a possibility. I'm sure there are lots of people around here who would go with you… Not the science students, though. They're too busy trying to find the missing formula to 'zom-B-gone,'" Jordan said, inclining his head toward a group of students at another table, writing intently on stacks of diagrams. One of them looked up from their huddle, only to glare at them, as if they could steal ideas from across the room in a noisy hall.

Denny chuckled, in spite of herself. "They're not zombies, Jordan, as much as you might want them to be. They don't eat people."

"And I say, I've studied zombies all my life. Think about it…they appeared suddenly, they're reanimated corpses, they're causing widespread societal havoc… They're clearly zombies."

Denny rolled her eyes. "I sincerely hope not. We'd better hope the scientists can solve this mess, or I'll never get the cops to look for Dad."

Jordan made a chopping motion with both hands. They had taken a course together once, during undergrad, and he had been exactly like this—completely unwilling to give up a point. "Look, I've made a career out of this shit, and I say Screamers are zombies. I'd say I've earned it. All my life, I've had people screw

31

up their faces when I tell them what I do for a living. You probably know the face. The one where they're betting themselves over whether or not you still live in your parents' basement. Well, maybe the world has finally encountered a problem that people like us are equipped to solve."

"Then by all means," Denny said, "get up there and solve it. Remember me when you're a millionaire, will you?"

She looked over Jordan's shoulder at the clock on the wall. Ten minutes to class, and she hadn't even touched her pizza.

"Crap, I gotta eat and run," Denny said. "See you later?"

"Yeah, call me. We'll do something on the weekend."

"Sure," Denny said, knowing she wouldn't. Four years of friendship and Jordan had never even seen her house. He seemed content to see her at school and ignore her quiet refusal to hang out anywhere else. As she shoved her way through the halls, scarfing down pizza, she felt a vague regret that Jordan would never meet Geoff or the Mandrakes…although Yasmeen wasn't such a loss. Not calling people, waiting for them to talk to her, was just a reflex that she had picked up over the years, as natural to her as breathing. As she got closer to the seminar room, and her head filled with thoughts of lesson plans and poets, the regret gradually faded into the background of her mind and disappeared.

It wasn't until Denny got home at the end of the day that she thought about calling anyone, and it wasn't Jordan. She trudged up the front steps of old number one-thirteen, smelling wood smoke and dirty diaper from the backyard, and opened the door. Thunder rumbled in the distance.

Geoff was there before she made it past the knee wall, wagging his whole bottom and turning in the little circles. Denny dropped her bags by the shoe rack, kneeled down and rumpled up his facial fur. Geoff, in turn, wetted the end of her nose with a kiss.

"Orf," he said, Geoff language for "My eyeballs are floating."

"I'll be with you in a minute, buddy," Denny said, flopping into her phone chair. "You know the routine by now."

Denny didn't need to look at the phone book to remember the number. She punched it in without thinking. This time, someone picked up on the other end almost immediately.

"Hello, this is Felicia Dennigan…"

"I know, Miss Dennigan. There's been no news on your father yet. Listen, we've got a high volume of calls coming in lately, what with the refugees and the crime spike. We need to keep the lines free for emergencies. In the future, please wait for us to contact you. Thanks for your co-operation, Miss Dennigan."

"Wait, I…" Denny began to protest, but the click of the receiver on the other end cut her off. A malignant moth fluttered to life in her chest, flooding her cheeks with blood.

"That bitch," she said. "Uncaring assholes, the lot of them."

Mom wouldn't care about this. Nobody would care, except her and Geoff and maybe Jordan, but Denny needed an outlet. If she didn't talk to someone about this, she would skip town, or tear her hair out one strand at a time. Anything to distract from the anger and frustration. She picked up the phone again and punched in a very long number—an international long-distance number.

Her mother's voice answered on the other end amid dense static, sounding a few dimensions removed from this world due to the crappy long-distance service to Florida these days.

"Felicia? Is that you?" Her mom's voice was both worried and accusatory, as usual. This was not Denny's usual calling time. This was undoubtedly about her estranged husband—again. This call would have to be truncated.

Denny heard all this in her mom's voice, but she didn't care. This time, Mom would listen.

"The police told me to stop calling. We have to do something," she said.

"What, precisely, would you like me to do for you, Felicia? I'm in Florida, thousands of miles away, stuck in the middle of the third tropical storm this month... I've got enough to worry about, and so does poor Mario. These storms are ruining all of the crops and, as a distributor, it's Mario who is going to pay the price."

Felicia rolled her eyes. Mom made Mario's business sound so legitimate, it was almost believable. That was, unless you'd had a look at the guy. And then there was the way she was always making him sound like the greatest martyr of our time... After Dad had left, Mom had given up on love. That was all there was to it. She had gone looking for a provider, and what better provider than a guy with a steady stream of protection money coming in?

"Listen, Mom, I need your help. They're never going to find Dad at this rate. *Never.* I can't sleep. I barely eat. Phoning the cop shop was the only way I felt like I was *doing* something, and now I don't know *what* I'm going to do."

On the other end, Mom sighed. "I'm not the best person to ask about this, Denny," she replied.

"No, Mom, I have to. You're the only one I can turn to. Nobody from the family lives around here anymore. Most of my roommates are gone, and I barely have any friends. Dad was one of my few lifelines to the world outside university. I have to find him. I have to."

Another long pause. "Your father...gave up on himself a long time ago. Sometimes you just have to let people go. He wasn't willing to get better."

If her mother had been standing right in front of her at that moment, Denny would have had another opening with the cops— a domestic violence call, to be exact.

"And what about you, Mom? Is that what you do to people who become inconvenient? Just forget about them? That's what *I* am to you too, isn't it? Just another inconvenience, calling and calling about a past you'd like to forget. Well if you don't want to hear from me, fine. Enjoy the silence."

Denny hung up the phone, then threw a pillow at the receiver. She walked to the hall closet, threw open the door, and pulled out a length of nylon rope she'd been using as a leash. Geoff sat in the hallway and watched her yank it from the top shelf, pulling down an old bike helmet and a couple of scarves as she did. He tilted his head at her and pushed his ears forward, his eyes wide and worried.

"Come on," Denny said to him. "Let me get at your collar. I need this walk just as much as you do. And let's hope for a good stiff rain while we're at it."

LIFE, DEATH, AND A FLICKERING TV STATION

For the second time in as many days, Denny knocked on the door in the corner of the Pop Culture wing bearing the gold nameplate. This time, Jordan opened the door and peeked out a crack, his pointed goatee making him look, to Denny, like a hipster version of *The Wizard of Oz*'s doorman—ain't nobody sees the prof, no way, no how. He scrunched up his brows.

"Hey…" he said.

"Can I come in?" Denny countered, keeping her hand on the door.

"Sure, but I'm a little confused. It's not Wednesday, and it's not lunchtime. My best guess would be that you forgot something yesterday, but then I remember that you never even entered the office."

"It's complicated. Just let me sit down," Denny said, pushing her way into the room. Inside, fluorescent lights shone down on two neat, grey, carol-style desks covered with Formica and term papers, staggered at a polite distance from one another in a cramped little closet of an office. A banana plant sat in a plastic pot in the corner, alongside Jordan's prized cardboard stand-up of

Freddie Krueger. He had bragged more than once to Denny that it was an original, bought on eBay. How an original of a mass-produced cardboard cut-out could exist, Denny thought, would be a great subject of debate for the postmodernists, but she let Jordan off without a debate. There were several reasons that Denny never developed feelings for fellow students, but trivial conversation was one of the main ones. Once they had a few beers in them, university men cared more about arguing a point than in assessing whether or not anybody cared about the answer to the debate. As a result, if a guy really cared about impressing you, you could bet on listening to an hour of half-drunken ramblings on whether or not the Care Bears counted as cyborgs, in the French feminist sense.

Jordan had never pulled out the high-class conversation filler while in her presence. Jordan was married to a man.

Mary, the other prof sharing Jordan's office, was out. Jordan pulled out Mary's chair, and Denny sat in it, reaching down into her bag as soon as her butt hit the cushion. She opened a manila file folder and pulled out half of the stack of papers wedged in it. She had printed them off last night, after a long walk with Geoff through the storm. She handed them to Jordan.

"I was hoping that you could help me photocopy these. I wouldn't ask except that it's important."

Jordan nodded. Denny tried to gauge his reaction by his expression but gave up after a few seconds. She had picked the most endearing photo of Dad that she could for the poster, the one they had taken in the gazebo at Montebello Park during the Folk Arts festival. Dad had been holding up a Lebanese flatbread of some kind, meat dangling out of the open end. Geoff stood at his feet, fixated on the sandwich with the kind of hope only a dog can muster on an hour-to-hour basis. Dad was laughing, and his jeans were clean and new, just bought at Walmart the day before. He looked the way Denny saw him always—sweet and fun-loving. Not homeless. Not crazy.

"You're offering a ten-thousand-dollar reward?" Jordan said, both eyebrows raising, "Are you filthy stinking rich? Have you been holding out on me all this time?"

Denny set her jaw. "I'll find the money, as long as they find him."

"Denny, you know they have a lot of rules about stealing photocopies. And I have a feeling you'll need a stapler that isn't tethered down in the library, too. There are plenty more people in line for my job. Last I checked, the department's waiting list—just for this department—was set at fifty-four people. Fifty-four people who would gladly leave the office supplies in their place, if only the University would let them use their degrees for something other than toilet paper. Hell, you know. If you weren't bloody brilliant, you'd have been passed over too."

"He's my father. What would you do if it was your father who was missing, and the police wouldn't do anything about it?"

Jordan's normally impish face fell just a little. He looked at his Freddie, over in the corner. "My father and I don't talk. He didn't even come to see me when Kyle and I got married."

Denny pursed her lips. Clearly, she was not the only one around with family problems. While she sympathized, she needed Jordan. She had to find some way to get through to him.

"What if it were Kyle, then? Wouldn't you do everything that you could to get him back?"

"Not fair," Jordan said.

Denny met his eyes, hoping that her concern and love for her father telegraphed in her expression. "I only speak the truth."

As they sat there, facing off, the latch clicked. Mary entered the room, shutting the door with her rear end while balancing a precarious stack of brown, interdepartmental envelopes. Jordan nodded to her. When Mary turned around, he picked the stapler up off his desk and shoved it into the inside pocket of his blazer without a sound. Denny grinned, picturing a young Jordan, still with the goatee of course, taking a five-finger discount on comics.

"Right, Denny, I'll be ready to go as soon as I finish these photocopies," he said.

"Go where?"

"Well, if I'm going to be investing in this business, I want to see the returns. Plus, I want to meet Geoff. All you do is talk about him. As your bestest buddy in all the world, I'm getting a little jealous."

"Right…okay…if you really want to…"

"That I do. And, I believe that after I have trekked around with you in very wet weather, doing idle chores, you will owe me a delicious beverage of some kind."

Denny smiled a little, in spite of herself. "The Fine Grind?"

"Indeed."

Three hours, seventy-two posters, and several shoefuls of puddle water later, Denny, Jordan and Geoff stood outside their last downtown stop, watching the rain fall from beneath the recessed doorway. It had been a used bookstore—a bad financial choice for Denny.

"I knew I should have waited outside," she said, holding up an unmarked plastic bag weighted down by a volume of Gothic ghost stories and a nicely bound copy of some Beckett plays.

Jordan untied Geoff from a nearby fire hydrant, then gave him a boisterous, fur-ruffling scratch. Geoff responded by shaking himself, adding dog hair to the muddy water stains on Jordan's khakis. Denny smiled. She almost laughed.

"Don't think about the books too hard, Denny," he said. "You could use a little bit of mirth."

"I guess that's why you've been clowning around with the dog all night then, to cheer me up?"

"Hell no. I'm just trying to give my work pants a much-needed makeover."

This time, Denny did laugh. She unfurled her umbrella and stepped out into the rain. Together, they travelled the block and a half down to The Fine Grind. She hadn't wanted to invite Jordan. She had feared she would break down or just give up entirely and want to go home, feeling overwhelmed and upset. Instead, Jordan had been comforting, in his own, quirky way, taking care of Geoff and schmoozing the more reluctant shopkeepers into putting up her posters. She felt another pang of regret for not doing this sooner. No disaster had happened on their walk (at least, not any worse than what had already happened in the past week) and in a way, Jordan had kept disaster at bay, rather than causing her more pain.

They approached the café through the blue haze of late evening, the yellow light from the open door cutting a bright swathe through the murky street. At the risk of using a much-hated essay opening, The Fine Grind had been St. Catharines quintessential student coffeehouse "since the beginning of time." It was located in an old, white-painted storefront, a throwback from the 1900s, with column facades and cornered windows. St Catharines had a lot of these, but most of them were crumbling and graffitied. The Fine Grind wasn't perfect—what building could be after that long with the same façade? But it had a dinged up sort of dignity, at least. Since it was a Thursday night, and growing late, there were only two people in there: Dave, the ever-constant bartender slash owner, and a sullen-looking young man with long, dark hair pulled back in a ponytail, nursing a cappuccino. The café was divided into two parts, with a soda-fountain-style bar and tables up front, and comfy couches, books, and board games in the back. In the far corner of the bar area, a television hung suspended in a corner, blaring out a sitcom on FTMN: The Foster Towers Media Network.

"You want me to turn that off?" Dave said, passing them a couple of menus. "I just had it on for company."

"S'okay, leave it on." Denny replied, choosing a seat near the bar. Geoff had come in with Jordan, unremarked upon. Now Dave peered over the counter, scrutinizing his soggy fur.

"He gonna shake off?"

As if in answer to Dave's query, Geoff took a long look at him, turned around once, then laid down, thumping his tail once against the linoleum as a symbol of good faith. Denny brought him in here once a week or more, when she had a few pennies to spare for a milkshake. Geoff enjoyed the outings, as he liked to people watch, and, more commonly for a dog, he also liked to suck up for cuddles.

"Nope," Denny said. "I think he got all the shaking out of his system back at the bookstore."

Jordan let out a single bark of laughter at this. As the sitcom on the television shifted to the over-dramatic opening theme of the news, they studied the menu. Denny usually had a strawberry milkshake or, on occasion, she would imbibe an herbal tea. The

Fine Grind had some of the nicest hand-blended tea varieties in town, and she still hadn't made her way through the entire list. Tonight, though, she found her tastes wandering to less summery fare.

"I'll have a hot chocolate, with extra whipped cream, a cherry, and a sprinkling of chocolate shavings," she said.

"Why not? Christmas is right around the corner, after all," said Jordan, adding that he would have a blueberry smoothie.

Ouch. Denny wondered if she had been too quick to trust someone else with her own personal laundry.

"Oh, shut up. It was my dad's favourite drink, okay? I just thought it might bring us some luck."

Denny's regret dissipated when Jordan hunched over a little, growing pink around the cheeks.

"I hope someone calls," she said, breaking the silence for both their sakes.

"So do I."

Denny went silent then, staring at the news on the TV but not really seeing anything that was going on onscreen. For the millionth time since the whole ordeal had started, she played with her hands, unsure of where to put them. She kicked her legs under the table like a little girl. The worst part about the last month had been the waiting, that impatient feeling that she should be doing something now, that if she was doing that nebulous something,

Dad would be home safe, and that there was no way to figure out what that nebulous something was.

Jordan let her be silent. He stirred his drink and picked up a newspaper. When her hot chocolate arrived, Denny devoured the top part quickly, then blew on the rest. Above her, on the TV, images flickered by. Someone in Toronto had started a fire in their townhouse, and it had spread through the complex. A newsstand clerk had chased down a mugger. A special report waxed poetic about whether or not fat people should automatically be investigated for resource hoarding.

Denny took a tentative sip of her hot chocolate. Like the other beverages offered at the Grind, it was delightful. In one sip, she was back on the December morning when she was seven or so, under a grey sky, listening to choirs sing at Niagara-on-the-Lake. Mom had loved choirs back then. They had walked all over town, listening to the music, Denny perched on her dad's shoulders with a big paper mug of hot chocolate in her hands. There had been a children's chorus, playing bells. Dad had broken out the old chestnut that he mentioned every year at around this time. Every time a bell rings, an angel gets its wings.

And then, as if the memory had crawled out of its grave, she heard singing—not sweet choral notes, but a rough, grasping melody, the song of a decaying siren shrieking over a storm-tossed sea. They were playing footage of the Screamers on the news.

There, in clear, crisp, and brutal high definition, a thing, half skeleton, half tarry darkness and air, lurched toward the camera. It was missing half of its right shin, and a lock of dirty hair of unidentifiable colour hung down from one side of its skull. It hovered in front of the camera, swaying, like a cobra facing a threat. And it sang…oh, the terrible song it sang. Its words, if words they were, babbled from a slack, unmoving jaw, overlapping one another like a chattering stream of nonsense.

Someone behind the cameraman was urging him to keep steady. The camera stayed locked on the Screamer for a few more seconds, then went into a deadly shake and refocused elsewhere, then cut out completely.

"Authorities are now saying that the Screamers vary in size, shape, and disposition, depending on the location, and that they may not be as easily contained as we had hoped. This next footage, from an undisclosed location, illustrates this disturbing trend," said the female voice-over.

Denny saw a vista of hills and scrub, caught in the dying light of dusk. Along the sides of the hills, unnatural lights flitted—lights with eyes, lights with faces. The camera turned, and where it came to rest, Denny saw a figure standing in relief against the last rays of the sun. He was made of darkness, but it would take more than darkness to stop Denny from recognizing him. The bomber jacket, the curly hair, the slouchy stance… Dad.

Denny shook Jordan's arm.

"Jordan! Jordan! Look! Dad's up there with the news crew! He must have gotten a job without telling me! He must've…"

The figure turned toward the camera, revealing a sunken-in face, obscured by darkness. The front of his bomber jacket was torn away, revealing an exposed ribcage with a glowing yellow heart pulsating within. He slid along the ground, faster than a blink, until his hollow eyes filled the camera lens.

As his screams began, the song twisted Denny's heart into something that she couldn't bear to feel beating within her. Every nerve in her body caught fire and made her gasp for air, and she began to scream too.

"Oh my God," Jordan said, finally connecting what had happened. "Come on, Denny, we'll get out of here. We'll go home."

Denny sank to her knees.

"No! Dad, no! Dad!"

She kept repeating those words, over and over, sobbing, curling up into a ball and protecting her arms from Jordan. He wanted to touch her, to help her up, but she wanted to stay there…stay there forever, until she became a Screamer herself, scaring people out of their homes and throwing her anger at the world.

In the background, she could hear Dave scrambling around from behind the bar.

"What's wrong with her? Should I call an ambulance?"

"I don't know…" Jordan answered. "Denny? Denny!"

With the first wave over, and many more devastating waves of grief to come, Denny pulled out of herself enough to notice that the room had gotten quiet. Someone had turned off the TV. They were all staring at her. They all knew.

Denny stood up on shaking legs. She held out a hand, still grimy from being on the floor to Jordan.

"Give me the dog. I'm going home."

"It's ten o'clock at night, and you're in no state to be walking alone."

"Now, Jordan!"

"No. I'm coming with you."

Denny, her vision still blurred with tears, shoved into Jordan, wresting the leash from his hands while he struggled to regain balance. Geoff pranced and circled on the leash, his tail low. When Denny gained the lead, Geoff trotted ahead of her, eager to be out of the conflict.

She took long strides, pushing herself into a fast walk that, by the time she reached the end of the block, had her taking fast gulps of humid air. She heard the splash of someone running through the puddles behind her. No, Jordan, no. Just go home.

"Denny, come on," he called, now just a few sidewalk segments behind her. "Let's go to the bus station. You're gonna get mugged out here."

Denny turned around to face him. Fine. Let him see her red, streaming eyes. Let him see her messed-up hair. She'd never told

Jordan the whole story about her dad, but she was sure that if he kept after her, she'd spill that, too. And then any ounce of professionalism she had managed to protect at school would fly out the window. She had told a manager once about her dad. She had missed a week at work when he ended up in the mental ward at North Bay. From then on, all of her reports had read "volatile temper" and "problems with authority," as if Dad's illness had somehow rubbed off on her. As if those were really the symptoms of mental illness and not some excuse to punish her because they were afraid of her dad's diagnosis.

No, she would not go back to the bus station, despite the shadowy figures standing on the next corner and in the stairwell of the dive down the street. At this time of night, people were going home from night classes and heading out to the bars to meet their friends. She almost always saw students at the bus station coming home after marking.

"I need air," she said.

"You're not getting rid of me," said Jordan.

Denny bit her lip as a fresh bout of sobs rose up in her throat. She convulsed a few times, but the tears stayed in. "Fine, just...give me space."

Jordan gave her space, all along the hour and a half walk from downtown to one-thirteen George. Denny cried in silence, keeping her back to him so he couldn't see, but she knew he knew anyways. With the sun down, the rain tapered off and a chill wind

49

replaced it, freshening the long tracks down her face and neck. She shuffled along, like the corpse of a murdered child she'd seen in a movie once, waterlogged from falling into a well.

People didn't just die and show up as ghosts. Ghosts were a manifestation of the subconscious, the return of the repressed. The suffering of ghosts represented *our* suffering and the painful secrets we hide.

But Dad had been real. Dad had been too badly damaged to be alive. His heart was glowing. *He* was suffering. If cultural knowledge held on the subject, Dad *would* suffer, for all eternity. Dead would have been better. Dead, at least, would have meant an end to his suffering. Dead would have meant a chance for him to be with God, to be saved and purified of his demons.

Demons. Ha. Funny given the circumstances. What were the Screamers? Was it really Dad, or just Dad's body, animated by some force of nature?

The twist in Denny's heart squeezed tighter as she remembered Dad's song, that hell-coal of a melody that had set every nerve ablaze and skimmed along the edge of her ability to understand. There had been meaning in that song, but no key in the human mind would unlock it. In one verse, it had conveyed all of the poison in Dad's soul and his vain struggle to extricate it from his life. He was suffering. Suffering still.

Denny reached the darkened porch of number one-thirteen and rummaged around in her purse for the key. She found the fob and yanked it out of the top of her bag. A half-full package of Kleenex spilled out onto the porch. She shoved the key into the lock and wrestled the latch open. Jordan got there before she could pull Geoff inside.

"Good night, Denny. I hope you decide to talk to someone about this, even if it isn't me."

Denny let Geoff in and came out on the stoop. She threw her hands up in the air.

"Why talk? A picture is worth a thousand words, and there he was, on national television, his glowing heart beating for everyone in the nation to see. After that, I don't know what more there is to say."

"I'm not going to tell anyone," he said, coming a little closer. "We faculty have to stick together, especially the expendable humanities dabblers. We're like red shirts on *Star Trek*, for Christ's sake."

Denny let out a dry laugh. They had just remade the *Star Trek* TV series a few years back, to outstanding critical success, and so Jordan's vintage TV knowledge had begun coming in handy with the students again. Damn him, he was calming her down, despite the ache in her chest still lingering on. She sighed. "I just...don't want people to think I have issues."

"We all have issues, Denny. You're just more adept at hiding them than most. Do you want to let me in, or are we going to stand around here all night?"

"I-it's already past midnight. We've both got work...well, you've got work tomorrow."

"I'll live."

As it turned out, Jordan lived until about quarter-to-four in the morning, when he got up from the kitchen table, plodded over to Denny's prickly, old, beige armchair, and arranged the throw pillow beneath his head. He hadn't pressed her for more information than she was willing to give; rather he let the conversation ramble wherever she took it, usually in circles that ran from sadness to anger to denial and back. They had probably rehashed the same information about twenty times, but in that time, Denny had gotten a chance to think things out.

"Leave phone numbers of people who can cover for you on the counter, along with the course codes. I'll get someone to come lead your seminars," he said, yawning.

Denny did this and headed for the stairs. Geoff trailed behind, with the stiff gait of the very, very sleepy. She was halfway up the stairs when Jordan called out to her again.

"What do you think you're going to do?"

Denny paused, letting a long silence drift between them. By the time she answered, Jordan had probably already gone back to sleep, but she needed to say it, if only for her own sense of resolution.

"I'm going up there after him. I'm going to find out how he died and find a way to free him."

"What?" said Jordan, and loudly. Talk about a light sleeper.

"I've also made up my mind. I want you to find out who's next in the seniority line after me. I want to know how much they'll pay for my job."

"Denny, you can't…"

"Good night, Jordan. And this time, I mean it."

NO EASY CHOICES

"Another butter tart, Miss Vandersam?" Denny asked as she brought a pitcher of cold milk out of the fridge.

"Please, call me Amelia," said the blonde strip of a girl sitting, hands in her lap, at the kitchen table. She had to be at least twenty-eight, and Denny spotted a wedding ring on her index finger, but she had big, Dutch blue eyes that gave her an innocent look and a nearly flat chest.

If they had met under other circumstances, Denny might have confessed her jealousy. Sometimes her double Ds had her back screaming at her to think about a breast reduction and a diet. As it was, though…

"Professor Carapelli told me that you were interested in quitting your job. I wanted to know what duties were involved," Amelia said, shielding her eyes with long, blonde lashes. Denny had served up tea and canned ham sandwiches, but the girl hadn't touched them. Denny forced herself to eat half a sandwich, although she wasn't very hungry either. She took a swig of over-steeped tea and remembered Dad's song. She had to keep the song and the suffering present, or her conscience would give her away.

"There's no reason to mince words," Denny said. "No one is home, and I have nothing to gain by telling on you. I'm getting married, and my husband wants me to stay home and have children. He's in real estate and, as you might suspect, he makes a good wage. I don't really need the money anymore."

Amelia's peaky shoulders rolled forward. Her lips pursed a little bit. She needed the money. She probably needed the ham sandwich more than she let on, as well.

Denny continued, "But, don't let that convince you that I'm eager to get rid of the job. If a decent offer doesn't surface, I'll stay right where I am, for as long as it takes to get what the job is worth. It's good work and, frankly, Geoff wants me to retire more than I do."

"How much?"

"Seven thousand dollars. Think of it as an investment in your future. I've got three courses, two seminars apiece. You'll make it back in a couple of months." That, at least, was true. Miss Vandersam wouldn't be living at the Ritz, but with Denny's job, she could expect to make ends meet with a clean apartment and a plateful of vegetables gracing the table once in a while.

Yes…comfort… Denny would miss that when she got back to town. For about the fiftieth time today, Denny wanted to take it back, to tell Ms. Vandersam to leave and forget it all. But then that shaky camera shot, the glowing heart and the song, came back to her, and she knew again why she did it. Dad would have given anything for her. No one else had understood him. If she didn't find him and help him, he would stay up there forever, singing that terrible song.

Let McDonald's trap her for the rest of her life. She'd gladly work in a hotel, or a bar, or a gravel pit until her next chance came along. And next chances always came along, even if it took fifteen years. She'd get her name on every seniority list going. She had one chance to do this, and it was now.

Amelia must have sensed her hesitation. She gave a half-smile, saying, "And what if I tell the department that you're accepting money to deliver up your job?"

"I'm already on the way out. Telling will only hurt you. The department can let me go, but they won't hire you in my place. You see, they seem really big on rules, but only when it suits them. You make trouble, you blow whistles? They won't want you in a million years. Whistleblowers cost money, and I think we both know that nobody has enough of that lately."

Amelia sighed. She pulled on a lock of her hair a moment, then dropped her hand to her leg with a clap. "Fine. I'd heard this might happen, so I've put a bit of money away for the occasion."

Denny gave her what she hoped was an appreciative, understated smile. "Thank you. I'd like cash, please, by Sunday or the deal is off. You can drop it off at Professor Carapelli's office in an interdepartmental mail envelope."

"But it's Friday now!"

And Dad couldn't wait. "It's your choice," Denny said, standing up from the table, "but this job could be your ticket to a better life. With teaching experience, you could save up, do a concurrent PhD, and set yourself up for a profitable career. Once you're in the system, it's much easier to stay in."

"Whatever, I'll get you the money by the end of the week. Just quit pretending to be my guidance counsellor, okay? This isn't something I would normally get involved with."

Denny nodded. She was tempted to say that yes, Amelia probably would do this if she were in Denny's shoes, but she held her tongue. The house of cards about the husband was missing a couple of aces as it was—no need to draw attention to it. By the time the girl suspected anything, she'd likely be stretching out in her shared, broom-closet office, and Denny would be long gone. Denny ushered her to the door, insisted that she take a ham sandwich to go, and headed back into the cool of her kitchen. It was just past noon, and the sun had reached its hottest, the air its most unbearable humidity. In a few hours, it would break into another rainstorm, but for now, it hurt to breathe. The air tasted of ozone and well-used kitchen.

Denny walked over to the refrigerator and rested her forehead on the freezer door. There. She'd done it. She'd gotten the money. Now on to the next task.

Out the screen door and down the steps, Mrs. Mandrake was patching up a hole in the lean-to's roof with the battered, old lid of a Rubbermaid tub and some rusty nails. The whole thing shook as she leaned on it, bashing the nails in with the heel of her shoe. It was just her and the baby home at the moment, with Jason off at school and Mr. Mandrake in the peach fields. Baby Randolph sat in a makeshift crib of foam-topped chicken wire, gnawing on the ear of a threadbare lion.

"Mrs. Mandrake?" Denny called over the pounding. She stopped hammering, put her shoe back on, and climbed down from the crate she'd been standing on. She approached Denny with the posture of someone trying to gauge the temper of a new animal. It wasn't rent day. Nobody ever visited except for rent day. Or if Yasmeen was threatening to evict them over the smoke, or the crying, or any number of things her delicate disposition couldn't take.

"What can I do for you, Denny?" Mrs. Mandrake said. "Hammering getting to you? I can stop for a while, but I was hoping to patch the roof before the next storm."

"No, nothing like that," Denny said. She went to the stoop, sat down, and motioned for Mrs. Mandrake to do the same.

Once they were settled, Denny said, "I'm going up north soon, and I don't know when I'm going to be back."

"Your father?"

Denny nodded. "Things… I think things went wrong for him up there. I'm taking some money and some supplies, and I'm going up there to find out what happened."

"Denny, you can't just up and leave! You don't know what you're up against. The North's no place for a nice girl like you. The only ones left up there now are those as want to be left alone...bandits and crazies and militant Native groups like that Verity Twoflower's bunch... Oh, I've heard about them on the radio news. The lot of them are trying to take back the North, stake it out as a separate country, not just a separate province. They're calling it a potential war..."

Denny cut her off with a raised hand. "I know, believe me, I do. But I'm going just the same. I'm in the process of quitting my job at the university, and I'm going to be paying Yasmeen my next six months of rent upfront."

Mrs. Mandrake pursed her lips but said nothing.

"While I'm gone, my room will be vacant. I want your family to move in and live for free for as long as I'm gone. It's not much, and you'll have to confine yourselves to my room for the most part and stay out of Yasmeen's hair, but it will give you a chance to get back on your feet. Maybe you could even save enough money to get a place of your own."

Mrs. Mandrake's hard, drawn face lifted into a big, tearful smile. A flush rose in her grey cheeks and shoulder blades. She drew Denny into a hug and held her there for a full minute. Despite living outdoors, and having few changes of clothes, Mrs. Mandrake smelled sort of nice, like old wood and dusty bookshelves.

"You're a gem, girl. We'll never forget this."

"Invite me over for a barbeque when you guys get that house in the country you've always wanted," Denny said with a grin.

"That'll be a while yet. But what about Yasmeen? Did she really give permission for this?"

"My room, my money, my choice. If you keep the common areas clean and keep the kids quiet, she'll have no say in it. The landlord just cares that the room's paid for and the neighbours don't complain. Nobody living here has the right to kick anybody else out. Besides," Denny said with a wicked grin, "Yasmeen should be happy that the smoke smell is gone."

Denny went out that afternoon, to the hardware store, the pet supply store, and the hiking supply store down on Fourth. She took the stolen shopping cart from the backyard with Mrs. Mandrake's blessing, and by the time the rain broke she had it all stacked up in her room, ready to be packed. She had put all of the supplies on her credit card. She knew she would be in trouble if Amelia had second thoughts. She didn't care. If the North really was a place for outlaws, as Mrs. Mandrake said, what would one more outlaw matter? She would wait until Sunday to leave, but she wanted to pack everything now. She wanted to make the hard decisions before her shock and anger wore off. Plus, it felt like doing something, and activity would stave off the jitters that set in when you're close to your objective, but not close enough.

Denny opened the extra-large hiking backpack that she had bought at the hiking store, a moss-green contraption on a metal frame. She loaded the emergency materials into the front pocket— first aid kit, water purification tablets, flares, bear spray—and then began loading the food into the bottom. She had bought a combination of canned and freeze-dried food, enough to last her a month, as well as a supply of dog food for Geoff.

Yes, she had decided to take Geoff. She would need a friend up there to watch her back, and Jordan had a considerably more demanding schedule. Not that he hadn't tried to bargain her out of it again, several times, on the phone, in exchange for a trip during reading week. On the whole, Denny thought the dog would give her a lot less back-talk. Plus, Geoff had spent more time with Dad than anyone else. He wasn't trained or anything, but maybe, just maybe, he'd pick up on Dad's trail, or unearth some vital clue.

At the moment, Geoff was laying on the rag rug at the foot of Denny's bed, his adopted relaxation spot. He raised his head, gave a wide dog yawn, then started to pant. Denny knew how he felt. The upstairs was stifling in the late afternoon, after having had all day to warm up.

She went back to packing, loading her self-charging flashlight, map, trail shelter, and sleeping bag in next. With all of those supplies packed, there was very little room for clothing, toiletries, or personal effects—depressingly little, in fact. She jammed a couple of pairs of jeans and several t-shirts in as far as she could get them, a pair of running shoes, underthings, a bubble vest, and a winter coat. She had bought a utility belt as well, with an axe, compass, and water bottle holster, but she kept that hung over the edge of her bookcase.

The very last things to go in, simultaneously the most and least important, were the books. Denny had four bookshelves full. Most of them had been pulled from deep piles in the backs of used book stores, where she exclaimed at her luck for having found a volume that almost no one knew existed, for the low, low price of a dollar. She loved them. She loved the smell of them, and the way they looked on the shelf, a crowd of titles and differently textured covers. She had read each and every one and taken something away from most of them. She picked up her volume of Sherlock Holmes stories, feeling the roughness of the real cloth binding and the embossed cover. This one was heavy, but she'd take it anyway. She had a feeling she'd need a little bit of Holmes's indomitable rationalism by the end of this.

She pored over the next choice for a while, before pulling a small, red Gideon's Bible out of her shelves. Most people at Brock didn't seem to believe in God anymore, seeing him as a barrier to rational thinking. Given the fanaticism of the campus "Christian" fellowship, who opposed a unisex bathroom on the grounds that trans people *might* use it, Denny understood where the doubters were coming from. But she was neither a born-again zealot nor an atheistic woman of science. She just believed in God. And if God was behind this phenomenon in the North, she wanted him behind her, too.

With the Bible and the collection of mysteries packed away, she could fit just one more book into the top of her backpack and still close the drawstring. One book, out of her vast store.

Denny pulled the copy of *Songs of Innocence and Experience* that Dad had bought her off of the shelf. Her initial impulse was to grab it quickly, pack it away, and then look at it on the train, if need be, to try and glean any hidden clues about what could have led Dad to that area, and how he could have died. Instead, she opened the front cover and stared at the postcard from Sudbury. She flipped it over and passed her fingertips over the bumps made by his handwriting. They were like braille impressions of his last living months.

She had held steady all day, but now an aching sickness crept up beneath her ribcage. Her arms went heavy and her hands trembled. She sat down on the edge of the bed.

The North was ahead of her, a vast expanse of chaos, the wild West with a different compass direction, and somewhere in it, like a tiny beacon in a stormy sea, was a mystery that only she could solve. She, who had still gotten lost in the Mackenzie Chown complex at school until her third year of undergrad. She, with few friends and no functional family.

Geoff sat up, sidling toward Denny and the book. He stuck his nose between the leaves, giving the postcards a sniff large enough to pull the stack toward his nostrils. He pulled away, leaving a nose print on one of the pages.

Denny gave him a quizzical look. "Can you still smell him? You haven't forgotten him either, have you?"

Geoff laid his head on her leg, giving her the "pet me" eyes. His tail thumped on the hardwood. She stroked his head, and he let out a deep sigh through his nose, one of those "ka-fuff" sounding noises that dogs often let out while having a nightmare.

"What did you see, boy? I wish you could tell me," Denny said, closing the book and laying it aside.

As Denny stroked Geoff's head, the wave of depression that had struck her eased off into a vague feeling of fatigue. Maybe the North was vast, and maybe there were monsters roaming the wastes, but as long as she was with Geoff, there was a chance that his nose and his memories could lead her through. Dogs never forgot kindness, and Dad had been kinder to Geoff than he had been to himself.

Another thing kept her moving forward after that, as well. She might be the only human being on the planet who missed her father, but his dog missed him too, and somehow, that made her feel a little less crazy.

She picked the book up off the bed, placed it in the backpack, and then pulled the string. Everything was wrapped up. Everything was final.

And still, nothing was solved.

LAST NIGHT IN PARADISE

Jordan showed up on Denny's doorstep Sunday night wearing wellies and a long, oilcloth raincoat. He peered out from under his hood at her beneath the porch light, like Aragorn entering the Prancing Pony.

Denny knew she looked awful, wearing wrinkled old pyjama bottoms and a tank top with faded blue stars all over it, but her fight with Yasmeen that afternoon had knocked all the energy out of her. She had hoped that Yasmeen would go out during the delivery of the money, as she did most weekend nights, but she had stayed in tonight.

Denny motioned with her thumb upstairs and mouthed "Yasmeen" before even greeting Jordan. He grimaced.

"Do you want me to just hand you off the envelope then? I'll see you at the bus station tomorrow, anyway," he said in a hushed tone of voice.

Denny pursed her lips. Yasmeen sitting upstairs, especially in the state she had left the argument in, was a scary prospect alone. Sitting downstairs, waiting for her to emerge, felt a little like sitting at the bottom of a mountain watching the avalanche roll in.

"I'd prefer some company right now," she said. "I had a rough afternoon."

Jordan came in, discarding his boots on the plastic mat at the door while Geoff crowded him for attention. Jordan patted him the way a ten-year-old with the flu might. He frowned. "Your room?"

"Just for a minute, to make the exchange behind closed doors... I don't want to be up there long."

"God, what happened? Did you threaten to kill her firstborn?"

Denny shook her head. "Come on, let's talk up there."

The two of them skirted Yasmeen's room like an unarmed villager in India probably skirts a tiger's den—walking on the outsides of their feet and barely breathing. Once inside her room, Denny threw on a bedside lamp that cast a yellow glow through the space.

Jordan handed Denny the envelope. She opened it and counted the seven thousand dollars with no small measure of relief.

When she had stowed it away in the front pocket of her backpack, Jordan leaned toward her with his chin. "So?"

"So, Yasmeen didn't take it very well. I knew she wouldn't. I just didn't know she would yell for so long before letting the Mandrakes move in. She should do opera. She's got the volume, now all she needs is the pitch."

"She's got bitch...is that the same as pitch?"

Denny cringed.

"Quiet! You say it that loud, and she'll come charging back out here. Now let's lock up and get downstairs. I still have some food to use up before I leave."

"I really can't talk you out of this, can I?" said Jordan as he sat down on the prickly yellow chair again. He had a plate piled up with leftover butter tarts, an end of bread with peanut butter smeared on it, and a glass of sugary imitation cranberry drink. Denny sat on the ottoman, nursing the last glass of milk from the fridge.

"No, Jordan. The job's gone. It's final."

"I'm not even talking about the job anymore. Screw the job. You're going to get yourself killed up there. You'll be a target for all the outlaws and sickos roaming around looting."

"Why? Because I'm a woman?"

"Partially, and also because you're a pampered academic who's never set foot in the wilderness before."

"Pampered? Please, I've been camping. Mom took me in high school. And I never expected any sexist bullcrap from you, of all people."

"I'm just trying to be realistic, and you should be too. Otherwise, you could be in serious danger," he said, setting his plate and glass down beside the phone. "You're so caught up in your loss that I wonder if you're thinking any of this through."

"I'm an academic, Jordan. They pay me to think." Denny realized after the phrase was already out of her mouth that she hadn't been modulating her voice for several minutes. Neither had Jordan.

"No, they pay *you* to parrot the opinions of other academics. They pay me to think...some of the time, when it suits them. And you know what I'm thinking? I'm wondering why you're willing to give up everything for someone who visited you twice a year if you were lucky. What are you hiding, Denny? What's the deal?"

Denny looked down into her milk glass, now empty. She sighed. Jordan had been a good friend to her, especially in the last few days. Perhaps it was time to explain.

"Her father was batshit nuts. Certifiable," said a voice from the stairs. Yasmeen walked down into the kitchen, a sneer on her face and a stare full of hatred directed at Denny burning in her eyes. "I bet half the time he didn't even know where he was. That's why he was always roaming around, never coming home, never supporting his family. He was dirty, too. Had my family been here, they never would have let someone like that through the door."

"Get out of here, Yasmeen," Denny said, low and dangerous. She stood up, and Jordan tilted forward, as if unsure whether to get up or stay put should there be a fight. "You need to shut your fat mouth when you don't know what you're saying. Dad had post-traumatic stress disorder from watching my stepsister burn to death in a car accident. He wasn't crazy, and he wasn't dirty. He was one of the strongest people I ever knew. So you'd better fuck off back upstairs, princess, before I decide to give you some trauma of your own."

"You're just like him," said Yasmeen. "Just look at how you're following in his footsteps: leaving your job, giving away your home... You'll end up the same in the end. I've slaved away in the cafeteria nights and weekends, taking courses to raise my grades, having to keep begging my parents to help me get along, but you...you walk into the school for five minutes and they hand you a job teaching. I know you sold your job...and that makes you just as crazy as him."

Denny threw her milk glass against the wall behind Yasmeen. Jordan yelped and ducked away from the flying shards. Geoff scrambled to his feet and fled halfway up the stairs.

"I'd be proud to be like him!" she yelled, as Yasmeen fled back up the stairs to her room, wide-eyed. "At least he cared about something other than himself!"

Denny covered her face with one hand and sat back down on the ottoman.

Jordan crept over and placed a hand on her shoulder. "You're not crazy, Denny."

Denny gave a sigh from deep within her that closed tighter with every breath. "Yes, I am," she said.

SEABURN'S STASH

Denny trundled down the front steps for the last time the next morning, listening to the deep creaks they made under her weight. She had grown considerably heavier with the added bulk of her utility belt and the pack on her back. Geoff padded down the steps after her, wearing his brand-new heavy-duty leash and harness set.

Since it was ungodly early, the sky only barely pink with the coming dawn, she spied a couple of construction workers across the way smirking at her on their way to work.

"Going mountain climbing?" one of them said in a pseudo-flirtatious manner.

"Going north," she said. That shut them up, but quick.

Denny stayed on her side of the street, heading in the opposite direction from the workers, toward the bus station. At first, the air felt dewy and cool, breezing gently against her face, but as the sun rose, the air grew heavy, humid and hot. The smell of exhaust fumes soon drifted into the mix as she moved deeper into the city centre. By the time she crossed the last intersection before the bus station at King Street, Geoff was panting heavily and she had stains spreading out from her underarms where the straps dug in. She unclipped the water bottle and tin cup attached to her utility belt and squirted some water into the cup for Geoff, then squeezed a mouthful for herself. Geoff lapped the water up, then stared at her for more. He had stopped panting as much, though, so Denny didn't feel bad about reclipping her thermos to her belt and picking up the cup.

Up ahead, a familiar figure slouched against a cement column... Jordan. With him stood an unkempt, shorter man of about their age with a bushy beard and red plaid shirt. As Denny drew nearer to them, she saw that the man's shirt, as well as his jeans, were faded and pilled.

Denny forced herself to hold out a hand, wondering if the grip that met it would be clammy, or callused, or worse...sticky. The man had the look of a hunted animal about him, exacerbated by his wasted features and thick glasses that gave the impression that he had small, shiny eyes like a rat's.

"You must be Seaburn," she said.

The man pulled away from her hand.

"Yeah, some people call me that," he replied. "We've got to get going soon. You got the cash?" Seaburn-of-the-many-names had a voice that seemed to cringe mid-word, as though everything he said tasted bad.

Denny pulled a wad of cash out of her pants pocket.

"You get half now and half on arrival."

Seaburn scowled. "All right, you gonna pay for gas?"

"If you run out of cash, and we need it."

Seaburn heaved the kind of deep, rattling sigh that only a chain-smoking man-child can manage, took the cash, then turned his back on them.

"I'll go get the car out of the parking garage," he said.

When his plaid-clad back had disappeared behind the ticket booth of the garage across the street, Denny grimaced at Jordan.

"Are you sure about him?"

"As sure as I can be about a friend of a friend of my cousin's...yeah. Just remember: don't let him see you take the rest of the money out of hiding, and don't let him drive if he's been off in the woods by himself for a while. He's an okay guy...he's just got a lot of really pathetic addictions."

Jordan finished talking, and silence fell for a few seconds. A breeze blew between them, spattering Denny's left cheek with a thin layer of grit. Standing there, in the shadow of the pillar, he looked almost as stable to her, almost as strong as the cement. For a moment, she reconsidered. For a moment, she wondered what life would be like if she were to stay here and anchor herself to Jordan in the sea of uncertainty, make him her new family.

But no... Jordan had a family of his own, and a husband to think of. Someone had to stand up for her small family, and Denny was the only one left alive to do it. She drew near to Jordan and hugged him. He smelled like aftershave and tea tree oil.

"Thank you," she said, and for a moment, she remembered what it was like to matter to someone. In the anticipation of her long solitude, she basked in that rare feeling, until the screech of brakes from across the street broke her out of her reverie. Seaburn had emerged from the parking garage behind the wheel of a beat-up green sedan, after skidding to a halt in front of an unexpected traffic control bar. He pulled a sharp turn across three lanes of traffic and ground to a halt in front of Denny and Jordan.

Jordan let her go with a smile and a hair rumple.

"Since I can't convince you not to go, all I can do is beg you to come back in one piece. Without you, I lose the one person in the entire world who not only knows my work but gives a shit. True story, Dens," he said, with tears in his voice.

Denny gave him a reassuring smile that felt like it took every muscle in her face just to uphold for three seconds. She tossed her pack in the back seat, loaded Geoff in, then got in the passenger's side next to Seaburn. The car smelled like wet upholstery and old incense. She cracked a window and leaned out.

"Don't worry, I've got Geoff with me," she called as the sedan swerved away.

An uncomfortable, twitchy silence hung over the car as they pulled out onto the QEW, punctuated only by Geoff's panting. The dog kept laying down, then pacing, then laying down again, panting loudly. He reminded Denny of a little boy: Are we there yet? Are we there yet?

There was no doubt that the dog was feeding off Seaburn's energy, as well. Hunched over the steering wheel, he never stopped moving in some small way, twitching his brake foot or drumming on the steering wheel with his fingers. He also seemed to let out sighs at intervals, as if he were about to say something but thought better of it. They were barely on the highway five minutes before he reached into the glove compartment and pulled out a cigarette. Even with the windows open, Denny ended up bathed in the smell.

At least the day was turning out sunny… A perfect driving day, despite the constant mugginess. The air coming in the window was thick, but it was moving and that was a pleasure that most people treasured. As a kid, when there had been more cars, when they had run on gasoline and electricity, she had relished the wind on her face but taken it for granted. Then fuel had run out, and the government had disallowed the use of gasoline for anything but transitional work for the state, and electric and hydrogen fuel cell cars had become expensive. Now, the only people who had cars were real estate brokers, entrenched executives and managers, and, of course, drug dealers. It made for far less traffic on the highways, at least, but it also took a chunk out of highway policing and maintenance budgets. Over the past 20 years, the QEW had gotten bumpy, patchy, and just plain dodgy in places.

Still, despite the unexpected lumbar massage offered by the pavement and the nasty smells wafting from the driver's seat,

Denny found herself happy to be back on the road. It reminded her of the trips her family used to take to Hamilton and Oakville, to hike in the woods and feed the birds. Some of the same landmarks were there, despite the intervening years... The old hotel complex at Vineland, which once held a waterpark, a miniature village, and an antique shop, the clusters of vineyards along the escarpment tapering off into the subdivisions surrounding Hamilton.

As the city loomed up around them, all drip-stained cement and decaying balcony railings, Denny shifted in her seat, staring half at the glove compartment and half at the road ahead. Spray-painted on a gritty grey overpass in DayGlo orange letters were the words: *The Screamers Are Coming*. A crude drawing of Edvard Munch's scream face floated beside it. All around them, empty overpasses snaked over the landscape, remnants of a time and a culture lost to the tides and wind. Half of them were closed now that the government had no reason to maintain them but no real reason to tear them down until they started falling apart.

Seaburn slowed down as they approached a steep, hastily constructed earth berm, sided with sandbags that sprouted out of the original road. Reed beds closed in on either side of the highway, marking the edge of the deep pools where Lake Ontario had flooded over the original highway. The car's tires spun a little at the bottom of the hill where the ground was wettest.

"I hate this fuckin' thing," Seaburn muttered around the blackened stub of his latest cigarette. "Gives me nightmares. Just get me the fuck over it to the skyway. Rather fall from high up than drown in the mud. You better pray we don't get a washout after all this rain."

When they reached the top of the berm, it widened out to about three car-widths of gravel-strewn earth. As they chugged along, stones pinged off the underside of the car. Denny understood why Seaburn might feel a bit antsy. Water stretched out for kilometres on either side of them, flat, silver, and placid but for the reeds blowing in the breeze. On one side, rows of flooded-out cottages and a collapsing sound barrier stuck up out of the water, blocking most of the view of Toronto. On the other, long-abandoned chemical silos swam in Hamilton Bay, and behind them stood the remains of the steel company, a forest of smokestacks and rusty warehouse roofs. Denny also caught what might have been the tops and bumpers of unfortunate cars poking out of the water at intervals, but she deliberately blocked those from her mind.

Luckily, Denny's prayers were answered. The earth berm held and, with the exception of a few chunks of debris hitting the underside of the car with a rather alarming clang that elicited more swears from Seaburn, they managed to make their way around the long, shallow bend leading to the Burlington Skyway.

Since the original entry to the bridge was buried beneath the earth berm, ten feet underwater, the berm had been shaped in such a way that it deposited them halfway up the bridge. It was a much smoother transition than getting onto the berm had been, and Denny didn't notice much change to the bridge since she had ridden on it as a child. There wasn't even any vandalism up there, because it was too long and dangerous a walk.

Despite the better road conditions, Seaburn still puffed on his cigarette, then let it dangle from his shaking hand. Denny felt obligated to calm him down.

"So, we made it, and it looks like the road is improving..." she said.

Seaburn chuckled twice, a strangled sound.

"Yeah, once you get to Burlington you're okay. On that side, they had time to build dykes. Water level was lower over there, and they had the levees at the harbour. Say, you smoke weed?"

"Um, no..."

"Well, I'm going to pull over the minute we get out of cop country. I need a little herbal relaxation... I'm going nuts here."

Denny remembered what Jordan had said back at the bus station.

"Can't you wait until you get there?" she said. "Then you can do whatever you want, and I don't have to wait for you."

"No way, man... Once we get up there, I'm on business. And the RCMP are the only ones around right now, and they're, like, super cops or something. I've gotta pull over."

As Seaburn said the last sentence, so intent was he upon its import that his eyes had drifted completely away from the road and locked onto Denny. She grimaced, then pointed back at the road. Time to try another tactic. When Dad was having an anxiety episode, the best thing had always been to keep him talking. Maybe if she could hit on something that Seaburn felt passionate about, she could keep him distracted enough that he wouldn't have to pull over for a puff and leave her in the middle of nowhere while he wandered around high...or worse yet, fell asleep.

"So you really like to smoke weed, eh? How'd you get into it?"

Seaburn gave that little cough of a chuckle again.

"That is quite an interesting story...in fact, it kind of goes along with the time I puked in the punch at my middle school graduation, but my buddy Skankfish tells it better than I do... At least he did before he did too much meth and went all catatonic on me... Man, Skank used to be the best. But anyway, one day me and Skank were hanging out at the back of the schoolyard by the fence..."

As it turned out, it didn't take much to keep Seaburn talking if the topic was drugs, the details of various friends' arrests, or who punched who at what party. He seemed to want to talk in a long, nervous stream, and Denny let him, doing her best to look interested and prod him in whatever direction she thought the longest-winded anecdotes were going to come from.

They passed along a worn and ash-smelling road through Toronto, that great beast scarred with train tracks and long-neglected superhighways, and as the sun began to set, they worked their way further and further north. The trees along the road gradually became less black-spotted maples and more leaning pines. Denny had never been up this far. She had been shown pictures, of course, of Algonquin Park (who in the Humanities hadn't seen a Group of Seven painting, she wanted to know) but she had never imagined the massive granite cliffs, the winding roads through tiny hamlets, the rolling ground covered with pines on the high end, and wide marshes on the low. Some of the marshes closest to the road had been heavily sand-bagged to the point that Denny could see the reeds peering up over them, looming over the road, but somehow it didn't make her feel as uneasy. Back in Hamilton, it had felt as though nature was the attacker, flooding through human growth and development like an inexorable cancer, but here...here it felt like she and Seaburn were the intruders, and nature was just claiming its own.

She had learned some interesting facts about Seaburn through their ongoing dialogue, as well. He thought he hadn't told her some of these things, undoubtedly, but he was wired as hell and lacking a few brain cells to boot. Denny could fill in the blanks, even if someone of Seaburn's own milieu might have been left in the dark. Seaburn worked for someone dangerous back in the city. He had been managing a secret drug stockpile in Sudbury for that someone when the Screamers rose. Being generally of a nervous disposition, and being more dedicated to saving his own neck than a pile of drugs (not his worst inclination, honestly), Seaburn bailed on the stash and fled south with throngs of others looking for refuge. He tried to skip the border, but his boss caught him on his way through town and set thugs to watching him. After things calmed down a bit, and the refugees slowed down to a trickle, Seaburn's boss paid him a visit and set him an ultimatum: he could either find the stash and return it in full, or he could forget about entering the 416, 905, or 519 area codes again. And considering that Southern Ontario was one of the few places southerly enough not to have Screamers, Seaburn would have a very hard time travelling through thousands of miles of no man's land to get to another border crossing.

After piecing all of this together, Denny understood the shake of Seaburn's hand a bit better and even, much as she hoped against it, his desire for one final puff before reaching his destination. It was either find the stash and dodge the Mounties, or stay in the wilderness for as long as he managed to last. Not much of a choice. But, like Jordan had said, anyone coming up here would have to be a desperate man anyway.

Night settled over them just as they reached a stretch of pine tree-lined road that ran downhill through a long, trough-like plateau. At the far end of the long, shallow dip in the road, Denny watched the last vestige of light slip into the crease between the trees. She hadn't seen any cars pass them in two hours.

As far as she could tell from her limited knowledge of the area, they had just cleared MacTier by about an hour. The trough was about eight or nine kilometres long, and here, no buildings dotted the landscape, only power lines and the occasional leaning pine jutting up above its shorter brethren.

They had descended about a third of the way down the side of the hill when Denny felt the sensation she had been dreading: Seaburn was putting on the brakes. He had just finished a lengthy story about how his ex-girlfriend had lost her kids one day at the laundromat and then later found them on the roof of their apartment building, throwing gravel at one another (as a corollary to the story of how she had gotten her eye patch), but he had gone silent for a few seconds, and Denny had not thought of another question to ask him quick enough. As the car slowed down, he slapped the dashboard once, with finality. The light from the instrument display gave him a greenish rim light, making him look like a particularly smoked-out denizen of the netherworld.

"Sorry, babe, it's been nice talking to you for all these miles, but I've got to pull over and take a puff. Not to mention a piss."

Geoff stirred in the back seat. The change of pace had woken him up. He pushed his paws out in front of him and stretched.

It was Denny, however, that let out a little squeak, trying to think of something to say that would stop him. Much as she didn't want to think about how many times Seaburn had cleaned his flannel jacket in the past month, she placed her hand on his arm as he reached for the door handle.

"Seaburn, please, don't go. I'm scared. It's dark, and there could be God knows what animals out there. What happens if a bear gets you? Who drives the car then? What if you trip and fall into a ravine? I'm begging you…stay here."

Seaburn paused with his hand still on the door. He drew in a ragged breath then sighed it out.

"Look, I'm…I'm really sorry, but this is a bad situation for both of us. Just hold tight for a half an hour. Just a half hour."

"Half an hour in the dark. Give me your keys, at least, so I can have some light!"

"There's a touch light in the door pocket. I've only known you for half a day, and I've got ten thousand sunk into this car. I can't let you have these keys."

By this time, Denny was almost yelling.

"Oh, so you can drop them while you're stumbling around out there high? I don't want your shitty car, I want to keep your keys safe!"

In the back seat, Geoff was looking between them, his tail between his legs, trying to back up when there was nowhere to go.

Seaburn was up and out of the car so quickly that when he slammed the door, he almost got Denny's fingers along with it.

"Fuck it. I've tried being nice. I'll be back in half an hour, and if you're not here, fuck you and fuck your dog," he muttered. Before he melded with the shadows, Denny saw him fumble a lighter out of his pocket.

MEETING THE WILDLIFE

As the instruments dimmed, Denny looked for the touch light in the door pocket beside her. All of the contents were obscured by shadow, and no way was she going to go sticking her hand into random crevices in Seaburn's car. For all she knew, he had old needles stashed somewhere unexpected. Denny pulled an old tissue out of her pocket. Better that than nothing. She poked once or twice on what might have been a couple of old cigarette cartons, then hit on something round. She pulled the touch light out of the pocket, laid it on her lap, and pressed the button.

A fountain of pale blue, flickering light sprayed out of the touch light. At first, Denny held it to herself like a treasured pet, but she soon realized that with the light so close to her face, she couldn't see out of the windows at all. Once she set the touch light on the driver's seat, she found that her eyes adjusted just enough that she could see the pale outline of the sky against the tops of the trees.

Having figured out her living arrangements for the next half hour or so (at least she hoped it would only be that long), Denny's inner monologue started up. Geoff was asleep on the back seat, and so she wouldn't wake him if she could help it. Tense, alone, and a little bit chilly, she tried to force herself to sit back in the seat and forget where she was. All she ended up doing was leaning back on her right arm and making it fall asleep, and counting the minutes until Seaburn was due back.

It had been at least twenty minutes when Geoff raised his head and growled. Denny looked back at the dog, then squinted her eyes, trying to see more of what was outside. Geoff never growled at people...even people he didn't know. He only growled when there were animals outside.

Denny heard a loud crack coming from in front of them and across the road. Something big was trundling through the underbrush, breaking things in its way. Whatever Geoff was onto, it was big. Denny grabbed Geoff's collar and shushed him, but Geoff was locked onto whatever it was and no amount of petting or shaking was going to break him out of it. He barked, and Denny cringed.

All of a sudden, she remembered the touch light on the seat. Whatever was out there would see that first, if it wanted to come looking for Geoff. She smacked the touch light, then huddled in the dark, staring out the window for any new information.

Please don't let it be a bear, please don't let it be a bear, please don't let it be a mother bear of all things ran through her head like a neon news ticker. She remembered a story that her dad had been fond of telling, about her great-grandfather. Apparently, he had been on a tour of the Rockies one time, in a car with roll-up windows. While crossing through Banff, he had been forced to stop for a group of black bears crossing the road. One of the bears, smelling the sandwiches in the car, had decided that it wanted a taste of the food…and stuck its claws under the rubber sealing on the window and pulled it down with nothing but brute strength. If it hadn't been for the timely arrival of a park ranger, as Dad told it, old Great-Grandpa would have ended up as dessert.

Geoff was still growling. As Denny's eyes adjusted, she could see the road, a vaguely reflective charcoal grey strip, and the black blocks of trees on either side. Up above, the sky was a deep blue, not quite black yet, and speckled with stars.

A shape emerged onto the tarmac, and as it crossed the lighter portion of the road, Denny could see that it was a huge animal, with long, spindly legs, a droopy neck, and bumpy, scoop-shaped antlers. A bull moose. Denny let out a sigh of relief as a small cow with two calves peeked out of the bushes and crossed the road. Geoff barked again. The bull turned its head, then quickly ignored him. After the moose family had disappeared into the forest, Denny heard a long, hooting call, and then silence reigned once again. Geoff relaxed. After ten minutes, with the exception of the nervous dog stink that now filled the car, Denny would never have known he'd gotten upset in the first place.

By the time the moose had crossed the road, Denny figured it had been forty minutes or so since Seaburn had disappeared into the forest. She gazed at the mottled charcoal grey wall of the forest edge beside her, waiting to catch a washed-out glimpse of his flannel coat in the moonlight. After what must have been an hour, she blinked to clear the impression of the window and the trees out of her eyes and tried to think of something else to do.

Almost without realizing it, she fell into her old trick from the doctor's office. Whenever she felt both bored and nervous at the same time, she had developed the habit of attempting to recite familiar poetry in her head and trying to remember all of the stanzas perfectly. Some people, she knew, did the alphabet backwards in similar situations, but she had worked that trick up to light speed years ago, along with much of Yeats and most of the prologue to *The Canterbury Tales*. She started out with something from the Blake book Dad had given her. It was the last piece of literature she had read, and thus the most likely for her to remember.

> *Tyger Tyger, burning bright,*
> *In the forests of the night,*
> *What immortal hand or eye,*
> *Could frame thy fearful symmetry?*

Okay, that was the easy part, the part they always quoted in textbooks. Now what was the next part again? Something about "skies" and "Burn the fire of thine eyes." "In what far immortal skies?" No... "In what deeps and in the skies..." still no, but closer...

Denny had almost cobbled together half of the second stanza (In what distant deeps or skies/ Burnt the fire of thine eyes) when Seaburn slapped the hood, startling her out of her memorization game. He slung open the door and slipped down into the driver's seat, spine supple as new rubber.

"Better?" Denny asked flatly.

"You know it," he said, breathing heavily for a moment, then, "Did the bears get you? How about the boogey man?"

"I survived," she said.

They pulled into Sudbury about an hour after midnight. Except for the multi-lane highway leading into the city being eerily empty, and a few pieces of debris strewn here and there, things looked surprisingly normal. A rather grey little city, set on a lake, it had small, rolling hills of Canadian Shield rock dotted with white Cape Cod style houses, not unlike those in the older areas of St. Catharines. The trees here were lower, cut off by the shallow soil, but there were still lots of them. The only really remarkable thing about Sudbury at this point was the lack of people.

"I'll drop you and the dog off a block away from the arena," Seaburn said, his usual cigarette trailing smoke out of the window as they took the nearest exit off of the highway. "The RCMP have set up an outreach station there."

"Will anyone be up to talk to me? I don't want to hang around downtown all night."

"Oh, don't worry... they'll be up," Seaburn said with as knowing a look as he could muster.

After turning down a few empty streets, Seaburn pulled into the lot of the Sudbury Community Arena. A brick-faced building with tall windows, it was surrounded by all manner of vehicles: police cruisers, motorcycles, humvees, vans, most marked with the RCMP logo. True to Seaburn's word, the lights were on, and Denny could see people, both in and out of uniform, pacing the long foyer in the front of the building.

Seaburn fidgeted a little. Denny tried to figure out what would be appropriate to say to him (thanks? best wishes? it's been real?) when he popped the trunk and tilted his head toward her, eyebrows raised. Ash from his cigarette fell onto his jeans and left a smudge there.

"One more word of advice? Don't try to find me if you get in trouble."

"I'd better go before you start to look suspicious," Denny said, stepping out into the night air.

The minute the seal on the door opened, the sound assaulted Denny's ears. Wailing from all directions, as if the whole city was mourning...but there was no one around out here. Denny had seen that on the way in. Then, around the rim of the parking lot, she spied a pair of glowing green fright-mask eyes, lit like someone had just opened the Ark of the Covenant. Geoff, still stuck in the back of the car, turned in a circle twice, whining as he did so. From the direction of the road, a lit figure glided out from behind a house, burning orange. Denny could see its ribcage silhouetted in the light.

She reached into the trunk, yanking her backpack out so hard that she felt several muscles pull out of alignment, including the one running up the side of her neck. She ignored the pain, flung open the door to the back seat of Seaburn's car, and pulled Geoff out by his collar. The frightful sound of the Screamers' songs ripped into her the same way it had over the television, strumming her nerves like violin strings. It sounded as though they were harmonizing, but the harmony made their music sound all the harsher, like wind blowing through an old, broken saxophone.

In the end, she didn't even yell goodbye to Seaburn. Instead, she ran as fast as she could, dragging her backpack alongside her. Geoff pulled so hard on her hand toward the arena that eventually she let him go, lest she be pulled over, backpack and all. He reached the doors long before she did and stayed there, jumping and barking and circling, cheering Denny on to hurry up. She didn't look behind her. She couldn't look behind her, for if those fiends caught up, she would become a terrified, gibbering wreck, and whatever they did to the living souls they caught would surely happen to her.

Someone inside the building, drawn by Geoff's barking, threw open a door. It was a lady RCMP officer, and when she saw Denny she gestured with a muscular arm. Geoff slipped in between her legs.

"Hurry, quickly, don't draw them in! Don't look back!" she said, caught between speaking loudly for Denny's benefit and obviously not wanting the monsters to hear her. Chest heaving, heart pounding, Denny ran the last few steps to the door, bursting through into the bright light of the arena foyer with the female RCMP officer's arm around her for support.

"It's okay," said the officer. "It's all right. They don't come in here with the doors closed, and that's the way we're trying to keep it. What's your name, ma'am?"

"Denny... Felicia Dennigan."

"Denny will do fine," the officer said, leading her over to a worn table made of lacquered plywood with a bunch of papers stacked up on it. "Let's get you signed in."

"Signed in?"

"Yeah, you need to sign in to be able to access shelter services," she said, pulling out a moulded plastic chair the likes of which Denny had not seen since middle school. "I'll need you to write your full name and address, and your reason for coming to the shelter on this form here. The one underneath it is a sworn statement of your criminal record so that we know how to sort you once you get in. If you have no criminal record, check that option, but I'm instructed to warn you that lying about your record is a federal offence. When we process your background check, and we're pretty quick about that sort of thing here, you'll be fined ten thousand dollars if we find out that you wilfully neglected to disclose anything on the sheet. In the instance that you can't remember all of your charges, please let us know and do the best you can."

"I'm not a criminal," Denny said, pushing the forms back toward the officer. She had finished them while the officer was talking. Innocence made background checks really easy.

The officer shrugged. Now that Denny's heart had slowed down a bit, and she was surrounded by the familiar smell of...was that stadium hot dogs? she noticed that the woman sitting across from her was blonde and pretty, her highlighted hair tied up in a neat little bun. Her badge identified her as Officer Menken.

"Most people aren't criminals, but I have to ask. It got pretty lawless around here as people were clearing out of the city, and even though we know most of them won't come through here, we don't want people coming in to rob and take advantage of the refugees. Not a lot of walls on the arena floor," she said.

Denny noticed a gently curving row of windows running behind the officer. Behind them, she could see a peaked roof with a lot of conflicting rafters running across it, and row upon row of multi-coloured hockey and lacrosse banners, complete with that tacky gold fringe they always seem to have. Denny stood up just enough to see the arena floor. It was bare down to the cement and covered in bedrolls. On the side nearest them, there were only men. A stretched-canvas divider in the centre of the floor guarded by RCMP implied to Denny that there were women and children on the other side.

"There's not a lot of ice on the arena floor right now, either," she said. "Is this all that's left of the people of Sudbury?"

"No," said Officer Menken. "We have a few other shelters...but there aren't many people left, that's for sure. We're down to an estimated ten thousand from a previous population of over a hundred and fifty thousand. With most of the industry and services in town shut down, and the Screamers driving people out of their homes, most people have to come here in order to stay."

Officer Menken picked up the papers that Denny had filled out. As she read, she said, "So, you're from the Golden Horseshoe. Me too. You coming up here for the reward money?"

"No."

"Looking for a family member?"

"Nobody living."

Officer Menken drew in her lips and lowered her eyes.

"Ah," she said. "I can get someone to direct you to the coroner's records, if you like. They're not complete, but they go up to about halfway through the crisis, when the coroner... Well, that

93

was a messy business. Jumped off the roof of the municipal building. Said the Screamers had him surrounded at night, wouldn't leave him alone. At the end, he wouldn't even enter his own office. He was convinced that something was just going to reach out of the morgue and..." Officer Menken mimed a raking grab, like a zombie coming out of the earth in an old horror movie. Oh Jordan, thought Denny, you would have been in your element here.

Well, she would just have to summon as much of the knowledge that Jordan had instilled in her over a thousand lunch hours and departmental movie nights as she could... Hopefully the master had trained her well.

But this wasn't a movie. That coroner had been a real person, and whatever those things were lurking outside the arena, whatever poor Dad had turned into had driven him mad, possibly killed him. Who knows if they had mind control? Or some sort of pheromone, like in a horrible Mark Wahlberg movie she had seen once... If the dead could rise and walk, anything was possible.

"I don't think I need medical records," she said, "but I'd like to know everything that I can about the Screamers."

Officer Menken's expression darkened. "Just who are you looking for? Those things aren't to be trifled with...I hope you know that."

Denny looked the officer up and down. She looked pretty perfect, very put together...but she was from Niagara... Maybe she'd get it. And she was a police officer. She might have seen him sometime in all the chaos. She might even have seen the same thing that Denny saw on TV.

It was still like pulling an anvil out of deep mud to dredge the story out of her mind, to a stranger. She sighed.

"My dad was homeless. He disappeared up here sometime between one and six months ago. I saw him on the Foster Towers News. He was a Screamer."

"Is your dog trained?" asked Officer Menken.

Naturally, this was not the response that Denny was expecting, but after a pause, she said, "More or less."

"Then come with me. Now that you're officially checked in, there's someone you need to talk to."

RED ROSE JENNINGS

Denny followed Officer Menken down the length of the long foyer at the front of the arena, purposely avoiding the darkness that stretched beyond the glass on her right. She noticed others, officers and shelter patrons in grubby church bin clothing, doing the same. A little girl on the way to the bathroom tried to press her nose against the glass. Her mother yanked her away hard enough to dislocate a shoulder. This place seemed to be a place that people shuffled through, unwilling to stay for long.

Officer Menken opened a service door and led her down a set of stairs lined with rubber to protect the floor from ice skates. From there they passed through a boiler room with a washer and dryer in it, where about thirty people waited in line with armfuls of laundry. Two appliances for thousands of people... No wonder they were up all night waiting. Then again, nobody here really seemed to be sleeping well.

After the boiler room came a long hallway with locker rooms. More lines stretched out of these, people waiting to use the showers and washrooms. At the end of the hallway, they turned left and entered the arena proper, through a stand of bleachers. Officer Menken opened one of the several scuff-scarred doors in the wall leading to the rink. Denny stepped through. Menken placed the same hand on Denny's shoulder that she had done upon her arrival, but this time it was more the hand of a consoling relative at a funeral than of an official herding shell-shocked survivors from place to place. She grabbed a bedroll in her other hand from a rack along the wall as they made their way to the far corner of the rink.

Denny looked around her night's accommodations, thinking how similar this place was to Burgoyne Arena in St. Catharines, where she and her friends had gone to amateur hockey and lacrosse games in their teens, to eat crappy food, ogle the boys, and cheer on the fights. Somehow, even without the rink filled, the place still managed to smell like ice, nachos, and old sports equipment.

Most of the arena floor was taken up with other sleeping bags, but Officer Menken directed her over to an empty spot. Beside where she would be sleeping sat a girl in a white shift, who had her back to them. She had thick, dark hair with a light halo of flyaway fluff. When she turned around to look at them, Denny placed her in her early to mid-teens. She had a common sort of face, with a rounded nose, small, close-set eyes and thin lips: the kind of girl you'd expect to work the night shift with at Tim Hortons or the Walmart Christmas sales. She had seen things. Even without a wrinkle on her olive skin, she had a hard-bitten look about her.

"Denny, this is Violet Jennings," said Officer Menken. "I think you two should have a talk before tucking in for the night. Now, I've got to get back to the intake booth. If you need anything, talk to one of the officers along the wall and they'll do what they can."

Denny thanked her, then started unrolling her bedroll. She had been allotted just enough space for her bed to fit between Violet and an old lady who was snoring deeply.

Violet spoke first, as Denny had been prepared to let her do.

"So, what kind of a name is Denny? You a dude?"

Denny fluffed up her pillow and avoided eye contact. She had worked enough crap jobs to know how this went.

"What kind of a name is Violet? You a house plant?"

"No, my mom liked flower names. Good thing she only had girls...if I'd had a brother, she might've named him Juniper. I know she was planning on it, and it's only fifty-fifty Aunt Norrie would have talked her out of it."

When Violet talked about her family, she looked off into the distance. It was like she was telling the story only for herself, embroidering little flowery medallions in the scrapbook of her mind. She smiled a little while she talked, and not the jaded smile Denny was expecting. She looked at Denny as if she wanted an excuse to go on, to dwell on happy memories, but Denny couldn't think of anything to ask her but the one question that she suspected Violet had been subjected to many times.

"So where's your mom and your aunt now?" she asked.

Violet smoothed her hair with both hands, but it came back just as flyaway as ever.

"That's a long story, but I know that's why Menken sent you to me. It makes me sad that nobody ever wants to talk about Mum's flowers. She did paintings, you know, awful flat things that I always made fun of her for, but she put them up all over. Not because she thought they were good, but because they reminded her of us. She was always really into all that Celtic nature stuff... She called us her flowers. Like we'd grown out of her life and made it beautiful."

Violet's eyes welled up for a moment, but she rubbed the tears away quickly with the sleeve of her night dress. When her arm lowered again, that hard look had returned to her eyes.

"Your mother sounds like a really caring person..." said Denny, unable to help but feel some of Violet's emotion.

"She was," the girl replied, "until the night she killed my aunt and uncle."

"She what?"

Violet waved a hand. "Like I said, it's a long story. Finish up with your bedroll, get comfortable, and then I'll tell you."

Denny felt a little uncomfortable sitting in her sleeping bag listening to Violet tell her story, but the girl insisted. Still, it was a little too much like a ghost story at a sleepover for her taste. Those always gave her the creeps, even when she *knew* they weren't real. At least all the lights were on in the arena still.

"When I was eight," she began, "my older sister disappeared. Rose was twelve, and we did everything together. Except for that one day. I was kept behind at school because I hadn't done my math homework, and my teacher wanted to go through it with me in detention. Rose decided to walk home by herself, and nobody stopped her. Teachers tend to think that twelve is kind of the cutoff age for adult involvement, you know? They can babysit, they can walk home by themselves. At least that's the logic.

"Anyway, Rose was last seen by a few friends heading in the other direction about five minutes after she left school. Somewhere between there and home, she disappeared. They put out an Amber alert, scoured the neighbourhoods, plastered it up all over the national news...but they never found her. Everybody at my school felt guilty. If one of us had stuck with her, or maybe if we could remember some key detail of the days leading up to her kidnapping...but we were just kids. And none of us had really seen anything.

"My mom wasn't the same for a long time after that. She would just sit at the window all day and break into crying fits every night. She didn't sleep much, and she didn't eat much. She stopped doing her paintings for a few years. Dad's a deadbeat, living in Australia now, I think, so we knew he wouldn't be much help. The only one who offered to do anything for us was Uncle Maurice and Aunt Norrie. 'Come and live with us,' they said, 'and we'll help you take care of Violet. Just pay us rent and we'll take care of the rest, so you can recover.' It was the last chance we had, so we took it. Mom needed a change of scenery and more good company. We moved in with them just over two years ago.

"For a year and a half, it seemed to be working. Mom was perking up again, sleeping and eating better, and she'd even started to do her paintings. We hung out a lot together, and I stopped feeling like I was just a replacement for Rose. I think she started to be really thankful that she had me, and that I *was* me."

"So what changed?"

"The Screamers came. They ruined everything. It was probably around three in the morning when it started...that time of night when you wake up and feel like there's something watching you from the blackness in the hall. It was the month when they started sandbagging, too, when the rain started getting really heavy and people started losing property if they were near the water.

"I woke up in a cold sweat, my heart pounding. I felt like I couldn't breathe, like I couldn't even move or anything. At first, I didn't know why. It looked like any other night. My curtains were blowing in the breeze, and I could hear the rain on the sidewalk outside my window. My nightlight had gone out, though. That was the first thing I noticed that was different.

"The voice started out like my mother's, but younger, like she was in the bathroom humming a lullaby. It had that echo to it. I listened, trying to calm down, trying to remember that she was here with me. And that's when the song changed."

"Do they all sound the same?"

"No. They're all different, but this one cut me more than anything else ever could. Picture the saddest, slowest love song you've ever heard, and then imagine that every few bars, it rises into a screech so terrible that it's like someone getting their eyes cut out. I don't know how, but all at the same time it managed to be mournful and angry and even a little bit proud. Don't tell me how I know, I just felt it."

"I felt it too," Denny said, feeling a little bit of half-healed ache spread within her at the recollection of Dad's song.

"I couldn't understand any of the words, but I knew they *were* words, too, and that somebody, somewhere could understand them. It wasn't exactly like listening to a foreign language…more like listening to somebody talk while you're still asleep. You form your own words, in your head, but you know it's not what you're really hearing, if you could just wake up.

"I wanted to stay in bed. I wanted to stay there, pull the covers over my head and try to wake up from whatever horrible dream I was having. I swore to God in that moment I would never try pot again… I'd done it at Christie's party that night, and I thought then that it had been laced with something, acid maybe, and I was having a serious freak-out. Then Mom came stumbling down the hall in her nightgown asking where that sound was coming from. She was calling for me, and as much as I hated to leave my bed, I was all she had.

I tiptoed out into the hallway, where I saw Mom heading for the stairs. She was holding the steak knife she always kept under her pillow, just in case. Once you live at Jane and Finch for a while, like she had, I guess you never quite got out of the habit. At least, that's what I thought at the time. She asked me if it was intruders. I said no, at least I thought not. She asked me if someone was maybe blasting 'the young people's music.' I said hell no. Even the death metal bands of old would have heard this voice and ran for the hills.

"Somehow we ended up on the patio. I think it was because one of us saw the light and decided to follow it. It was a dark red light… Yeah, dark, and still a sort of light, like a creepier version of blacklight. It was the colour of a 60-watt bulb being shone through a bloody tank of water. It rippled like water, too, up over the patio furniture, onto the back of the house. The whole backyard was filled with rays of that light, flowing through the air like strobe lights without a source.

"The song, which had kept going, got much louder. Something moved, in the bushes, at the back of the yard, and lurched out into

103

the open. Even in the darkness, I could see that it was wearing sort of a cape…but by the sight and the smell of it, I knew the cape was blood. Then I saw the face…and I knew that it was Rose. It had her nose, her eyes (only one eye socket was left covered with skin but that was enough), and a chunk of her hair. Our nose, our eyes, our hair. She was the one singing. And it only got more horrible when she saw us. Her blood cape flew up around her, and streams of it came out of her… Well, you're a girl, you know. Only her…parts weren't there anymore…just bits of bone and a huge hole in her stomach. I was afraid she was going to touch me, so I crouched down on the ground and started pushing myself away from her.

"My mother had tears in her eyes when I looked at her. She put the knife on the patio table and reached out her hands like one of those Jesus freaks on TV. She kept calling out, 'What is it, baby? I love you! Rose!' …those three things over and over, in no particular order. Eventually, the screams got too loud for me to hear much of what Mom was saying. They bit into my ears, and I felt like something was squeezing my heart until I must have passed out, because when I woke up, Rose was gone. I still smelled blood though. Mom was covered in it, and Uncle Maurice and Aunt Norrie were lying there, on the patio stones, their guts spilled all over. She wouldn't look at me, only at them and sometimes at the fence by the bushes. I grabbed her face and made her look at me. I screamed at her to tell me what happened, to tell me what she did and why. All I wanted was for her to tell me why. But all she would keep repeating, with her eyes blank as a static TV screen, was 'You're safe now, honey, you're safe.'"

The bitter look in Violet's eyes had brimmed over long ago into tears.

"She sacrificed my aunt and uncle to keep that…thing that my sister had become from haunting me for the rest of my life. Stay away from them…they're demons. They'll snap your mind like a twig and make you kill the things that you love most to survive."

Denny had begun petting Geoff while Violet was telling her story. He had gotten concerned by all the sadness in the room and cuddled up to her, butt first, as was his way. Violet broke down crying then, and when she did, Geoff flopped across the divide between their two sleeping bags and rolled over a bit, tongue lolling out. Violet reached down and stroked his soft fur.

"He's a good dog," she said.

"He always works for me when I'm sad," said Denny. "Something about that goofy grin, I think. And the way he tries to get in your good books by sitting on you."

Violet smiled, although Denny didn't see much happiness in the gesture. Just a willingness to be friends. Geoff sidled his rear end up to Violet, and the "canine mutiny" was complete.

"You can sleep there with him if you like," said Denny. "He doesn't roll around much."

"It's okay, I don't sleep at night anymore. I'm not sure I can. You sleep, and I'll make sure he doesn't wander off. We can switch in the morning," said Violet, leaning down affectionately toward Geoff's face, which was licking the air as she got closer. He had rolled upside down now, the silly sod, and was wiggling with the scratches. Who could look at that face and not feel better? Not even Violet was immune.

Denny lay down in her sleeping bag and covered her head. Once there, she lay there, pretending to sleep for a very long time. She had learned long ago, with her mother, that you don't contradict people when they're in pain, but there were so many more questions that she wanted to ask Violet. She believed the girl had seen everything she claimed to have seen…if there was no evidence that what she said was true, then why would Officer Menken rely on her testimony? But still, something just wasn't ringing true. If the Screamer formerly known as Rose had wanted Violet's mother to kill the most important things in her life, why wouldn't she have killed Violet, too? No, Denny knew what years of living in a dead sibling's shadow felt like and the kind of things it caused you to do, without even realizing it. One of those things was to de-value your worth to your family, to erode your faith in their love for you in little ways, every day, until you were utterly convinced that you were not important to them, and that you could never measure up to what your sister would have been.

Violet's mother had heard something that night from Rose...that much was undoubtedly true. But had it really forced her to kill the most important people in her life, and caused a psychotic break just with its powers alone? Denny doubted it. Denny thought that perhaps, just perhaps, Violet should suspect her late aunt and uncle as authors to her mother's madness, rather than Red Rose. But these were things that she could never say...not to a casual acquaintance and probably not even to a lifelong friend. If she ever figured out how to free her dad, though... If she ever broke the code shrouding the Screamers' shrieks and jabbering, she would come back here. She would find that yard, and she would try to give Violet some peace.

Denny finally fell asleep while listening to Geoff's snores. When he was contented in this strange place, it almost felt unnatural for her not to be. She drifted off into a long, dark hallway, and there she heard another song calling her away.

WILD WEST, WITHOUT THE WEST

When Denny woke up, around noon the next day, Geoff was warming her legs. She packed up her bedroll quietly so as not to disturb Violet, who had fallen asleep sometime after the sun rose. As much as she appreciated the safe place to stay, she had decided not to impinge on RCMP hospitality for another night. She had a lot of travelling to do if she was going to make her goal by sunset.

Part of the night she had spent sleeping fitfully on the cement floor of the arena, unable to find a position that didn't either squash her chest or cramp her shoulders. The other part, some three or four hours spaced out over the course of the night in which she temporarily despaired of sleeping, she had spent deep in thought.

As much as she respected Violet and what she had been through, she just couldn't bring herself to believe that the girl's interpretation of events was the correct one. If only her mother had been somewhere closer, and if only she could convey what had happened to her, what she heard…but an incomplete story was better than no story at all, and so Denny decided to learn what she could from Violet's story and move on to hear other opinions. Inarguably, the Screamers were dangerous. Undoubtedly, they played on people's emotions. But why they did this, and whether that motivation was purely sinister, was anybody's guess. Clearly, they were taking the forms of real people. At least, in a large number of stories, the people affected by the Screamers seemed to recognize them as someone they used to know. But how sure could you be about the floating pieces of a corpse? Perhaps they *were* just manipulating people, but if so, to what end? Denny had only dabbled in writing a tiny bit, in early undergrad, but she still remembered one of the key things she had learned about antagonists: nobody is evil for the sake of evil. Not even re-animated puppets of some strange supernatural force.

She had a lot of questions, and overnight she had also decided that she wouldn't find answers here. The people with answers would be the people on the front lines, the people at the camp of the Foster Towers Media Corp. They'd been documenting the Screamers all along... they'd have first-hand knowledge of their behaviours, the types of Screamers that there were, and maybe, just maybe, some insight into what they might be saying. Jordan had made her watch this really old movie, *Ghostbusters*, one time when they'd been doing a mark-a-thon in the TA lounge. It was silly, but she almost pictured the front-line people working on the problem to be a bit like that...off-the-cuff, brilliant without being arrogant, and just spontaneous enough to survive in a world where it seemed like anything could happen from moment to moment. Of course, since no one had found a solution to the Screamer problem yet, they couldn't know everything, but surely they knew more than Violet Jennings and the superstitious people flitting around the arena, afraid to go to sleep. And then, there was that fleeting chance that she could find the cameraman who shot that video of her dad and that he would remember Dad and where to find him.

It was with this determination in mind that she took her bedroll, backpack, and Geoff and made her way back to the check-in desk. She wasn't sure who would be there, but whomever it was would be enough to say goodbye to and maybe get some directions. To her surprise, when she pushed open the door to the main atrium and rounded the hallway to the admittance desk, Officer Menken was still there, a little more wilted than before but awake and alert.

"I thought the shifts would have changed by now."

"That'd be nice, but no. We work 48-hour shifts here, so the off-shift can get some sleep in the daytime. Are you going already?" asked Menken when Denny handed her the bedroll.

"I was only passing through," Denny replied, "but thank you for sheltering me. I don't know what I would have done sleeping outside."

"Well, you'd better get used to it where you're going," Officer Menken said as she pushed the bedroll under the table. When she came back up, there was a contemptuous curve to her lips.

Denny instantly resented her attitude. Why would no one here just *help* her?

"I don't have a lot of choice. He's my dad. He's all I have. I have to do *something*."

Officer Menken placed a tired hand on her forehead.

"Did you listen to anything Violet told you? Usually she turns people right around and sends them home."

"I listened, but I'm not convinced that everything she believes really happened. I don't think she's lying about what she saw...I just have a hard time believing that the Screamer *made* her mother do it."

Officer Menken gave a little grunt. Her expression was similar to her mother's when Denny was pressing a particularly undesirable point.

"Go home, Denny. Go now while you still have the chance. You have no idea what we're dealing with here. You didn't see what happened when the Screamers rose, the chaos and confusion. We couldn't rein it in for weeks, and I've seen mass protests with tens of thousands of people in them mopped up in a few days. Go home and enjoy what's left of your life...because I'm not sure we're going to be able to stop this from spreading. It's already moved further south in the past few months, to places ten kilometres down the road. The Screamers will reach St. Catharines, and when they do, your life will be pulled out from under you just like all of these poor people."

"And so your solution is to just turn tail and run, and hide, and wait for this plague to catch up with me? What kind of solution is that? I thought the government was paying people to come up with something."

"*We don't have a solution,*" Menken said, the power behind her voice speaking volumes about her frustration at being put in this situation. "The reward programs, and the news shows, and the big, bad old perimeter, and all that other lovely bullshit is just something the government cooked up to make people in Toronto and Ottawa happy and calm. Because as we all know, the basis of Canadian government is, at its core, to keep the stuffed shirts in Toronto and Ottawa happy and calm. These things don't follow our laws...making a police perimeter to keep them in is like declaring a no peeing section in the pool for Christ's sake! It's a wild west up here and you are one, vulnerable girl. If you go past the perimeter, there's nothing that I, or anybody that works with me, can do for you if you're raped, if you're killed, if your food all gets stolen, if somebody eats that sweet little mutt of yours (and it's been done, believe me)... Think for a second, please!"

Denny looked down at Geoff. Geoff kissed her hand and leaned into her, as he always did. Geoff wouldn't give up on her, or Dad, and neither would she. For all she knew, Geoff had already risked a lot to even get to her. She faced Officer Menken, making sure to keep any anger out of her voice, but replacing it with a whole lot of determination.

"I do think, Officer Menken. Every day I think about my dad. I think about how lonely his life was… I often wonder how he died, and if he was alone then, too. I think about the night I saw the monster that he had become, and how I heard his suffering. I can't let him suffer anymore. He's had enough sadness in his life… I have to put him to rest! Yeah, I'm a little crazy… I'm Sean Dennigan's daughter, and nobody that knew him will ever say he had all his bricks in a row…but I could really use some help right now, and I'm going to try and do this, no matter how many people refuse me help. Please… don't you know anyone who could at least help me to get to the Foster Towers Media camp safely? If you're concerned about me, you can at least help me make it that far."

"I know somebody who works security on the perimeter, doing permissions for the Foster Towers supply trucks. Every week, a food truck goes past the perimeter and up to the camp by a bunch of old logging roads. If I can't persuade you to turn around, your best bet is on that truck. Offer to watch the load in the back and you'll be set. You'll have to wait another night, though…the food truck only goes up on Thursdays."

"Thanks, Officer. If that's the case, I can stay another night. The food is free, and I think Violet will want some more time with Geoff."

The truck jostled to a halt, its frame leaning one way, then the other as though it was navigating some giant mud ruts. After a few moments, the truck driver slid half of the back doors open, letting in a shaft of cold, overcast light.

"Ah, you're both still alive in there. I heard the dog sliding around and I was a little worried."

Denny tilted her head, unable to do much else considering that her right hand was holding Geoff, perched carefully, and quite uncomfortably, on her lap. His back legs had been digging into her knee for hours, but letting him go would drop him on the slippery floor on his side. So, he stayed, and Denny's leg fell so far asleep that she wasn't sure she had toes anymore. Her other arm was straight out, at an angle from her body, and as taut as a guy wire. One of the larger boxes beside her (evidently filled with a rare species of edible bricks) had started to topple when its downstairs neighbour developed a crinkled corner and threatened to fall over on her at the next bump.

It had been an interesting ride. Three hours in an airless tin box, clunking and banging along what had to be some of the worst roads in the history of the world. She had half-fancied that the driver was taking them on a shortcut through the bottom of a quarry. At one point, the truck had lurched over to one side and stayed that way for a couple of kilometres. More frequently, they had just gotten on a patch of road that was bumpier than a highway through a minefield. During those periods, Denny had found herself doing the posting trot while sitting on her bench, trying to deflect as much damage to her tailbone as possible.

The quarters had been no great shakes either, not that she had had any expectations on that account. The inside of the freight compartment was small for a truck, and square, lined on one side with metal racks stacked with crates of fruit and vegetables, instant eggs in cartons, frozen items in cold packs, and water bottles. The other side had a metal shelf, about the width and height of a bench, on which was stacked boxes of dry goods. When she got into the truck, the driver had simply skooched over a stack of toilet paper and paper towels and whatever was in the boxes of edible bricks to make a seat for her. There was no room for Geoff to lay down, unless you counted a mover's pad hung up on the wall and that was stuck behind the stacks and stacks of boxes. It was also quite chilly in there, on account of the food. Luckily, Denny had been warned and wore a sweatshirt. The stagnant air inside the compartment smelled of old vegetables and egg whites.

Once the van had started up, Denny held onto her seat for dear life. The paper towels fell over on her almost instantly, but she stood up and set them to rights, the bumps in the road jostling through her whole body. This wouldn't be the last time they would fall down throughout the trip, nor would the thousandth be the last time.

She sat down just as the truck had hit its first corner. She was okay, but Geoff slid and scrabbled on the textured aluminum flooring, unable to find any traction, even with his nails. On the next turn, he ran into the shelving, causing a resounding wobble to go through the whole thing that made Denny's heart stop for a moment, thinking it was going to topple over on him. She got up, helped him over to her seat, and kept a hold on him for the rest of the ride.

During the ride, she had also gone over her parting with Violet many a time. The girl had pleaded with her not to go, but Denny had forced herself to calmly reassure Violet that she would be all right. Even if she wasn't going to be all right, what would be the point of telling her? Violet had lost enough friends and family members. She didn't need to get attached to Denny too. That was why Denny didn't tell her the promise that was on her heart, that she would solve the mystery and come back and talk to Rose for her. Because if she failed, it would just be another failure heaped on Violet. And so, as the wordless promise had slipped by, unnoticed, she had left Sudbury, possibly forever.

With the grey sun streaming into the cab, and the driver climbing up inside to inspect the shipment, Denny pushed Geoff down off of her lap, stood up, and stretched as well as she could with her arm still holding up the box of edible bricks. She swayed a bit on her feet at the inevitable head rush, and after that…she noticed that her right leg was invisible. Or, at least, it was acting like it wasn't there for a moment. From the hip down to her toes, she was numb, and her leg just didn't want to hold up any weight. Fair enough. It had held up Geoff's weight for most of the trip. The only real problem was keeping her balance while still holding on to the box stack.

"Here, let me get them from you," the driver said, rushing to take over for her. He was a plain, oval-faced man, a little portly, and completely clean-shaven, including his head. He wore a black trucker's cap with the mesh in back, a leaf-stained apron, and an old jeans and button-down shirt combo. He lifted the brick box, knees bent, and set it down in the corner behind the food racks for a moment.

While the driver bustled around the back, Denny took a few minutes to let her leg regain its circulation. She tested her foot every few minutes, and when it burst into tingly, rush-y life again, she forced herself to walk around, making little "ah" and "ooh" faces periodically as she did. Finally, when her leg was back, a bit wobbly but definitely acknowledging its own existence, Denny started helping the driver unload the truck. There were only so many things she could carry, but the driver let her have them, and she gladly took an end on some of the pallets.

As they unloaded box after box, Denny used her time outside of the truck to scope out the encampment. She had expected to find them on the crest of some hill somewhere, tents pegged into the narrow bands of soil between the solid domes of the shield rock. Instead, the first thing she heard was a waterfall. As she walked around the truck, she looked back, to see where they had come down a dirt road, little more than two mud ruts in the ground, that at some point had been blasted out of a cliff face. On their side of the river was a gorge wall a hundred feet high, made of earth, with granite bulges sticking out of it at intervals, and various and assorted plants clinging to its sides. On the other, pine forest, as thick as Habitant Pea Soup straight from the can, stretched as far along the shore as she could see. Around a curve in the river, about a half-kilometre away, a tall waterfall and rapids flowed over a high precipice.

What she hadn't been expecting were the buildings. They had belonged to a hydro-electric dam once, but the part that held back the water had long since been pulled down, probably as a cost-cutting measure. The outbuildings, however, lingered on. Denny had never seen anything like them in all her life. Around the bend in the river, the rocky cliff face rounded out somewhat, forming a horseshoe-shaped depression likely carved long ago by erosion. The cliff wall there sloped up at perhaps a sixty or seventy-degree angle—not enough to allow people to easily climb up, but certainly enough to build on, for the ingenious architect.

There, on the sloping cliff before her, sat the strangest jumble of buildings that Denny had ever seen. At the bottom was a mausoleum-like structure of grey limestone, not unlike the Sir Adam Beck plant at Niagara Falls that she had seen on many a school trip in her youth. It had a neo-classical facade with columns, giant, seamless bricks, and long, yellow-tinted ripple glass windows with heavy metal grating imposed over them. Built directly on top of that was a long, forlorn-looking office building type structure, with vertically ribbed white siding streaked with rust in most of the visible places. It looked as though someone had taken a trailer office, magnified it twenty times, and placed it on top of another building. Further down the river, where the limestone building ended, the office trailer extended down and elongated the whole complex. Yet further up the hillside, a confused jumble of tanks, rusting catwalks, and corrugated tin buildings led to a carved stair that surmounted the top of the cliff. The whole thing struck Denny as though a giant bad idea had struck an otherwise stately historical building sometime in the nineteen-sixties.

Denny set down a box of apples, then went back for a couple of bags of power bars that had been left at the back of the truck.

"That's the last of it," the driver said, swinging back up into the cab. "You're on your own from here. I told them that you're here to stay awhile, and they said it'd be fine. I didn't make any introductions, though. I'll leave you to do that yourself."

With that, her last link to the world she had left drove back up the shelf cut into the cliff and disappeared over the top of the hill. Only the sound of his engine revving and his shocks clunking lingered as evidence he had ever been there.

When Denny came back to the delivery pile with the power bars, a group of young men were hovering around the crates, picking out the choicer bits for themselves. They chuckled and jostled one another.

"Hey, Sarafian, quit hogging all the Cheerios. We *all* need the essential vitamins and minerals that are part of a nutritious breakfast, *thank you*."

"Aw, fuck you, Georgie, who's hoarding all the Tang?"

"Yeah, and who else really wants Tang?"

One of them, the eldest looking, who Denny estimated was probably close to thirty, if not beyond already, looked her up and down and up again. Denny watched him out of the corner of her eye, as he "appreciated" her breasts. Oh boy. One to avoid. Why did they always come out when the company was limited? She stood up and looked him in the eye, forcing him to do the same for her or risk her "figuring out" what he had been up to. God, these types were stupid. Any woman with half a brain who had developed big tits for more than a year could just feel guys' eyes on her the minute he started acting creepy. Call it woman's intuition…it was certainly more real than that motherly crap they peddled as women's intuition. Or you could just as easily call it rape-dar. Sadly, Denny had been forced to develop her senses early, as she had developed early.

"Felicia Dennigan," she said, pushing her stiff hand toward him in the most brusque, business-like way possible.

"Georgie Foster," he said, pasting a big oozing grin on his face that he obviously thought was charming. "Producer for the Foster Towers Media Corp. Don't tell me you've come all this way just to get in as a weather girl?"

Really? Wow. Denny forced herself to be polite. For Dad. She needed to know what this guy knew, especially if he was the producer. Then she could move on. Quickly. For a moment before she replied, she checked him out as well, briefly, although certainly not with the ardour that he had bestowed upon her. He was a taller man, around six three or so, with the babyface and ruddy brown crew cut of the perpetual undergraduate. The others with him wore various combinations of tracksuits and hiking clothes, but not Georgie. No, he wore a wrinkled, yet still expensive-looking pastel pink dress shirt and designer jeans, the kind that are designed to look like dress pants, even though everybody in the free world knows they're not, and never will be, dress pants. Sort of the Eliza Doolittle of pants, if you will. All in all, Denny thought he looked like a self-important douchebag.

Through all of this, Geoff had been sniffing around the river's edge. He gravitated a bit more toward them now, keeping his eyes on the men.

"I'm not from the media. I'm looking for my father. He passed away recently, and the last known footage of him comes from one of your cameras. I just need some information on where you were when you took that video and what information you have on the Screamers that might help me, and then Geoff and I will be on our way."

"Geoff...that's a cute name for a dog. You name him that?"

Argh. Just...argh.

"No, my dad named him."

You know, my missing dad? Denny thought, before continuing, "Geoff showed up at my house without Dad one day, and that's when I knew something was wrong."

"Wow...that's just like that movie... *Homeward Bound? The Incredible Journey?* I used to watch that thing over and over as a kid! What an amazing dog, to be able to find his way home like that."

"He was thrown out of a car, actually. But yeah, that was a pretty good movie."

"Well, *Felicia*," he said as though her name was a secret she had just let him in on, "you're welcome to stay here and talk to my people as long as you like, but I just need you to keep in mind that they are bound by a confidentiality contract...there are some things that we've done and taped up here that we're just not allowed to talk about to the public."

Denny wondered what those things might be, but her mind just wandered to Scumbag McGee over there making a sex tape, and so she dropped it for the moment. Georgie continued.

"So, find out what you can, and don't dwell on what you can't. Most of our confidential information probably doesn't concern you anyway."

Denny wished that she could talk to somebody else. Anybody else. The pudgy guy with the long hair in a ponytail or the olive-skinned guy with the big nose that Georgie had called Sarafian... Anybody but this creepy, overgrown middle-schooler who somehow managed to get a job as a producer... Oh no... Foster? *Georgie* Foster? Denny remembered where she had heard that name before. The Fosters owned the Foster Towers Media Network, and Georgie was the heir to the throne. According to the rival networks (although admittedly they had a stake in making the Fosters look bad) Georgie was a notorious playboy, a college dropout, and a frequently sighted guest at all of the latest night clubs, where he was usually plastered and clinging to a large pile of equally plastered women. He also frequently got arrested, in a highly publicized manner, for dangerous driving (also while plastered). No wonder he had expected her to be impressed with him... Oh well, tough nuts. She still thought he was a pus-dripping scumbag.

Georgie put his arm around her, touching the small of her back in a way that he no doubt felt was erotic. Denny pulled away under the pretense of fixing Geoff's collar, hoping he would take the hint. Luckily, this time, he played ball.

"C'mon, boys," he said. "We didn't come all the way down here to sit pretty for the lady. Let's haul these groceries back up to camp. Felicia, you follow us, and we'll get you set up in a tent just as soon as everything's put away."

He had called her Felicia three times now. As much as she itched to correct him, she felt like giving Georgie her nickname at this stage in the game would be like giving her real name to the fairies...a license for more mischief. Besides, it might make him think she trusted him. No dice there. She strapped on her backpack, which until now had been sitting with the other supplies, picked up the power bars that she had only recently stowed on the pile, and followed the three men upriver toward the power plant.

As they grew closer to the buildings, the roar of the waterfall drowned out all other sound. A thin mist hung in the air all around, nearly invisible to the eye, but not to the touch. It clung to the fine hair on Denny's face and eyebrows like dew on a blade of grass, frosting her white.

"I bet the ice is bad here in winter," she said.

"Very good observation," Georgie said to her, as if she were a third-grader who had just mastered long division, "but this isn't our winter camp. The truck would never be able to reach us down that slope. When November hits, we'll move up into the hills, into one of the old mines that the corporation has staked out for the purpose. It won't be as homey as the old Upper Duck, but it'll be a lot warmer and safer."

Upper Duck? Denny was confused only for a moment, until she saw, carved into one of the huge footstones of the limestone building, the words *Upper Duck River Power Plant, 1927.*

They turned left under the limestone columns and the Greek temple overhang in the facade. The air under here grew cooler and mustier with every step.

Sarafian pushed open a tall set of metal doors, brown with age, that sported the same type of corrugated grating as the windows. As they moved inside, she could see that the entire interior of the limestone building, with the exception of a few offices at the back, was one big, flat warehouse, dotted with the footings from several old generators, which had been removed when the dam was torn down. One lonely generator remained, rusty and disused, in a far corner. From the looks of it, it had been too damaged to salvage.

All across this wide expanse of floor, people bustled about in between instant-assembly dome tents, like the ones they used to use to camp in church basements when Denny was in Girl Guides, with tension-mounted frames that didn't require any tent pegs to stay up. There must have been thirty or forty people in all. Because the power station's tinted windows kept the interior of the building gloomy and grey, glaring square work lights had been attached to many of the railings surrounding the generator footings, giving the place the aspect of a permanent night construction site. From somewhere beyond a partially-opened door, Denny could hear the hum and splutter of a gas generator.

The guys led her over to one of the back offices, the smaller one on the left. Georgie paused in front of it for a moment, pulling a jumble of keys out of his pants pocket. He unlocked the door, and everyone moved in. There was a small refrigerator in one corner, and lots of supplies piled up on white-washed plywood shelving throughout the room. It looked like an old break room. A door out the back of the room led to a mudroom type of place, in which she could see, beyond the glass window, stacks and stacks of gasoline canisters.

She set down the power bars, then stood there, waiting for their next move. To her relief, Georgie said, "Sarafian, why don't you take our new guest upstairs and get her a tent?"

Sarafian lowered his bushy black brows. "I'll put her with the girls," he grumbled, tilting his head forward slightly, in a way that left Denny wondering if he meant to be portentous, or if he was just naturally serious.

"I hardly think it's necessary to put her in the pink ghetto," said Georgie. "There's more than enough room over here, and none of the girls will have any information for her."

"I'm sure she'll enjoy seeing some girls up here, though," said the big guy with the ponytail. "Once she gets out of here, it's a Wild West, without the West. The only other bitch within two thousand clicks is Verity Twoflower, and I doubt she'll want to sit down and swap make-up tips."

One of the other guys chuckled.

"Yeah, this one doesn't look like a dyke. She won't be interested in Twoflower."

Throughout this, nobody even asked her. Nobody even looked at her. She started a sentence several times, only to be cut off by the next guy to speak or their laughter.

Sarafian slunk in between them, as they continued to rip on Verity Twoflower. His shoulders were hunched, and he spoke quieter than the rest of them. He wore a green fishing vest with lots of pockets, a white t-shirt, and cargos.

"Come on," he said, "they'll be at this for quite a while."

Sarafian led her out of the office and back across the floor of the main building, weaving back and forth through the tents. Denny saw a man on a cell phone talking to somebody in Toronto, arguing about advertising revenues. The phone probably cost double a year's tuition. They passed a bank of camera batteries on a cart, charging in their docking stations. Somebody else sat cross-legged in the entrance of their tent, writing madly longhand on a ringed pad of Hilroy paper. The whole scene reminded Denny of a busy metropolitan newsroom transplanted into a Boy Scout camp.

Some of the men responded to Geoff as he strolled by with a "Hey Pooch!" or an invitational whistle or cluck.

Sarafian led her to the end of the mausoleum nearest the waterfall, where a peeling, white wooden door with a glass panel led into the other part of the building that looked like an office trailer. Inside was a wasteland of torn-down cubicles, old scattered papers, and dust, layers of thick dust, white like the mica from inside of drywall. The dust began about twenty feet from where they stood.

"Do yourself a favour and don't kick that up," Sarafian said. "We had a guy try to clean out here in our first week, and three days later we were sending him home, breathing at fifty percent lung capacity. We think there's old insulation in it. It seems to stay put if you leave it alone, though. Nobody's had any problems since."

Geoff walked over to the edge of the dust and tried to give it a sniff. Denny pulled him back.

"Geoff, no!" she said, speaking as sternly as possible in the hopes that he would understand the gravity of the situation. He left the dust alone for the time being, at least, and followed along as they turned left, heading up a flight of stairs that were of the same stone as the mausoleum, and probably were rather dashing in their day. At the top, some forty stairs up at least, they made another left turn into a set of double doors, the only doors on this level.

Inside was another vast room floored with old wood. A few lopsided old desks lurked in the shadows along the edges, but other than that the room was empty, except for a large pile of supplies thrown in the centre of the dusty floor like bodies after a disaster. The light coming in the windows on the left side of the building flickered with the movement of the waterfall and the swaying of branches on the side of the hill, as though it were perpetually raining outside. The items were all normal things...a tent in a bag here, a set of summer clothes there, but there was an eerie quality to the way they had been locked away and tossed aside.

Sarafian led Denny to the pile and handed her a tent. The side facing her had a stitched-on label. *Suzie Thompson*, it said in black sharpie letters. Sarafian raised an eyebrow when Denny hesitated, jostling the bag in front of her. She frowned at him.

"Why are you handing me someone else's stuff?"

"She didn't need it anymore," he said, his scowl deepening. "Take it before I drop it. I don't like touching Suzie's stuff as it is."

Denny took the bag. Sarafian was off like a shot for the door.

"Ohhhh, I see," Denny said, trotting up behind him as he walked away. "You had a crush on her, and she had to go back South for the big story."

Sarafian gave a loud huff of air, almost a snort. He stayed silent after that.

"Nell, we've got a visitor."

The girl that poked her head out of the leftmost tent gazed out at Denny in surprise but not much joy. Denny understood, to an extent. There were only six women here, in a group of tents huddled closest to the outer doors. If it was this hard for women to get into the news business to begin with, she could understand why they would view the arrival of another woman, especially a woman they didn't already know, as an unwelcome source of competition. For all they knew, she could be some hard-hitting, nasty status-seeker from head office who had come in to separate the wheat from the chaff, so to speak. She could be there to replace one of them as the token female anchor.

Nell emerged from the tent. She was taller than Denny but still not very tall all told, and so thin that her knees and elbows looked a bit knobby. It didn't seem to Denny, though, that she was doing any augmenting of her own skinniness, however, but more that she was just naturally so. She had wild, red, curly hair that was more or less pulled back into a bun at the back of her head, and a funny, bumpy nose that probably would have looked terribly awkward on anyone who wasn't already so quirky looking. She wore a blue and white yoga suit with short pants and slip-on amphibious shoes.

"We weren't expecting any visitors," Nell said, walking up to Sarafian with an accusatory tone in her voice that she was clearly trying to hide for Denny's sake. "We have all the people we need. We sent them a memo. We *told* them not to send any more…"

Sarafian held out his hands in a placating gesture. Denny had noticed that he talked with his hands a lot, especially when he was trying to explain something.

"Felicia was an *unexpected* guest. She came up here with the food truck. She's looking for some information from us on her dad, and then when she gets it, she's going to move on. No harm, no foul, right Nells?"

Nell pursed her lips to one side and narrowed her eyes.

"As far as I can tell, yes," she said, "but you had better remember..."

"I remember, I remember. Let's set up Suzie's old tent, okay? Might as well make her comfortable while she's here," Sarafian said, turning on his heel before Nell could say anything more. He was across the floor and into one of the office rooms at the back before Nell said anything to Denny.

Nell gave Denny a much shorter, much cooler appraisal than Georgie had, but that look still left her feeling ripped-open and off-balance. Her lips raised into half a sneer.

"Come inside for a minute," she said, "I've got some supplies you're going to need."

Nell didn't wait for Denny to reply. Her warm, wiry hand gripped Denny's wrist, pulling her into the tent as fast as she could without Denny stumbling. With a final, cool look out onto the generator floor, Nell zipped up the flap.

"You idiot!" she hissed, her freckled face growing pinker by the second. "What are you doing up here? Did you not talk to Officer Joyce?"

Denny shook her head.

"How about Officer Menken, then? I've got one of my girls posted at every outreach centre, trying to keep air-headed little idiots, like you, and their purse dogs away from this place! Wasn't the testimony enough for you? It's genuine, oh yeah. The Screamers are going to blow your mind. But there's so much more up here awaiting a sweet little morsel like you that I bet you didn't even think of. Tell me something…who benefits most from anarchy and chaos?"

"Criminals?"

"Uh-huh. Robbers and murderers and rapists. *Ra-pists.* Do you hear me now, princess? I mean, do you even have a gun?"

Denny felt her cheeks flush. She had never learned how to use a gun, and she had been a little scared of them. She was ashamed to admit that she had not done everything possible to ensure her safety on this mission…mostly out of fear that she would hurt someone, even Geoff, by accident. Still, Nell's tirade had broadsided her, and she found herself wanting to say something cheeky back to dull the sting.

"No, I don't have a gun," she said pertly, "do you?"

Nell pressed her lips together, her eyes filled with cold rage.

"No, but I wish every day that I had brought one. Those guys in the office, they have guns. And they've used them. Not just on deer and gophers, either. But, of course, I don't want to scare you." she said, lip snarling.

"What…happened here?" Denny said.

"More like what's still happening. We tried to stand up, and people started dying. Suzie was the first. She broke into Georgie's office, looking for evidence we could send to the RCMP. Georgie's boys were watching. They shot her in the head. Buried one of the leading investigative journalists in North America in an unmarked grave."

Denny pushed her hair back out of her face. Suddenly, it had gotten uncomfortably hot in the tent, and small.

"Best we can tell, we think they're after a drug stockpile. Something to do with Twoflower's militants. Foster… Garrity… Sarafian… they're all in on it. Rumour has it that the Natives have a massive stockpile of drugs they stole from all the other northern dealers, and anybody that gets their hands on it will be a real rich bitch…not that the Fosters need any more money. Wouldn't be surprised if Georgie just wants to put it all up his nose. Mommy and Daddy sent him to rehab a couple years ago, but that was about as effective as teaching long division to a banana."

Denny fell backwards out of her crouch as a large, square hand rapped on the side of the tent.

"Come on, ladies, some of the other campers want to get a load of the noob," said Garrity. "You can do each other's hair after the tents are set up."

Nell gave the side of the tent a big old double finger.

"Just getting her a toothbrush, Garrity," she said.

Nell pulled the tent out of the fabric tube it was wrapped in and flipped it up into a dome the way an expert waiter flips a cloth over a table. She zipped the front flap open, brusquely, and gestured inside.

"There's your home now. I tried to help you by feeding the RCMP as much anonymous information as I could and getting my contacts in the right places, but you're stuck here now. Play dumb and they might not hurt you, but they're not gonna let you leave."

Denny looked over the top of the tent, toward the door. Sarafian had just finished threading heavy steel chain through the handles. He locked it in place, with a clank that resounded through the room. Trapped. She had come up here suspicious and wandered right into a nest of drug lords masquerading as journalists.

 Denny had a horrible, sick feeling building in her gut and a sensation like she was falling from a very high cliff. They couldn't have...but then again, they had left all the constraints of modern society, of Canadian law, behind them when they crossed that perimeter. By the time any of them managed to escape and report this, it could be years later, if they survived at all... All of a sudden, the weight of what she had done, how far she had come, and the very real risk she had taken crashed down on Denny. She had crossed the border into a lawless territory, completely unprepared, like a lamb to the slaughter. And she had thought herself so savvy, so knowledgeable and wise. Wisdom from a book, maybe, but could she really shoot a gun? Into another person? Thoughts spun through her head, glancing from one horror, one fear to the next. She did the only thing she could do at that moment...she crawled into her tent, crouched on the floor, and cried.

Through it all, Geoff curled up at her feet, and stayed there, his nose pointed toward the door.

DENNY GETS HER GUN

After Denny took Geoff into the little tent, along with her backpack, she huddled there for a long while. It grew hot when the slanting rays of sun from the long windows drifted over the tent, but she didn't undo the door flap. The only other person there was Nell…and she didn't know what else to say to her. What did you say to someone who had gone through what she had gone through?

She didn't know. Part of her couldn't even process the things that had happened to her today, let alone what might be in store for her once the sun set. And Sarafian…that bastard had sold her out. He had locked her in. If she ever got hold of a gun, he would be the first person she would test it out on. Target practice, yeah. She spent some time raging, imagining what she would do to him, what she would make him and Georgie do to *each other*, if she had a gun. If she only had a gun. But she'd been too scared to pack one. Now she was a mouse, a trapped mouse.

She felt even more trapped when the others started discussing her as if she couldn't hear them through the polyester walls. It didn't take them long to notice the extra tent.

"Someone new?" said one woman.

"Oh no, they've started kidnapping people now."

"No," replied Nell's voice. "She came here on her own, without a gun. Something about her lost father... I think he might be a Screamer."

"Without a gun?" A groan went all round. "She's a Toronto runaway, isn't she?"

"Worse...a sheltered grad student."

"Fuck. They're not going to let her go, are they? Just what we need, some entitled twenty-something mooning around getting in the way."

"She won't last that long," said someone else. "Georgie will 'put her to work' on one of his assignments up in Native country, and she won't come back. Just like Bilodeau, and Singh, and Shaughnessy. She's got an English degree. On the off-chance she lives through a scrape with Twoflower, she might get some use out of it."

"Deceiving the masses. That's what I'd always dreamed of doing with *my* degree," said one of the men.

One of the classes Denny had taken as an elective in undergrad was a history course about war diaries. It had been a fascinating course, stretching back to the Victorian period, but it had also given her frequent nightmares. In them, she would sign up for battle, thinking that her father, who was usually a decorated officer or a hero, would keep her safe. Then when she reached the point where she met with the others and had to ship off, she would realize that she had been put in with the common foot soldiers, and there was a good chance that she would die in the war. At that point, utter panic would overtake her as she realized that she was about to be crushed in a machine or mutilate herself trying to get away.

It had been then that she had first experienced the feeling of sitting in a waiting room, knowing that you'd signed up for something, but not really knowing the extent of what you'd signed up for, and learning the terrible truth that you were caught, that things were getting real and there was no way to recede back into the fantasy. Only those times, during those dreams, she had awakened, in her own bed, safe at home, and thanked God none of it was real. This time, she had no such luxury. Nauseated and trembling, she pulled out her father's final postcard and held it, the corners growing soft from her sweat.

They had killed. They were going to trap her here at best, send her off to die at the end of a militant's rifle at worst. She was a literature major...not a foreign correspondent. She had never even taken a business writing course. It had been all fiction and history, all the time.

But if there was one thing she had learned from that course, from those brave people who had faced impossible odds, it was that sometimes the only way to deal with violence and chaos, and live, was to run straight through it, no looking back. Suzie had died because Georgie was protecting something in that office, and she had a pretty heavy hunch that whatever it was, it would have information on taping locations and dates. Suzie had also thought that he was hiding information that the RCMP needed. If she could grab the information and escape with it, she might just have some powerful people on her side, if she could contact them. There were plenty of working landlines up here still. The north had never fully integrated with the wireless revolution, which was just as well when society reverted back to wires a hundred years later.

She paused a moment, mid-thought. Was she even really thinking this? How was she going to get into the office? How was she going to get out of the building once they were on to her? There was every possibility that if she just sat tight, ate their food, and did as she was told, she could ride out the crisis in relative safety.

Yeah, right. Because appeasement worked so well for England.

But she had fought this far, hadn't she? She had gotten here and fought her fears all the way! In thinking back on her past, Denny realized that she had something she could use in this fight: willpower and stubbornness. And, in all that time, she had acquired something else powerful, as well: some serious brainpower. If she could balance six courses while TA-ing for two, if she could hold her own among a crowd of hundreds of other students who wanted her status, her grades, and her eventual job, then she could at least try to formulate a plan. But to do that, she would at least need a little more information. And to get that, she would have to do something that always made her cringe: she would have to open up.

Denny made sure to bring Geoff out of the tent with her as she made for a circle of crew people, Nell included, who were now sitting around the work light, eating and talking as the last of the late afternoon sun began to fade into dusk. Her plan worked like a charm: the crew might think many things of her, but she'd bet her boots that they hadn't seen a sweet, cuddly dog in a while. Several of them duck-walked toward him, crouched with their hands out.

"Awww, who's this?" said a brunette with a long, sharp face and big eyes. "Who's a puppy?"

Geoff licked her face.

"Oh, somebody's giving me kisses, isn't he? Come here, sweetie pie!" she drew him over, sat down on the ground and pulled his butt onto her lap. She hugged him and petted him, and the two others centered around her, petting his head and kissing his face. Geoff gave a big, doggy grin, panting. For him at least, this was heaven.

Denny sat down quietly and let the girls enjoy him for a moment. She waited for them to acknowledge her.

Eventually, the sharp-faced girl asked, "So what's his name?"

"Geoff. We go everywhere together."

"I'm surprised they didn't turn him loose. I guess they didn't see him as much of a threat."

"Honestly...he isn't. I've never seen him attempt anything mean, except if you count death by licking."

The girl gave Geoff an indulgent look, like a mother to a small toddler, then said, "Why did you come up here?" as though she had told Denny, and told her eighteen times, not to undertake a dangerous sub-arctic trek to find her dead father's reanimated corpse.

"Well, I came up here in general to find my father's body and put it to rest. I came here, specifically, because someone on this crew shot footage of him, and I need to know where that was. Otherwise I'd never know where to start looking... I could look forever. I thought I was prepared for whatever might happen. Turns out I was pretty wrong, eh?"

The brunette gave a terrible, anxious giggle, one that sounded more like pent-up pain bubbling up from inside of her than any real laugh. She didn't say anything for some minutes, but Denny waited nonetheless.

Denny settled down by Nell. Most of the rest of the group had gravitated toward Geoff by this point, and he was being his usual, charming self. The perfect point man.

"Suzie was your friend, right?" she said, low enough not to be heard by others.

Nell narrowed her eyes at Denny. Slowly, she replied, "We were going to blow this thing wide open. She didn't give me up in the end."

"Who is 'we'?" Denny said, feeling bold.

Nell took a mouthful of stroganoff.

"Who says there's more?" she said. "Look, I know you're going to try and get that info. It's your neck. Just don't involve me in it...and enter through the loose window pane on the right-hand side of the office. They can't lock it, and they don't bother trying, because nobody's small enough to fit through. But I'd wager you are, if you wear a tight enough top."

"Really? It's that simple?"

"No, but I bet if you show up there after everybody's in bed, you might make a few discoveries."

Denny tried to catch Nell's eye, to gauge if she was serious, but Nell's face was angled squarely toward dinner. She shovelled a few mouthfuls in quick succession, as if to drive home that the conversation was over.

Nell had good instincts, it seemed. Georgie and Sarafian ducked out from behind a tent a couple of rows away and joined the crowd around Geoff. Denny tensed. What were they playing at?

Georgie crouched down and put his hands on either side of Geoff's head, then ruffled his fur. Denny could tell that he was pressing too hard. Geoff flinched away, but Georgie just moved onto his neck.

"Oh, goo'boy, goo'boy..." Georgie said. Sarafian just stood behind him like a grumpy troll.

"Aww, come on, Sarafian," he said. "Get in on this. Didn't you ever have a dog?"

Sarafian reached out one hand, gave Geoff's head a quick pat, then put his hand back in his pocket.

"No," he said, "I had a sugar glider."

"Oh yeah," said Georgie. "You were into all that exotic nature bullshit, weren't you, Raffi?"

"Not much of that left anymore, though," Sarafian said. "People are wild enough for me these days."

Georgie stood up and gave a fake stretch.

"Well, I for one could use a furry friend in my life."

Sarafian grabbed hold of Geoff's collar. Geoff looked back at her with wide eyes and whined. Denny stood up part of the way, but a wiry hand shoved her back onto her butt.

"Not now," Nell hissed in her ear.

"You bastard!" Denny said, trying to burn a hole in Georgie's head with her eyes. Sarafian tugged, and Geoff got up, reluctantly, and followed.

"I won't hurt him," said Georgie with a smile. "He'll be my little buddy, and have the best of everything. Unless, of course, you decide to make trouble. Then he might just get caught in the crossfire. Goodnight, princess! Welcome to the team!"

Denny nodded, her eyes tearing up. She slunk back into her tent, alone. Nell didn't try to stop her this time. When she got inside, she dug into her backpack, pulling out piles of clothes, boxes of food, and various instruments that she wouldn't need in a million years inside of a limestone power plant. Finally, she found what she was looking for. It looked like a longer, thinner version of one of those glasses cases that people put their money and small items in while they go on water slides, with a smooth outer casing, rounded at the ends. Halfway down its length was a seam, held together by a sturdy set of plastic snaps.

Denny pressed on the sides of the case and pulled it open. It took a great deal of strength to pull the two halves apart. So much the better. Half of the case was a handle, and the other half was a small, serrated hunting knife. On the back, elastic straps hooked under two loops in a groove. She pushed it back into the case, made sure everything was secure, then pushed it down into her cleavage. That was one of the few true advantages of big boobs. With the right bra, they were locket, wallet, and stash all in one.

She repacked her bags, then lay down on her side, on the plastic-covered concrete, feeling the weight of the blade pressing on her breasts, her pulse spilling over it, beating against it. Her heart had been replaced with a blade…and it felt so hollow, and so sick, and so right. Her heart had been ready to stab someone for a long time. She had just been waiting to find out who, and now she knew. Sarafian. Garrity. *Georgie fucking Foster.* There was no rehab for what she was going to do to that fucker if she had the chance, oh no. In the most primal part of her, she hoped that they would try to stop her. The guns were still a problem, though. She'd have to sneak around, at least until she found one. They had to have one or two in that office of theirs…

The lights outside faded to black, and slowly the squiggly dome-shaped lights on the walls of her tent went out as people retired to their bedrolls for the night. After the last stragglers had turned out their lamps, Denny waited. Then she waited some more, crouched by the door. A set of footsteps passed by the back of her tent. They had guard patrols going. No big surprise there. The next time the steps passed by, she slowly, steadily zipped the door of her tent open, just enough for her to crawl through, her fingers on the mechanism to muffle the ticking of the zipper.

Outside, she could see the silhouettes of the other tents outlined by a pair of dim security lights trained on the door of the office. The window Nell had told her about was in relative dark, but she would have to be careful. She made her way slowly, carefully along the edge of the tent cluster, following the direction of the guard. He looped around the edge of the room and came to a stop at the door to the office. As he scanned the room, Denny ducked behind the nearest tent and didn't move until she heard his footsteps start up again.

There was a good twenty-foot gap between the office and the nearest tent, most of it illuminated. Once the guard was out of sight, and no more came along for some minutes, Denny button-hooked around the security lights and into the shadows behind the far corner of the office. So far so good. She paused to catch her breath for a moment. No turning back now.

A shadowy figure plowed into her in the dark, grabbing both her wrists and pinning her against the wall. Before she could react, a pair of lips mashed into hers, forcing her mouth open. She gave out a squeak, which under the circumstances came out as more of an "Mmmph!" Shit. Nell hadn't been kidding about there being rapists up here. Denny started to struggle, and the lips pulled off of hers. A hand quickly replaced them, muffling any attempt at noise.

"Just go with it," whispered a familiar voice in her ear, "guard coming."

A flashlight appeared around the back corner of the office trailer. Although it made her cringe to do this with God-knows-who, it appeared that God-knows-who was trying to help, for the moment. She grimaced, then returned the kiss. The guy didn't have bad lips. That much she'd give him. Rather supple, actually, for a dude. It was still extremely disorienting and weird.

A flashlight beam shone in her eyes. She squinted, and broke the kiss. In the light, she could see his face...Sarafian. Holy God. She had kissed Sarafian.

He shielded his eyes. Apparently the eyebrows didn't do a good enough job.

"Shit, Maryfield, why you always gotta be a killjoy?"

"She's supposed to be in her tent," said Maryfield, a solidly built guy in his late forties.

"I went and got her. She deserves a hearty Foster Towers welcome, am I right?" Sarafian said, grinding his hips against her. She hoped that was his handgun she was feeling. She smiled lasciviously at Maryfield, gave her best porn star sigh, and topped it off with as air-headed a giggle as she could manage. She nibbled on his neck, just for effect.

Maryfield sighed.

"How come I never get the cute ones, huh?"

"I might share," said Sarafian with a wink, "if you can get the two of us some privacy. Ever heard of the rotisserie? It ain't gay if you've got a chick in the middle, man."

"I've gotta stay on guard if you're in there, but when Garrity comes on shift at three...I can probably make it in. Just don't rough her up too bad, okay? Foster's an animal. They're no good to anybody after he's done with 'em."

"You get me into the office, to a decent bed, and I swear, you'll never even know I was in there."

Maryfield moved to the front of the trailer, and Sarafian followed behind, pulling Denny along by the hand. The vacant effect wasn't hard to achieve, as she was still kind of floating in shock.

Sarafian closed the door to the office behind them and locked it. The place was a mess, clothes strewn everywhere, like the room of an overgrown child. Dishes were stacked up in a corner, and they stank. Obviously, Georgie hadn't been too quick to adjust to not having a maid. The only exception was a large, old-fashioned desk at the other end of the room, stacked with papers and homemade booklets stuck together with bull clips.

Denny yanked her hand away from Sarafian, pulling out her knife with the other.

"What are you playing at?" she hissed.

Sarafian approached, hands outstretched. Denny stepped backward, stumbling slightly on a pile of crumpled magazines. She jabbed the knife at him.

"I could ask you the same thing," he said, "but I think I know the answer. The papers you want are in the purple binder marked *Documentary*. Take the shotgun as well and as many shells as you can carry. You're going to have to shoot your way out."

Denny kept the knife pointed at him as she inspected the desk. There was the binder. She flipped through it. It was full of pictures and what looked like a TV script. She tucked it inside her sweatshirt.

"Hurry up," said Sarafian, "Georgie's passed out in the back room, and he could wake up any time."

Denny gave him a quizzical look, eyebrow raised.

He gave her the crossing guard keep-moving motion.

"Less questions. More action. Come on! I've got a lot riding on this."

"*You* do!" Denny gave a quiet snort.

Beside the desk, leaning on a bookcase with a carton of shells was...the shotgun! Denny dumped the contents of the carton of shells into the front pocket of her sweatshirt. She picked up the gun and slung the strap over her shoulder, just as a groan and some rustling came from the back room. They both went stock still. Denny looked at Sarafian. His dark eyes were wide, his spine rod-straight. He raised a hand to his lips, very slowly, then pointed to the door, followed by a bashing motion. Denny nodded. She got low and scuttled over to the far side of the door, plastering herself against the wall when she got there.

The door creaked open and Georgie, eyes closed to slits, his clothes rumpled, shuffled out into the office. He noticed Sarafian and gave one of those drunk, blinky half stumbles that the truly inebriated give when they have an unexpected guest.

Denny seized her opportunity, raising the butt of the shotgun over her head in both hands, and slamming it down into the back of his head. Georgie crumpled to the ground, let out a sigh, then was silent.

"Get out now," Sarafian said, "and be prepared for an alarm. Take the back stairs, up and out of the roof. The doors are unlocked there."

"Where's my dog," said Denny, getting dangerously close to him, shotgun raised.

"Trust me," he said.

"I don't...trust...anybody," she replied.

Denny looked at the door, breathing hard and anticipating her escape. Before those goons outside figured out what was what, she wanted to have the gun more or less figured out. She'd seen people in the movies flip the barrel down on shotguns to check if they were loaded before, so she tried it. To her relief, it was loaded. If she could get out of here on two shots, then she could learn the rest later. If not...well, she'd just have to do it on the fly.

She flipped over the deadbolt on the door and cracked it open, the gun barrel preceding her. Then she kicked the door all the way open. Couldn't hurt to shock 'em a little. Heart pounding, she stepped out into the atrium and pumped the barrel.

A ring of five men stood around the entrance to Georgie's room and their stances betrayed surprise.

"Stay out of my way, fuckers, or I'll shoot," she said, backing away as quickly as possible, back to the wall, toward the set of mesh stairs leading to the warrens on the upper floors.

One of the men reached for his pocket, and Denny could see the butt of a gun jutting out from it. Without allowing herself to think about it, she aimed and shot. The recoil of the gun knocked her back, bumping her head against the wall, but the other guy got it worse. The left side of his chest exploded in a spray of blood and bone.

Denny felt the back of her heel hit the bottom stair. She brandished the gun around one more time.

"Anybody want some more? Huh?"

One of the thicker men tried to run after her as she ascended the stairs, moving faster with every step. She shot again, nicking a hole out of the pavement in front of him, and he fell to the ground. Unfortunately, so did Denny. She even slid down a couple of steps for good measure. For a moment, she watched in shock, out of ammo, head aching, as more men boiled up behind the one who had fallen. The entire encampment was out in full force, now, and more guns were being drawn all over the place. Denny tried to push herself up, to run away as fast as possible, but she used her shotgun arm, and the gun slipped on the stair, causing her to fall back down again.

A shot pinged off of the railing a foot from her head. In the moment, Denny abandoned all pretense. She covered her head and screamed.

Her scream was echoed by another one from the mausoleum floor. Gunfire exploded out of the other end of the room, mowing down several men in the process. Bullets flew through tents, smashed one of the windows of Georgie's trailer.

"Take that, you fucking bastards!" yelled Nell, amid the war-whoops of her companions. Someone had given them guns. Denny had a sneaking suspicion she knew who. She took her chance, pulled herself to her feet, and ran headlong toward the upper floors, not even daring to look back.

Denny wrenched the flimsy door at the top of the stairs open, then slammed it behind her. Beyond it, everything was black, and she could taste the dust in the air. Her heart pounded up in her ears, and her legs felt numb and wobbly. Had she just shot...no, no, not now. Not now.

The sliver of light from under the door illuminated the bottom of another staircase. This one creaked as she climbed, and she prayed for no missing stairs. The floor underneath was the same limestone cement of the mausoleum, not very friendly to skulls.

She hit another door. This one didn't have a knob. Instead, her fingers clutched on a ring of soft, rotting wood. She shoved her way into the next room. This one was a storage room of some kind, filled with old tools and parts and strange machines that Denny couldn't place. Moonlight shone through the high windows and through the opening in a door across the way...a door leading to the outside. Denny reached it, opened it, and found herself on the rusty catwalk she had seen earlier that led to the top of the cliff. The sound of the waterfall was everywhere and, despite the rust coating everything, she found the path slippery.

Once she slipped, her shotgun flying over the void by the strap. When her weight shifted onto the railing, it groaned and leaned outward. She stifled the urge to scream, dropping down to the catwalk and pulling her shotgun back in. She let out one sob, then choked back the rest. Above the waterfall was another noise...barking.

"Geoff... *Geoff!*" she said, finding a second wind. She clambered up the final flight of stairs to the top of the cliff, lungs heaving, legs screaming, scrambling on her hands and knees over the last few steps. She could see now, in the light of the moon, that her hands were covered in mould and grime, her arms stamped by dirty door frames and the rust on the railings.

At the top of the stairs, a group of old antennas clustered toward the sky, speckled with rusty cow-splotches. Geoff was tethered to one, and her supplies were hanging from the cross-piece of another. Geoff's hind-quarters shivered, and his tail hung between his legs. At home, he would hide under a chair if someone dropped a pot on the floor. All of the gunplay downstairs had probably not been to his taste.

Denny wanted to hug him, to reassure him, but instead she unhooked her backpack, slung it on, and untangled Geoff's lead from the antenna bundle. He was as eager to be off as she was, pulling at the lead the minute she got him free.

At the top of the cliff was a clearing of Shield rock, covered in lichen and small bushes which ran for about fifty feet. On the right, the Upper Duck River churned toward the falls, deep, wide and uncrossable.

Denny had no idea where she was going...she just needed a place to hide long enough to look over some of the information she had stolen from Georgie and figure out how to get help. Up ahead was a jagged wall of trees, almost a flat green-black cut-out in the dead of night. A howl, not wolf, not elk, drifted out of the trees. Denny wanted more than anything to run the other way but forced herself to move forward, toward the darkness. If she was afraid of the woods, chances are they would be too. She hadn't seen any evidence that the Foster Towers Media Corp had learned how to subdue the Screamers, and so they would stay away.

Geoff balked at the darkness lining the edge of the woods. He sniffed the air and sneezed. All Denny could smell was pine. She strode in between the first trees, tugging him along with her. She would stick to the river, in case at some point she found a way to cross and throw them off her trail.

Once under the cover of the trees, she found herself stumbling over every rock and exposed root. She yanked her flashlight out of her utility belt and clicked it on.

So much for the light providing warmth and familiarity. Sure, she could see more details of the trees, but it was a cold, ghostly highlight which made every low-hanging branch and vine into an unfriendly clawed arm reaching out to touch her, every breeze-blown leaf cluster in the distance into a rotting zombie bear circling her trail. She shivered, a cold sweat breaking out on her skin and soaking her clothes. Her legs began to ache, and her arms grew heavy, expressing all of the stress and fatigue that had built up in her over the course of the evening. She wanted to stop, pitch her tent, and curl up in a warm sleeping bag, but she forced herself to push onward…

Surgite...the famous last words of Sir Isaac Brock. *Push Onward.* Just what a good disciple of the general would do. She pushed onward over rocks, between scratchy bushes and through a couple of near ankle-twisting holes, letting those words swirl in her head. His famous last words, hopefully not her obscure last thoughts.

After an hour of shivering, stumbling, and more false alarms than she wanted to remember, she came to a sandy place along the river surrounded by dense bushes. She would only have one avenue of escape if she camped here, but similarly, her enemies would only have one avenue of approach, making it easier to guard. Better to only have to listen in one direction. The first thing she did, after shoving her way through the bushes with many a poke and scrape, was to pull some of the shotgun shells out of her front pocket and reload her gun. She was fairly certain she did it right...mostly. But it was dark. She took the rest of the shells and shoved them into a plastic baggie, then put the baggie into a zipped pocket in her utility belt. One thing about having a homeless father was you learned the value of baggies right quick. They're cheap, they're less obvious than a wallet, and they protect your cigs when you're stuck out in the rain without a jacket.

Denny tied Geoff to a nearby tree, then she doffed her pack and pulled out the tent. Lucky for her, she'd bought the kind that flips open almost instantly, so aside from a little wind that threatened to pull her and the tent off-balance in mid-flip, the thing was out and the pegs hammered into the ground in an amount of time that almost seemed tolerable even to someone in her hyper-aware state of mind. She kept the axe that she used to hammer in the pegs out of her pack, just in case she really hadn't loaded the gun correctly.

Next, she walked back through the bushes to see if the tent was visible from the other side. The cover wasn't great, but if her pursuers didn't have good flashlights, or if they were a fair distance away, they probably wouldn't spot her. The tent was low to the ground, just high enough to sit up cross-legged in, and so it sat below most of the brush line. She returned to the tent, lugged her pack inside, then led Geoff in and zipped up the door. Inside, it smelled like the hardware store. Inside Denny, it felt like being dropped off at the orphanage. Alone at last, with no clue as to her whereabouts, in this tiny capsule of warmth and wind-resistance...what a farce this had all been. She rolled out her sleeping bag and got in. Geoff stayed watch at the door, alert and tense.

Denny noticed a lump when she lay on her stomach, and remembered the book she had grabbed from Georgie's "study" on the way out. She pulled the dog-eared, coffee-stained volume out of her shirt and ducked her head into the sleeping bag to read without shining a light into the forest. Perhaps there was something in here that would help. Knowing where she was going tomorrow would help her to stop feeling like an out-of-control boat adrift on the current.

DISTANT EARLY WARNING

Documentary Commentary on Far North Screamer Activity

Narrator: With no urban population left to speak of and Native tensions rising, it is crucial that you, the viewer, have all the information on the Screamer threat. The courageous crew (ha) *at Foster Towers Media Corp have braved the melting North and stared danger in the face to bring you the following documentary footage and gathered information on the Screamers.*

As far as our researchers (double-ha) *can tell, the Screamers are demons, sent from hell and not resembling anything even close to the humans that they were in life. Their words are nonsense, and, upon their return, they appear to be killing people that they once loved more than anything in the world. Experts are saying that their arrival may herald the Biblical end times and the final battle of good versus evil.*

But wait, Denny thought...some of this doesn't add up. Aside from their spurious claims to be actual researchers, and their Biblical rhetoric (clearly intended to rile up the gullible), their information on the nature of the creatures was just an outright lie. Violet had told her that she had recognized Rose as the same person she knew and loved. She had also said that her mother could hear Rose talking to her. And Rose never killed their mother...she may have induced her to kill her aunt and uncle, but the whole thing seemed too subtly executed to just be a killing

157

mission from Hell. And how did that explain all of the people who had seen Screamers and lived, like Violet?

They hadn't done any research. They didn't know anything. They had just holed up in that power station of theirs and occasionally struck out to tape a few monsters roaming around. She should have known that those cowards wouldn't want to actually get their hands dirty.

Denny flipped through the rest of the book, hands shaking, looking for the mention of a location, a specific event or case study, but it was all the same authoritative brand of non-information, like a third-grade presentation on AIDS. You could tell them how it works, but not the crucial information on how you get it. She slammed the book down on the ground, pages first, then cringed, realizing that she had made a noise.

When no one came charging through the bushes at her after fifteen minutes or so, she stopped sitting up, alert at every sound, and allowed herself to lay down again. She tossed and turned for a while, trying to plan her next move but unable to think very clearly and then, finally, against her will, she drifted off into a dizzy sleep.

As the first pink of dawn crept over the tent, she awoke to the crunch of boots coming through the bushes.

SINGING TO THE BONES

Denny sprang from her sleeping bag and grabbed the shotgun, which she had kept right next to her pillow all night. It had better be Georgie. She hoped it was Georgie. She'd kill him and then string him up as a warning to the rest of 'em not to follow her trail. Nevermind that she pushed the memory of the last guy she's shot out of her mind constantly…this was war. What was one more assault after the first one? She would still probably go to jail, regardless. And it was still self-defense.

She unzipped the door of her tent, and Geoff was off like a shot, barking and growling at someone behind the tent. Her cover was totally blown now. Better get the gun out before they shoot the dog…

Denny spun around, shotgun cocked and resting on her shoulder, and found her assailant, hands in the air, behind her tent. Sarafian.

This made it harder. He wasn't one hundred percent scumbag, because he had saved her, right? But he had let Suzie get killed, and he had come along for the ride as Georgie plotted his takeover of the Native drug empire. He had forced himself on her without permission. And he had seemed to enjoy it. He had better keep his distance.

"What the fuck do you want?" she said, raising her gun higher.

He sounded out of breath. His shell jacket had scuffs and stains on it that it hadn't previously had. There was a cut in his jeans, and under that an oozing cut in his thigh. His hair was almost comically tousled, making him look like a browner version of Bert from *Sesame Street*. "I'm coming with you. I would have found you earlier, but I had to get them off your trail," he said.

"Keep on walking. Maybe you'll get to someplace where they give a shit, but up here, I doubt it."

"You need help."

"I've got a dog. He'll be better help than you. Better conversation, too."

Sarafian reached into his jacket.

"Hold it! I'll shoot!" Denny barked, in her best impersonation of a police officer. What would Officer Menken have done?

Sarafian held up his other hand and slowly produced a beaten notebook and a data stick. Denny's heart skipped a few grooves. Maybe it was the lack of sleep, but she was feeling more than a little dizzy.

"I have information that can help you…" he said.

"And if I shoot you and take the stuff anyway?" She wasn't even sure if she'd do it… \but it was a possibility. Maybe he'd drop the info and leave.

"It's more complicated than that," he said, with an apologetic grimace, as if he knew what a pain in the ass it was to put up with him. "I'm a cameraman. I was there when we shot the video of your father. Most of what I know is all up here. Besides that, I suspect that there are big events in play here...larger than you or anybody else not living in that power plant knows. If you don't have me, you'll never find him."

"And what's in it for you?"

Sarafian pressed his lips together, then hissed breath out between his teeth.

"Redemption. That's what's in it for me. I stood by while many people died, when I could have done something. If we don't do something now, many more innocent people will die or rot in jail. Please."

A clear plea to her emotions. But what clues had he really given her as to his honesty? Georgie and the others could be waiting just around the river bend, with a burlap sack and a club. She had almost gotten killed back there. She had the gun...she would make the rules, or she wouldn't play.

"Tell me more. I want more information. And you're going to tell me where Georgie and the others are and how to avoid them," she demanded.

"Put the gun down and you'll have all the information you want."

What now? He wasn't backing off, but he wasn't armed, either. She wanted him, more than anything, to give her what she needed and then go, but she couldn't chase him all over hell's half-acre trying to get him to leave permanently, even if she did somehow manage to get the documents from him. Fear clenched the pit of her stomach. Danger. But if he did have more information on Dad, he could be her last chance to find out where he was...he could even be her last chance at getting home safely.

"You manage to get a tent before you left?" she asked, as if she preferred he shelter in a wolverine den.

"Tent, lighter, camera, but not much else," he said, twisting around so she could see the camera case and tripod strapped to his back. Possible bludgeon.

"I'm keeping my gun. I need to think about this. Geoff!" Denny said. The dog finally stopped growling and returned to her side. Sarafian's shoulders lowered from around his ears, and he let out an audible sigh of relief.

"What? I've still got the gun."

"Yeah, I know, but the dog had my ankle."

"I'm brimming over with pity," Denny snarled, backing her way back into the tent.

Sarafian pinched the bridge of his aquiline nose, pressing his eyes closed.

"You know what? I'll make this simple for you. After I left, Nell's people took over the power plant. Georgie and the boys fled south. If you want to go home, go back to them. If you want to find your father, the only way is through me. Get some rest and think about it. I'll give you until midnight. Then I'll leave, just like you want."

Denny gave him one last glare, then ducked into her tent, Geoff in tow. She opened the back window, gun at her feet, and watched him. She sat up and watched him as he pitched his tent and went inside. She hated him. Hated him for insisting on being present on her mission. Hated him for not being as hate-able as she had wanted him to be when she fled the power plant.

Denny had felt this hatred before and, if she was being honest, a lot of it was self-directed. She wasn't bad looking, all told, and she had never lacked for attention in high school, certainly, since she had developed curves early on (curves that could wreck a motorcycle, as Jordan would sometimes affectionately joke), but university had been a different story.

First of all, from the moment she had arrived, her first loves had been literature and grades. Launching herself into her studies had helped her to forget the turmoil of her teenage years and Dad's declining mental health. The resulting good grades had made her feel in control of her life and of other people's approval in a way that she hadn't felt in a very long time. She never felt worthy or able enough to help her father and never good enough to please her mother, who herself, as Denny had soon learned, was the queen of the double-standard. Compared to that, no boys seemed to offer her as much of what she needed.

There was also the fact that most university men expected *their* needs to be met right away, and Denny just hadn't been comfortable with that. Why should she give up the most personal part of herself to a stranger? It seemed like madness to her. It would have to be at least a year before she would even consider such a thing. I mean, they were talking about her *body*, her most precious and personal possession.

It wasn't that Denny was a prude, at least she didn't consider herself as such…as anyone who had taken a course in Christopher Marlowe could tell you, it was hard to be a prude and an English major at the same time. It was more that she had enough men flitting in and out of her life for five people, and she didn't want that feeling of being used, in the most intimate way possible, and then abandoned.

She had tried dating a couple of guys her way, during her pre-graduation who-am-I crisis in undergrad.

One of them was gorgeous and initially interesting, but all he wanted to do was drink, smoke, and well, you know, and when he found out that Denny did none of those things to excess, he tried to cheat on her with a mutual acquaintance, at a party they had been at together, and then never called her again. Denny had considered that a favour.

The second one had been strange, as relationships go. They had started out playing cards together at lunch and had quickly moved on to messaging each other on the computer at night while they worked on essays. He was a geology major of no particular distinction, and he was quirky and sweet, but a bit lost all told. They had played a lot of games, hung out with mutual friends, and he had seemed interested. Gradually, all his friends began giving her nudges and winks, and she thought some kind of relationship was imminent. But time went by, and although he never showed interest in anybody else, he kept his distance. Denny suspected that he wanted her to want to have sex with him, right away and throughout their relationship. She just didn't...couldn't. He was nice and all, but he wasn't someone that really excited her that way. Over time, they drifted apart, until one day, she tried to call him to invite him to a party, and he wasn't there. His friends said he had quit school and skipped town, wanting to tour the world and find some direction in his life. Nice of him to tell her. And what a great plan...living as a bum to find direction. She had a feeling she was better off.

A few years had passed, and she had been busy, and no better offers had surfaced. Then again, she hadn't really been looking, either. She hadn't thought her next encounter would be pressed up against a wall with a wannabe outlaw. He made her uncomfortable, in ways that even she found it hard to define for herself. Why did he have to keep showing up when all she wanted to do was forget him, as quickly as possible?

Denny lay down and watched the tent for an hour or more, waiting for him to come out and try to surprise her in her sleep.

Then, she listened to his snores for another hour before finally convincing herself that those were not fake snores. If they were, then Sarafian was hamming it up quite a bit. Sorry, but nobody would ever choose to have somebody think they snore like that. The flaps of the tent were practically breathing with him. After that realization, it was all downhill. She leaned on one elbow, then slipped down onto her forearm, then drifted off with her lips wedged in the crook of her arm.

It was dark when she woke up, a little river of drool having rolled down her elbow into the stuffing of the sleeping bag. Geoff was a warm lump beside her. He let out a long doggy snore when she turned over.

Light flickered off the walls in strange tree shapes. Sarafian had started a campfire. The smell of wood smoke drifted in on the breeze. It made her hungry…or maybe she had been hungry for quite a while already. Either way, it was time for some chow. She rummaged through her backpack until she came up with a tin of beef stew and a tin of dog food. After opening the cans, she crawled outside (shotgun still in hand) and sat cross-legged on the ground, facing the river. If Sarafian was going to try and kidnap her, she reasoned, he would have been a little more timely about it. Georgie and his boys didn't seem like the type to crouch in the bushes for ten hours or so.

She dumped the dog food out on the ground for Geoff, and he reduced it to a greasy smear on the sand in a matter of thirty seconds. Denny took a little longer. Vacuum-packed potatoes tasted gross when cold. After a few bites, it occurred to her that Sarafian might not actually be by the fire right now...but with her luck she'd spill stew all over his campfire and give herself away. She finished the stew cold and washed it down with a little bottled water. The packaging she washed in the river, then stowed it back in her pack. Maybe she'd find a use for it later, and besides, it was better than littering.

A scream cut across the leaf rustle of the forest.

"For the love of God, no! *Denny! Help me!*"

Sarafian. But not just Sarafian. Another sound rose behind him, both melodic and unbearably painful at the same time. She could hear the outline of the words in it, too, but they slipped past her, an inch away, without creating any meaning.

Denny grabbed her shotgun and ran past the tent, through the bushes and up the slight rise to where Sarafian had made his camp. The fire was down almost to the embers, his tent flap hung open, and he was nowhere to be found.

"Sarafian!" she called, "where are you?"

There was another glow, out in the woods, beyond the rim of the firelight. An angry red glow, like a day-old cut. Denny saw a man's silhouette stumble between the outline of two tree trunks, his hands pressed tightly down over his ears.

"Hold on," she called, running toward the glow with Geoff at her heels. As she grew closer, the Screamer's song grew louder, but as the shrill voice penetrated her eardrums, locked around her mind, this time it began to dissolve into meaning, like a glacier revealing an ancient, brutal animal, untouched by time.

You lived when I died
You did nothing
You said you cared
Now fall to nothing

Worthless…
Careless…
Hopeless…
My traitorous saviour

The edge of the clearing was like a tableau, an etching by Dore in a nineteenth-century novel. A blaze of crimson light, throwing everything into stark relief, Sarafian on his knees, one hand holding a knife to his own neck. From the centre of the light, a decaying young woman, clad only in leaves, stood lopsided, palm out, speckled with gunshots. She sang like a diva, hair flowing, revelling in the music she made.

Sarafian's hand trembled as he struggled not to cut himself.

"Suzie, no, please! I can change! I can help *her*. Let me make it right!"

The song went on.

You said you cared
Now fall to nothing
Fall to nothing
Fall to nothing…

Denny felt something well up inside of her…a new knowledge that she had never felt before. She gathered up all of the energy welling within her, and sang.

"Sto-op!"

The thing that Suzie had become pivoted toward her with an eerie silence. For a moment, she froze, but then, without thinking much about it, she continued singing.

He will help me
He will go,
Your friends are safe now,
All at rest

What will you gain
When he is dead
He'll be gone at most
Dead at best

He saved us all

169

And may save more
Before the judging at the last.

The Suzie-thing opened its puckered grey mouth and said two words, in a voice like a cloud of flies. "Guard him." It then collapsed into its grave, where the leaves folded over it and buried it once more. Its light faded out until all Denny could see was the firelight in the distance, and all she could hear was the sound of Sarafian's heavy breathing. She heard leaves crunching as he got to his feet and began shuffling back toward his camp.

"How did you just do that? How did you make it go away? No one can make them go away," he said, like someone delirious with fever or drink.

"I don't know," Denny replied.

WAYNE OF BARTON STREET

"Can you walk on your own?" Denny asked him. He hadn't moved for several minutes, only kneeled there, breathing hard. She didn't know what she would do if he couldn't get up. She still didn't really want to touch him, even to hoist him up. But she did feel a little bit guilty. His desperation reminded her of Dad, that day on the lawn when he couldn't take it anymore, when he left the first time.

Luckily, she was spared any more internal conflict when Sarafian hoisted himself up out of the dirt and began staggering toward his camp, nose to the light like a zombie in a video game. He wiped his brow and, even in the minimal light, Denny could see a smear of dirt marking his forehead. There was a sheen of sweat on him, too, and she could smell him.

Denny kept pace with Sarafian, Geoff circling around them both, until he reached his camp. He flopped down by the fire with nothing to sit on but a small exposed portion of Shield rock. Denny lingered just at the edge of the firelight, unsure of what to do or say. He was still covered in sweat, breathing hard and shivering. When he stared into the fire, nothing seemed to reflect back. His eyes were dark, hollow and haunted.

What harm would it be to give him a blanket? He didn't have any, and she had a sleeping bag that would protect her from just about anything. She weighed it for a moment, then went back to the tent and pulled out her emergency blanket, a thin square of grey fleece. Once back at the fire, she tossed it at him, then lingered on the perimeter of the glow again, unsure what to do.

Sarafian pulled the blanket around his shoulders. Before he could make eye contact, Denny turned right around again and began searching for proper kindling. The fire was getting really low, and if it went out, she didn't want to have to stay up all night trying to light it again. Bears and other beasties would be less likely to come sniffing around with a well-banked fire in the vicinity. Besides, moving around kept her nervous energy at bay. How did you interact with someone like him? How did you even get to civility? Denny grumbled inwardly. Of course she couldn't just get the information from the TV crew and move on. Of course they would turn out to be a crazed bunch of wild-west murderers and she would end up stuck out here with their cowardly cousin, too confused to know what he really wanted. Of course, in addition to wildlife, rough terrain, and a hoard of screaming, decaying monsters bent on killing people, she would have to travel with the one guy who could make it whole worlds of awkward, too.

Geoff caught up to her as she gathered another branch into the crook of her arm. He nudged her leg, and Denny felt a wet spot

172

from his nose on her jeans. She kneeled, and petted him, stealing a glance back at the campfire now that she was hidden by the shadows.

Sarafian slouched under her blanket, looking pale and sad. Even in the warm firelight, his normally tea-brown skin had taken on a grey cast. There, in the dark where she knew he couldn't see her, she felt another pang of sympathy for him. When had she become like this, so distant and unsure? It occurred to her then that perhaps she really hated people. After all, she would rather be around Geoff most of the time.

But no, that didn't make sense either. She still identified with people, she just...didn't get close.

And why did she feel so bloody lonely watching him sit there? She cursed inwardly. Fine. She would sit with him for a while. But she wouldn't say anything unless he did. Maybe he'd give her some more information she could use if she just listened.

Positive that she looked sour enough to be mistaken for another Screamer, she climbed back up to the fire and tossed in the sticks she'd found. Sarafian watched her do it, and she tried to pretend she didn't notice. Denny then plonked herself down a quarter turn around the fire from him and sat, knees up and arms crossed.

"You should probably call me Wayne," he croaked, gazing into the flames, "Sarafian sucks as a last name, but it sucks even worse as a nickname."

"So why did you let them call you that?" Denny said, still feeling a tad combative.

"Surely you've met gentlemen of their calibre before. They populate fine playgrounds everywhere. All you have to do is drop a hint that you hate a name they give you, and you've enshrined it as your nickname for all eternity."

"Well, mine's Denny, and I prefer it," Denny said, making a face. "Puh, *Felicia*, it sounds like some prissy French cat that lies around on a purple satin pillow all day. I'm sure it was my mom's idea. None of Dad's other kids had names like *Felicia*."

"Denny, huh?" He said it as though he was swishing it around in his mouth, seeing how it would taste.

Denny didn't know what to say after that. She looked at Geoff, laying beside her, and he thumped his tail twice, lazily. Apparently, he wasn't taking as well to their unorthodox hours the past few days as one might hope. Maybe it was time to go to bed.

Before she could budge though, he said, "I'm sorry about what happened back there. I'm sorry I touched you. I know that doesn't make it okay, but I have to say it. I'm not a bad guy…even though sometimes I am… I don't know. But you don't have to be afraid of me. I didn't kill anybody. I was trying to help them, in my own way and in my own time. You just kind of broke things open a little quicker than I was expecting."

Denny snorted."If you're such a great guy, then why did you stay with Georgie? You seemed pretty at home when I arrived."

"Home... I guess that's the problem. I don't really have one. At least not one I want to go home *to*. I'm from Hamilton. Only guy on the crew with no connections, no parents making six figures. I had nothing before I started working for Foster Towers, and I'd have nothing if I went home. Just a lot of guilt from my sisters, a severance check and a mouldy old apartment above a dive on Barton Street. That is, if Barton Street isn't flooded by now."

"It isn't," Denny said.

"Figures," Wayne replied. "You from the Hammer, too?"

"Nope. St. Catharines. More grunge, less water."

"Ugh. I went to St. Catharines once."

"Yeah, that's about the number of times most people go," Denny said. "They either show up out of curiosity and leave when somebody kills the cat, or they show up intending to stay for five minutes and get stuck for five decades. Either way, one visit."

"So why were you there, then? Get stuck?"

Denny paused for a minute. How much should she tell him? It wasn't like she was a spy or something, but a little worm crawled into her stomach when she thought of her life back home. It had been two years before she had told Jordan anything...and Jordan was a lot less threatening. Well, she could tell him the bare facts. It wasn't like she had to bare her soul or anything. Besides, if she was ever going to get to the bottom of what made *him* tick then, for better or for worse, there would have to be at least some minimal sharing going on.

"No, I stayed for the University. The only good thing in town. I had a good job there, and I left it. Sold it, more accurately. That's how I got the tent and all the supplies," she said, surprised at how much admitting she had left it all behind her still hurt.

"But why? Why not leave it to the authorities?"

Denny gave a snort.

"I tried the authorities. Who's to say Dad wouldn't rot, or melt, or disappear, or something before they ever even opened the case? I won't spend the rest of my life on hold waiting for them to get around to piecing the most sacred part of my life back together between doughnuts."

"You act like he was all you had."

Denny shot him the meanest look she could muster. What the hell did he have to be so critical about? You'd think a criminal on the run would have less discerning tastes.

"No, *I* was all *he* had. Dad and I didn't need anybody else."

"Okay…"

That was it. Right there. That look of incredulity, of criticism. She had been stupid to think he would understand. This conversation was over.

"I'm going to bed," she said, "and I suggest you do the same. You don't look so good, you know what I mean?"

"Well, thanks for helping me relax, Denny. You're a peach."

Argh! Cheeky bastard! One more quip and then she wouldn't answer him even if he screamed again. She took a few steps down the slope, then turned back halfway.

"I'm not your mother, and you pissed me off."

After the fiftieth turn in her sleeping bag, and the twentieth annoyed grunt from Geoff as she nudged him out of position, Denny flicked on her rechargeable flashlight and rummaged through her pack for something to read. The fire was still going, and whether or not Wayne was still sitting by it, she didn't care. So why wouldn't her mind stop going over there? She just had to get her mind back on what was familiar. Sherlock Holmes. Good choice. Maybe she could pick up a few pointers.

After reading the same sentence six times, only a paragraph in, the words went dead on the page. She tried another story, but to no avail. She pulled *Songs of Innocence and Experience* out. Too unsettling. She pulled out the Bible. Didn't know where even to begin.

It had been just her and Dad...all through everything. Sad that although he was around less than five times a year, he had been her closest companion. Why did Wayne have to remind her of the fact that he was gone? Why did he have to remind her of how futile this quest would seem to everyone but her, how futile it even seemed to a small, critical part of her that just wanted to be alone, that still blamed him for leaving her?

She could still smell the doughnuts in that little diner on Scott Street, with the bright red enamel tables, where they had gone out for lunch without Mom knowing. Where she had wrung the napkin to pieces, trying to explain through her tears that she was drowning…that she held her breath for the months while he was away. That she was only really gasping in air now and for the next few hours, and then she would go back to struggling for the surface again.

He had reached across the table and taken her hand (ink-stained, half picked-off clear sparkle nail polish) in his (meaty, slightly dirty, chipped nails) and looked into her eyes.

"We can stick together, you and I. Your mother don't get it, but you do. From now on, it'll be just us. We may not see each other all the time, but just knowing…just knowing that you're there helps me. And I can help you the same way. I may not be here, but I'm always *there*…know what I mean?"

That's what he had said, all those years ago, and Denny could still feel what happened next. It was then that she had split in two. Half of her had clung to those words as the board that would keep her from drowning, that would somehow carry her from the wreck of her childhood to the far-flung shore of adulthood (where, of course, all of your problems are magicked away by your boundless freedom to do anything you want), and the other half...had shrivelled a little bit more. Had become a little more bitter. A little more angry. That was the part that had said, over and over, that her dad had offered her a bad deal. That the affection that she clung to was only a tiny percentage of what she was entitled to, what most normal kids got every single moment of every single day of their lives. The part that wondered what was wrong with her. After that, there had been constant war inside her for a long time. The half of her that clung to Dad was forever at war with the anger, every day, stabbing away at it, killing it but never really putting it to rest. It had been painful, but over time she had convinced herself that it had worked. After a while, the part of herself that had doubted Dad grew quiet and stopped breathing.

But now he was gone, and Wayne was pointing it out. And it was night. And she was just tired enough to think stupid things. And the dead anger inside her had risen and was screaming at the top of its lungs.

Damn him.

CALLING UP THE RESERVE

She woke up to boots crunching around her tent, and a needle of panic went through her gut before she looked out the window and recognized Wayne's blue jeans and hard-soled boots.

"Hello? You awake? It's nearly noon."

Denny peeled herself off of the hard ground, her shoulders aching. Another pang of panic while she tried to remember whether or not she was wearing a proper shirt. Thank goodness, the answer was yes.

"Why didn't you wake me up earlier? I would have gotten up," she croaked as she stumbled out of the tent, zipping a loose sweatshirt on over her pyjama top.

Wayne had made his way around to the front of the tent, where he sat, dipping a stick into the river and watching the ripples.

"I didn't wake up myself until about an hour ago," he said, "and I wanted some time to think."

Denny remembered their previous conversation with a stab of aggravation and a little bit of embarrassment.

"So, where are we going?" she said.

Wayne let the stick flow down the river. He raised an eyebrow.

"I don't know, where are *you* going?"

"I'm coming with you. If you'll still have me," she said.

Wayne cracked a little grin.

"What?" Denny said.

"I can't believe you fell for that bluff in the first place. You're quick with a gun, but I thought you would have realized sooner that you've got all the supplies."

Denny felt her face flush. Not just because he had intended for her to come all along, but because he still hadn't forced her or stolen from her. He had let her make her own decision, even though her refusal to accompany him would mean that he couldn't get his revenge on Georgie and the others, or he would have to risk starvation trying.

"I don't have any survival training, and I'm not a hunter," she said. "I'm just warning you now."

"You've got a gun, if it comes to that. And I picked up some extra ammo on the way out. How much food you got in the pack?"

"Enough for a month for me...more if we ration it carefully. The dog has the same."

Wayne scratched his chin.

"Nice...we just might make it."

"Make it where?" She'd had about enough of his dancing around. If they were going anywhere, she at least wanted to know where. One amateur navigator would be bad, but two might actually stand a chance.

"Sit down," he said, pulling a folded-up map out of his pocket.

Denny sat near him, on the packed earth of the riverbank, and peered at the map. Wayne pinned it to the ground with one hand against the breeze and pointed with the other.

"We are here," he said, "at the southernmost tip of the Upper Duck River. We need to get to here," he moved his finger north a ways...quite a lot farther than Denny was comfortable with, actually, to a large golden blob on the otherwise green map. Denny read the text there, and her eyes went wide.

"The Hunting Bear Reservation? You've got to be kidding me. Verity Twoflower will have us hung up on the walls!"

"Don't believe everything you hear. Hunting Bear is where we find our answers. It's a risk, yes, but we have to go. Besides, right now it's the only other place (aside from the one you and I just trashed) that we can find food, shelter and allies in the North," he said, as if he were telling the story to himself more than to her. He didn't know if this would work either.

"You're not giving me a lot to go on here, Wayne. I've seen the news reports. They're a bunch of militants up there! They're trying to make a new country. They're crazy. That's why they stayed when everyone else left. It was a chance to establish their borders and fortify their location. I hear they're sending raiding parties out collecting weapons and supplies wherever they can..."

"But I'm not sure they're doing it for the reasons we think. This is going to be dangerous...there are no guarantees. Georgie and the higher-ups kept a lot of things from the technicians, but I have my suspicions. Something went wrong on their last trip to Hunting Bear, and I don't think the story they were giving on the news was the one that actually happened. The footage they got on that trip was also chopped up and used for various news reports on the Screamers, and that was where they got the footage of your dad, if I've got the air date calculated right," he said.

"But why would he be up there?"

"I don't know. I don't know if the Natives know either. But they might. And it's the best we have."

Denny paused for a moment, letting the breeze pull her hair back over her shoulder. Wayne's plan was crazy...and risky. But hadn't she packed for crazy and risky? Hadn't she bought into crazy and risky when she sold her job and left everything behind? What would she have if she went home? A job digging gravel in a ditch somewhere (at best) and a lifetime of regret. One thing about the Wild West...it sure lacked the bullshit the rest of society was slinging these days. And then she remembered Suzie's words: "Take care of him." Suzie knew something. Suzie knew that Wayne would need help to complete whatever mission he'd set himself. That it was just as far-fetched, and definitely more far-reaching, than her own mission.

"It seems like a long way, though," she said. "How long will it take us to get there on foot?"

"Well, it's 120 miles, give or take, few roads, and a lot of up and down. Realistically, walking all day, I would say...two weeks.

Once we get there, if we can get someone to help us, we could have access to ATVs, dirt bikes, trucks, you name it. Even if we got delayed, we'd still be far ahead of Georgie's crew. Of course, who knows what they'll be stirring up in the meantime. They've got to have material for the news, after all, and what makes better TV than poor defenseless Captain Trust Fund being run out of his roost by a bunch of ruthless feminist separatists?"

Denny grimaced and took a deep breath, then said, "We could even end up wanted criminals, but we can't worry about that now. There's nothing we can do about it. The thing you suspect is going on is much bigger, yes?"

"Yes."

"Then let's get packed up. We've only got so long to deal with this, and we're losing daylight."

After that, things moved on at a much more determined pace. There would probably be no more late mornings for quite some time, Denny reasoned, but after a day of walking over hill and over dale, she probably wouldn't have to worry about late nights, either. With Wayne's help, they had both tents packed up and their garbage buried by about two in the afternoon.

"We can take turns with the backpack, if you like," said Wayne as she lurched to her feet under the weight of all her supplies. "We might go faster that way."

Denny nodded, trying her best to seem hesitant, but inside she cheered. The backpack had been one of her biggest concerns if she were forced to travel on foot. She could manage, she had no doubt, but she had wandered around Toronto a half-dozen times with a regular school backpack on and ended the day with a sore lower back and pulled muscles across her chest.

Wayne had a smaller roll strapped to his back, consisting of his tent and his camera gear tied together with a net of backpack strapping. Denny guessed that he'd improvised it at some point during his career at the power plant because she hadn't seen anything like it in the camping supply stores. Once he had wangled everything into place, Denny reached into her utility belt and handed him her compass.

"Lead on," she said.

Wayne tucked the compass into his pocket, saying, "Well, first we have to find a place to cross this river."

They spent the next few hours following the river away from the dam, looking for a place where the water was shallow enough, or perhaps a fallen log or series of rocks. The river near their camp had been deep and swift-moving, with cresting waves appearing in the centre now and again. As they moved further away from the falls, the water calmed but showed no signs of getting any shallower. Nor did they come upon any convenient trees or rocks. They continued on, over small, shallow hills covered with pines that creaked in the wind, as the afternoon aged and the sun grew low. Geoff wandered alongside them on his retractable leash, sometimes ranging ahead, sometimes falling behind.

As the sun was setting, they came to a place where the river shallowed out, rushing over a bed of flat stones.

"Finally," Wayne said, "I thought we were going to waste the entire day finding a crossing."

"We better start taking our shoes off, although I hope we can avoid most of these pine needles...I got one stuck in my toe once and it's an experience I don't care to repeat," Denny replied.

"That's nothing. I got one stuck up my nose once."

"What? How?"

"How do you think? But I'll tell you one thing: my breath smelled piney fresh for a month."

Denny stared at Wayne, one eyebrow raised. She honestly couldn't tell from the smile on his face whether or not he was telling the truth, at least about the nose thing. She didn't have a chance to call his bluff, however, before Geoff pulled back on the lead, whining. He seemed to be shying away from the direction of the river, and before long, Denny realized why. Wayne followed her gaze across the river, where the bushes rustled as something heavy pushed its way through them. They stopped cold.

To her relief, not a bear, but rather a doe and fawn strode out into the stream, crossing tentatively toward them, their ears swivelling. The wind was at their backs. The doe caught their scent, bounding off into the brush with her fawn close behind.

Denny reached down to Geoff, scratching his head. She was surprised to find that, although the dog was steady, tongue lolling, her hand was shaking. Geoff, though, had held steady. He had warned them, but he hadn't given them away.

"Good dog," she said, "very good dog."

After that, they made short work of removing their shoes and socks and popping them temporarily into the centre of Wayne's bag. Since Denny weighed more with the pack on, she went first, so Wayne could grab her if he started to slip.

Denny slid a foot into the water and instantly her foot felt numb.

"This river is freezing," she said, thrusting her feet in with an effort of will: *ka-gloomp, ka-gloomp, ka-gloomp.* "I'm going to be tip-toeing the whole way!"

Wayne followed her with a series of *ker-sploosh*-es.

"Whaaaat? This is nothing. I used to go in the water at Centennial Park Beach in April! My grandparents couldn't keep me outta there! Little Wayne-a-roo, they used to say, hide of a polar bear and feet of a mountain gooohhhh-"

Big *Ker-sploosh.* Denny wheeled around to see if he needed help, but Wayne was already struggling back to his feet, his curls matted to his forehead, spitting out a stick that had made its way into his mouth. The pack on his back was dripping sheet rain down his legs. So much for keeping the shoes dry.

"Well?" said Wayne. "You gonna keep crossing or what?"

Denny kept moving, but replied, "I was trying to decide whether or not to laugh. It's still a toss-up. Please tell me your camera case is waterproof."

"I wouldn't float SOS messages in it or anything, but yeah, it's got a seal on it. It should be fine. We'll need to stop for the night on the other side, though. Walking in wet shoes will only set us back, and now the tent needs to open up and dry, too."

"Believe me, I had no intention of walking in wet shoes," Denny said, setting one foot, then the other, onto the shore. The pine needles were unfortunately prickly, and there didn't seem to be any clear places to wipe them off. When Wayne reached the shore, she motioned for him to give her back her shoes. She carefully dunked one foot into the water, then slipped her shoe on, then did the same with the other. It felt squelchy and awful, but it would have to do until they could find a campsite.

When they both had their shoes back on (such as they were), Denny looked up through the forest, where a narrow track had been beaten through the pines, running slightly uphill and due north.

"Looks like a deer trail," Denny said. "Maybe we can follow this for a while tomorrow to avoid the underbrush."

"Yeah, let's move up it a ways and see if we can find some open ground," Wayne replied.

After that, they spent most of the remaining light of day following the path through the darkening forest, looking for a likely place to settle in and build a fire. Soon, they found a little clearing in a ring of trees with some exposed dirt in the centre. Wayne set to work unpacking and opening his tent, and Denny pulled out her folding shovel to dig a fire pit. The ground turned out to be quite soft, due to the layers and layers of pine needles and little undergrowth. Within three-quarters of an hour, she had a nice pit dug, and by the time the last of the light faded, a fire was crackling away in it, and her tent was pitched nearby, across from Wayne's. She was mightily glad to get in there, take off her wet shoes, and get some fresh socks on.

Wayne had been in his tent a long while, she realized as she emerged, shoes and socks in one hand, bag of freeze-dried macaroni in the other. She placed her wet things on a clear space that she'd made after digging and sat down to eat her meal. She heard the snuffling sound of Geoff enjoying his behind the tent. After a few bites, the front zipper pulled down on Wayne's tent. Wayne's head popped out of the doorway, but he clutched the tent flap around everything else.

"Hey, could you lend me a hand here?"

Denny popped another forkful of macaroni into her mouth, chewed and swallowed.

"You're naked, if I'm not mistaken," she said.

"It was a choice between cold and wet or just plain cold. I made my choice, and I'll live with it," he said. "I just need you to put these out on a branch somewhere for me."

189

Wayne tossed a lumped-up ball of wet clothes out of the tent, where they landed beside Denny's feet. Despite his lack of organization, Denny had to admire that he had gotten the shoes to stay in the ball somehow.

"Just wait until I'm done my dinner. Then I'll hang these up and get you something to eat. What's your fancy, beef stew or chicken casserole?"

"They all taste like dog food, don't they?" said Wayne.

"More or less," Denny replied.

"Then by all means, surprise me."

By the time Denny wrung out Wayne's clothes, shook the sand off them, and hung them an appropriate distance from the fire, the last hints of orange drained from the sky. By the time she used the last of the boiled water to make him a container of beef stew, pinpricks of light lay scattered through the gaps beyond the treetops. A wail sailed over the rolling ground from far away. Denny quickly banked up the fire with the last of the gathered wood, bundled Geoff into the tent, and zipped up all of the windows behind her.

As the night filled with distant howls and trills, like a chorus of decaying wolves with human heads, Denny trembled beneath her sleeping bag. There was so much she wished that someone had been able to tell her, Officer Menken perhaps, or Violet... Could the Screamers travel? Did they enter buildings, or did they only inhabit human structures if they had risen there? She tried to sleep, but every time she started to dose off, she would picture a desiccated hand reaching in through her tent flap, or the brush of long, bony fingers along the nylon walls.

After a while, with nothing else to occupy her mind, Denny tried to separate the sounds, to distinguish the Screamers from one another. Back toward the river, but much further down, a high, piping voice, like a child's, was cry-singing something that, in tune, sounded like a broken Sunday school song. Another voice crawled over to them from the other side of the gradual slope they camped on, one long squawk and three chuckles in a repeating pattern that sounded like a parrot from Hell. Then there was another one, far, far away, perhaps down in the river basin by the power plant, that sounded more like Suzie. They all seemed to be repeating patterns, although the patterns varied in length and tempo.

Denny lay there for what must have been two hours at least, waiting for the Screamers to converge on them...but they never got any closer or louder. Either the Screamers weren't aware of them, or they couldn't (or didn't) move beyond the place where they had died. Perhaps, too, they only had an interest in speaking to specific people, even though they could be heard, in raw, untranslated form by everyone. But why could Denny hear Suzie's song, then? Was it because she was involved with Wayne? That couldn't be, because if the requirement were relation, then why couldn't Violet hear Rose's song when her mother clearly could?

And she had never, ever heard of anyone who could scream back to the Screamers. She had just done it when the time came...singing that song had been as natural for her as speaking, but it came from a different place. When she had sung, she had felt pushed forward by unseen hands, a vital seed borne by God's wind. At her urging, Suzie had gone to her final resting place. But what was the key to understanding these things? She couldn't understand any of the voices calling tonight.

Finally, without any answers, and unwilling to go trudging out into the woods alone to get them, Denny found herself drifting ever nearer to the shores of slumber. Geoff, too, settled down, only cracking an eye open now and again when something particularly loud happened. Just before she drifted off, she heard another voice join the mix. Male, young, sobbing quietly. It was going to be another rough night for Wayne.

NOISE AND SILENCE

The silence of morning pulled Denny from her sleeping bag as much as the soft light filtering down through the pine needles. The fire had reduced itself to a pile of smoky embers, which Denny smothered with a shovelful of dirt. Geoff staggered out of the tent with an apologetic doggy smile on his face, like a frat boy who'd just had a wild night.

Denny gathered Wayne's clothes off of the branch. They were still a little damp in places, but not so much that they wouldn't dry out completely after a couple of hours of walking. A snore drifted out of Wayne's tent. She felt a tiny pang of guilt for what she was about to do, remembering the sobs she had heard last night, but there could be no more late mornings if they were going to get to Hunting Bear in time. She whistled as loudly as she could. A squirrel in one of the nearby trees scurried away at the sound.

The snores stopped, but after several minutes, she still couldn't hear any movement in there. She grabbed one of the tent posts and shook it.

"Hey, you okay in there? It's morning."

"Ugh, just toss in my clothes," said Wayne. A hole opened up in the tent door and his hand poked out through. Denny put a ball of clothes into it, then stepped away for a breakfast bar.

Wayne emerged from the tent surly and silent. He said little more than grunts as they buried their garbage under the last of the fire pit dirt, tamped it down, and packed up the tents. By the time they had made it twenty minutes further down the deer trail, Denny had had about enough.

"I thought you'd want me to wake you up," she said to his back.

"Can we drop this, please? I just want quiet for a while," he replied, raising his hands.

Denny raised her eyebrows but said nothing more.

On they trudged for most of the day, through a stand of pine forest much like the one they had left on the other side of the river, only filled with more of the rushing of wind and less of the rushing of water. The slope they had camped on moved gradually up, reached a small hump of cracked shield rock, and then rolled back down again into a small glen with a creek in the bed. Most of the land they passed during the afternoon was a variation on this theme, fairly easy to pass and supplying good visibility in case an animal should cross their path. At one point, they reached an eroded ridge in the ground, draped with dangling tree roots, but they managed to find a way around it after a half an hour or so of looking.

As the sun faded in that subtle way that foretold the end of the afternoon in four hours or so, the ground began a gradual slope downward. By the time the sun was turning the distant sky creamsicle orange, they had reached a flat expanse of Shield rock surrounded by low hills. Grasses, moss, and small scrubby trees dotted the landscape, along with a few stands of wild blueberries out of season. Denny shaded her eyes and scanned the horizon. This landscape would go on for at least a day of walking. Hopefully the rocks and lack of cover wouldn't make it unbearably hot. In the far distance, what looked like an old tower loomed black against the horizon, along with the shimmer of water.

Wayne stopped a few paces onto the rock clearing and pulled out his map.

"That thing up ahead…it isn't on here," he said, voice wavering. Denny could see that the air was wavering, too, now that they were clear of the forest. It was going to be a long, hot walk.

"I'm sure there are lots of things out here that the maps miss," Denny replied. "Do we want to try and avoid it?"

Wayne sighed. "No, there's a lake on one side of it and a ravine that veers east on the other. We should be okay to go past it, but we'll either have to stop short or get well clear by nightfall."

Denny gave a dry chuckle, saying, "One advantage to travelling on hard rock, at least, is that nobody's likely to be buried here."

Wayne's brow darkened. He returned his map to his pocket and walked on. Denny felt a nasty comment bubbling up in her throat, but she pushed it back down. He'd had a hard night. She didn't have to take it so personally. But at the same time, it was hard to

195

deal with someone who treated you like you weren't worth talking to when you were also hot, itchy, and relying on the prince of grumpy for guidance through an uncharted wilderness. By the time they picked a camping place for the night, she was ready to smack him over the head with a tent pole if he gave her that look again.

They picked a place under a scrubby pine tree that leaned out of a crack like one of those skinny trees in pictures of the African Savannah pre-drought. Denny tied Geoff to it, then poured him some water.

When they pulled the tents out, they soon ran into a roadblock: the earth filling the cracks in the rock was too soft and shallow to hold tent pegs. Denny's tent was one of the newer kinds, a dome-shaped contraption with no real need to use tent pegs for stability (despite the higher chances of it blowing away in the wind). Wayne had just scrounged up whatever he could find and, unfortunately, the TV crew's backup tent was an ancient canvas thing with a peaked roof and thick plastic windows.

Over the next hour, as Denny searched around for rocks to build up a fire pit and sticks to fill it with, Wayne fumbled with his tent. First, he tried wedging his tent pegs in between the rocks. They fell out as soon as any weight pulled on them. Then, he tried tying part of his tent's guy lines to the tree in various places. The result barely resembled a tent and wouldn't pose any resistance to the kind of things that one erects a tent to avoid, and so Wayne

196

tore it down again with a swear. Geoff watched him, eyes wide, ears flat, tail down. Ultimate doggy disdain.

As Denny came back with the last armload of rocks for the fire pit, Wayne sat under the tree with Geoff, pushing the sweat and dirt off of his brow, or pushing them around, anyways.

"Do you want to try for the woods? It'd take us a couple of clicks out of our way, but you'd have a tent."

Wayne let out a snort and lowered an eyebrow as if what Denny had said was the stupidest thing in the universe. Denny threw up her arms and let them slap to her sides again.

"Okay, where you gonna sleep?" she said as if they had a spacious cabin just over the hill.

"Oh come on, are you serious?" Wayne said, the longest sentence he has spoken since noon. He stood up, and for a moment Denny thought that he was going to come after her, but instead he turned away, around the side of the tree.

Hot prickles climbed up Denny's neck. Her shoulders and jaw tensed.

"I could ask you the same thing. You really think that you're entitled to sleep in my tent after the way you've acted all day?"

"I've been helping you all day. Helping *us*! What have you been doing besides doling out the food?"

"And *you've* been doling out enough attitude for an army! What, you just expect to treat me like shit and then have me do you favours because I'm stuck with you? I have a compass. I have a map. I could still find my way back."

Silence between them. Somewhere, in one of the rock cracks, a single ragged cricket chirped. Geoff shifted his weight from one hip to the other. Great. Even the dog felt awkward. Wayne lifted one hand, just a little bit, and Denny noticed it shaking.

He said, "Well if they get me tonight…just you have fun getting back to town."

"I don't think they're out to *get* anyone, Wayne. The ones last night just kind of stayed in one place."

Wayne wrapped his arms around himself. He turned his head to the distant treeline. "That's because they didn't know we were there."

"Then how did Suzie know where we were? We were pretty far away from her grave, probably further than the Screamer over the hill last night, and yet she drew you in. I think they only bother people who have business with them, or maybe only people they think can help them, that they want to talk to. To the rest of us, their songs are just noise."

Wayne seemed to be relaxing a little. His next question sounded more like a child seeking reassurance than the sullen brat he'd been all day.

"So, what about all the people that went crazy or killed themselves? What's the theory on that?"

"I wonder, too, but I can only conclude that they must have had something big on their consciences. Thousands of square miles of wilderness hiding centuries of abuse, disappearances, unsolved crimes, runaways that met a nasty end...they'd all have something to say, and not everyone probably took the news as well as one would hope. I mean, think about it...one minute, you're taking a relaxing evening stroll along a ravine, and the next, the corpse of your missing sister climbs out to tell you that she was pushed in by her drug dealer. I think anyone might want to check their hold on reality after something like that."

Wayne came over to Denny's pile of rocks and started stacking them on the fire pit.

"Come to think of it, I've never really seen a Screamer attack anyone before two nights ago. When we were taping, we were all just so scared of them, and their songs were so horrible, that we just assumed that they were trying to hurt us. Too many horror movies, I guess," he said.

"Like I said to Jordan before I left, this isn't the movies," Denny replied. Since Wayne was working again, she decided that she might have some luck finding tinder and wood for the fire.

As she walked away, Wayne asked, "Who's Jordan?"

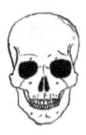

"Jordan was another TA that I hung out with a lot when I worked at Brock," she said, in between bites of some stuff that looked like waterlogged mozzarella. "I think he was the only person in the free world that actually got a little excited about the existence of the Screamers."

"He sounds like a sicko," said Wayne, sucking back a noodle from his freeze-dried stroganoff. The fire smoked and billowed in the other direction, the tiny flames barely leaping beyond the edge of the stones. They wouldn't be able to keep the fire going all night...bad news for keeping away the animals and, with blueberry patches in the area, even in the off-season they could be smack in the middle of bear country.

Denny said, "No, it wasn't like that. Jordan was a pop culture TA, with a specialty in horror movies. All his life, his family, his friends, just about everybody said he was too smart to be wasting his time on trashy movies, comics, and collectibles. They just couldn't see that those things were Jordan's passion, and that to him, they're just as worthy of examination and respect as Shakespeare. And to a certain extent, he's right...no matter what you think about pop culture, shouldn't its popularity alone make it important to talk about? It's what's in our heads, day in, day out."

"Yeah, but why would that make him excited about seeing people destroyed by a hoard of stinking corpses? Isn't he a human being, like the rest of us?"

This time, it was Denny that gave Wayne the lowered eyebrow. "He wasn't happy people were dying, Wayne. He was fascinated that, to him, the things that people had put him down and shunned him for enjoying had actually started to exist. He felt like, finally, all his education had prepared him for something that would matter to people."

"So why didn't he come up here with you and try to help you?"

"I think he wanted to...but he couldn't. When I sold my job and ran away, there was a chance I would end up living in a cardboard box when I got back. If Jordan sold *his* job and ran away, it would be him, his husband, and his son living in that box. Still, I wouldn't be surprised if he finds some way to involve himself in all of this, eventually," Denny said. For a moment, she almost expected to see his lanky, khaki-clad body stride out of the black woods on the horizon. She and Jordan had only really started hanging out in those last few weeks before she left. She hadn't expected to miss him so much.

"You know, I'm a bit surprised, too," Wayne said, leaning back with a mild smile on his face.

"What? Why?"

"You really seem to care about this guy. I kind of got the impression that you were a lone wolf. Didn't really need anybody else. I certainly didn't think you'd flip out today over a little silence."

Denny made a skeptical face, but she said, "I hate too much silence. I just have to live with it. I've always had to."

The two of them sat there, staring at the rising smoke for a few minutes. Geoff, having finished his own meal, came over for a pat from Denny. She slung an arm over him and he sat there staring into the guttering flames with them, panting all the while.

As the fire faded to the glow of coals, Wayne turned to Denny, looking her in the eye this time.

"Denny, I'm scared. I wish I didn't have to admit that, but I can't sleep out here on my own. Not after what happened with Suzie. Please."

His gaze was so intense, so sincere, that Denny averted her eyes. Seeing Wayne afraid only fed the fear parasite in her own stomach.

"It's not like I can lock the tent flaps," she said with a nervous half-smile.

The fear parasite had little fluttering babies that evening as Wayne rolled up in his blanket across from her. He still had all his clothes on, at her request, but he might as well have been stark screaming naked. Denny, too, kept everything on. It was getting nippy out anyway. Best to stay toasty and avoid colds. Geoff, with very little room for himself, settled down in between them at their feet by the door. Good. Any shenanigans and the dog would tramp all over her. No surprises. She also had her flashlight close at hand. And her pocketknife.

Denny fidgeted around a bit before deciding that she'd rather read a bit before bed, and let Wayne fall asleep before her. She shook her flashlight for a few seconds, then turned it on.

Tonight Sherlock Holmes held together better. As she read one story, then another, a mix of comfort and regret mingled in her. On the one hand, Holmes seemed to be able to make sense of anything…a trait she envied more than ever in the midst of this wilderness. On the other, everything in these stories had a rational explanation, no matter how haunting or uncanny they seemed. How did one produce a rational answer to a seemingly irrational problem? Organized religion had been trying to do that for centuries, and judging by the many religiously-based wars still raging all over the world, it didn't seem like anybody had come up with a universal theorem yet. How wonderful to live in Sherlock's world…a world of science and rationalism and *answers*. And yet, she had lived in that world before the Screamers rose. And in some ways, she supposed, that world had all been a lie. There had been something waiting just beneath the veneer of the visible world the entire time.

"Were you in English?"

Denny looked over. Wayne hadn't gone to sleep. Instead he'd propped himself up on one elbow and had been watching her read.

"What?"

"Were you an English professor?"

Denny gave an indulgent smile. Only someone who hadn't gone would think she could go through a PhD that quickly.

"No, I was a TA. I did all of the grunt work for the professors, but I also taught classes. I talked to people about books."

"Sounds pretty good," Wayne said, "so did you have a specialty?"

"Romanticism."

"Typical girl," he said with a chuckle.

"No, not Romance. Romanticism. The nineteenth century literature of emotion and personal expression?"

Blank look.

"Keats? Shelley?"

"Is Clancy in there somewhere?" Wayne asked, obviously trying his best for an endearing grin.

Denny sighed.

"No."

"Then you've lost me," he said, with a sheepish grin.

"Don't feel bad. That's most people these days. It's wonderful stuff, though. You should give it a look. Unfinished tales, mysteries lurking in the dead of night...the dawn of science fiction," she said.

Wayne chuckled, once. "So...according to you we need more mysteries lurking in the dead of night?"

"No, but we do need literature that helps us deal with them. Romanticism called me because, in many pieces, there are no fixed endings...only fragments, hints, and dreams. And the romantics...they believed in total expression. Imagine how much easier it would be for so many people to heal if they didn't have to feel guilty about their struggles, their depression..."

"You didn't strike me as the expressive type, at first."

"Chalk it up to a lack of good role models. Maybe it's always just been a dream for me, but being close to those authors, to their total freedom of expression, always made me feel a little bit better, like I was expressing myself along with them," she said, hugging her knees and dropping Sherlock on the sleeping bag. The book hit the side of Geoff's leg, making him twitch and grumble.

"So, why did you become a cameraman?"

"It was a paycheck," Wayne replied with a shrug. Denny inclined her head toward him, in the bullshit position.

"Okay, okay," he said. "I wanted to get out of Hamilton. When I was a kid, I wanted to be one of those guys on the *National Geographic* specials who waded through endless muck and reeds to get a shot of endangered elephants, or shimmied up trees to find the world's only wild albino python. I guess the best I could do was get up here, chasing Screamers and refugees."

Denny thought of where they were and wanted to laugh. She'd seen more wild animals since coming up here than in all her life before. Some of them had even been pretty strange and wonderful. "There's wildlife up here, too," she said. "Have you ever thought of capturing some of that while you're here?"

Wayne looked at the ground. "The point wasn't to focus on where I am. The point was to get out."

Denny thought about the day, the hike, the smell of the pines, the fresh air soothing her aches. If she had come here before the Screamers, if she'd even known what was up here, she never would have left. People on the peninsula never went much further than their own backyards, unless it was to Buffalo. And yet, on the full body of Canada, Niagara and all of the GTA were no bigger than a toenail.

"I think you'd miss it here. I know I would," she said.

A chorus of howls rose up around the edge of the clearing, fading up like a far-away air raid siren. Wayne's hand darted out, grabbing for the flashlight, but Denny clasped it, pulling it away.

"Turn it off,- turn it off!" Wayne hissed, his head jerking in the direction of the howls.

"Fine, just stop spazzing out!" Denny said, flicking off the light. The two of them became silhouettes as the moonlight seeped in through the tent walls. Wayne's silhouette dropped back. Denny heard the rustle of covers as he attempted to get comfortable.

"Good night, Wayne," she said.

"As compared to what, Denny?"

She didn't answer.

DAMN DOG

The sun rose, and the air in the tent got muggy. Denny emerged from the tent to a pale pink sky turning to blue, like a giant dome of cotton candy. She tested the air: fresh, moving well with a slight breeze, and tinged with the scent of pine and that strange sun-baked rock smell that was hard to put your finger on. Judging from the lack of clouds (a miracle on a fall day as warm as this), they would have a full day of clear hiking ahead of them. Soon after she emerged, Wayne and Geoff staggered out into the sunshine as well. Wayne gave a friendly wave and went behind the pine tree to relieve himself. For his sake, Denny turned around. That pine tree wouldn't hide a pencil. From the look of his hair, though, and the blanket marks on his face, he'd slept, at least a little.

They packed up in the shortest amount of time yet, and as the rocks heated up and the air got wavy, they began the hike again toward the tower in the far distance. Denny took a lot of long pulls on her water, hoping against hope that the lake up ahead would have a running tributary somewhere. She had filled up briefly at the power plant, but her stores were getting low. Her stomach turned a little at drinking water that had just been sitting around in the woods, but she'd just have to break out the purification tablets and hope for the best. She looked down at Geoff, striding along beside her with his tongue hanging out of his mouth. Oh, to have the stomach of a dog. He'd be able to drink just about everything, barring a serious case of industrial pollution.

As the two of them moved closer to the tower in the distance, Denny saw that it was an aged, wooden structure, the kind whose paint had all peeled off and whose boards had turned grey with age. They came over the crest of a slow decline that they hadn't seen in the distance, and she soon noticed that around the base of the tower was a jumble of buildings made out of more of the same weathered wood and corrugated steel. There had once been a chain-link fence around the whole compound, but now it slouched to the ground, worn down by years of wind and rust.

Wayne stopped when the rest of the compound came into sight.

"Looks like an abandoned mine. I know it's daytime, but all the same, I'd rather stay out. We don't really need supplies, and who knows what's in there, waiting around to get tripped on," he said.

Denny thought to herself that the only thing Wayne was worried about tripping on was another pile of bones, but she said nothing. No sense pouring salt in his wounds. Despite there being no real practical purpose to going into the mine complex, she had secretly been looking forward to checking it out during the day, ever since they saw the tower in the distance. All present circumstances aside, there was something fascinating about old, abandoned buildings…their age, perhaps, or the strange treasures from the past that still lingered in forgotten corners and piles of rotten wood.

"Yeah, as much as I kind of want to look around, you're probably right," she replied. "Let's head for the lake. I'm hoping the water there is clean enough to drink."

From the top of the slope, they made their way left of the mine complex, heading for the ring of tall, yellowed grass that surrounded the small lake. As they travelled, the Shield rock broke up more, becoming topsoil and small plants again. The wind blew against their faces, breaking up the sweltering heat and bringing with it the smell of fresh water. Certainly, poisoned water could smell fresh, but at least Denny could bet that they wouldn't arrive at the water's edge to find it choked with stinking algae. The edges of Lake Ontario stank so badly of it in the late summer and early fall that the people living along the waterfront planned to flee inland during those months. Combine that with mounds of goose poo from the giant flocks that covered the parks and, well, Denny had always felt thankful to live in the interior of the city rather than along the lakeshore.

They arrived at the edge of the lake at around three o'clock. With any luck, Denny would have time to test the water, then they could move far enough away from the mine complex by dusk to avoid any unpleasantness.

When they reached the water, Denny kneeled down and scooped up some of the water in her hand. There was no oil sheen

209

on top, and the water didn't feel oily or warm up, the way some chemical contaminants will do, when she rubbed it between her fingers. After a little boiling and some purification tablets, it would probably be fine. She took off her backpack, fished out her water containers, and dipped them, one by one, in the water until they were full. As she was loading them back into the pack, she felt a hand touch her shoulder softly, as if Wayne didn't want to startle her. A finger extended into her vision, pointing across the lake.

Slowly she turned. How they had missed the bear, looking back, she would never know. But there it was...larger than even she had expected, as big as a micro-compact car. It waded into the lake, its white and tan fur floating on the water as it sunk in. This was no ordinary bear. This was one of the polar-grizzly hybrids that had been proliferating ever since the Arctic started to melt.

So far, it hadn't noticed them.

Denny picked up her backpack, dropping it onto one shoulder. The weight of the pack caused a shooting pain to travel up her neck, but it would hurt more if the bear caught on. She groped backward, grasping onto Wayne's shirt, then pushing him back. They backed away slowly together for a few steps, until she remembered Geoff. His lead was on the ground to her right, and at the end of its vibrant red s-curve, Geoff stood at attention, tail up, neck straight, sniffing the air.

Denny reached down slowly for the lead. Her hand hooked around the loop after what felt like hours of groping around blindly on the ground. She pulled up on the leash slowly, steadily...

Geoff's license tags rang out like the peal of a bell on the silent plain. The pizzly's head twitched toward them, and its tiny, glittering eyes locked on them. It rose on two feet out of the water and roared, lake water spittle flying from its outstretched lips.

Before Denny and Geoff could react, the bear charged toward them, fast and direct as a freight train, its immense bulk flapping up and down with every bound. Denny fumbled for her gun, but her fingers were numb, frozen...by the time she found the stock and yanked it from its strapping, the bear was ten feet away and closing, and all she saw was teeth, teeth, and deadly claws. Wayne screamed her name and pulled on her, but that only caused her to stumble, suddenly off-balance.

A flash of black and white rushed into the space between them and the bear. Geoff skidded to a stop in front of her, barking and snarling, ears down, using all of his sixty-pound body to project aggression. Wayne yanked her arm then, and, as if smashed from a block of ice, her numb legs moved, pounding away behind him toward the mining complex in the distance. Denny turned to look back, not caring if she hit a rock or a gopher hole.

"Geoff!" she screamed, "Geoff, come!"

She knew he heard her, but Geoff stayed in the distance, a crouched figure blocking the bear's way, turn which way it might. Damn dog...damn loyal dog. She kept running, alternately thanking him and cursing him in her mind, tears pouring down her face as she commanded him, with her heart, to come.

A yelp cut through the air, and this time, she didn't have the heart to look back.

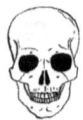

Denny's lungs burned and her lower back radiated with dull ache as they jogged over the old frost fencing ringing the rusted-out mining buildings. The whole place ran along a dirt track that was now barely two ruts in a sea of weeds. Denny and Wayne separated to try doors. The first building Denny came to had been secured with a rusty padlock. She rammed it with her shoulder, then kicked it, but the lock merely flopped up and down without breaking. Judging from the swears and clangs coming from the other end of the street, Wayne wasn't having much luck either. She ran to the next building, still terrified that the bear might be anywhere behind them, gaining on them with every lost moment. She spotted another building, two storeys with square windows and a covered staircase going up one side. This one had a steel door with a round knob and no padlocks in sight. She jiggled the handle, which squealed and resisted her. Using two hands she wrenched it around and threw her weight against the door. It banged open unevenly, sticking in one corner. Inside, the walls of the plain cement room were lined with old bunks, still strewn with mildewed mattresses.

"Wayne," she yelled down the street. "I've got the bunkhouse open!"

Wayne raced toward her as though a thousand Screamers were at his tail, button-hooking into the building by grabbing the door frame and swinging to save time. They forced the door shut together, sticky corner and all, then searched the room for something to block it with.

A huge, tan-and white back galloped by the building's rectangular windows, its footfalls shaking the ground. Denny sucked in breath so she wouldn't scream again. Wayne let out a tiny whimper. For a brief moment, they thought the beast had passed them by. Denny looked out a corner of the window, timidly, gun first, to see only an empty lane and a few drifting milkweed puffs.

Then, the pizzly sped out of the shadows of a nearby alleyway, slamming into the door with all its weight. The steel door bowed inward, but didn't open, yet. The bear backed up for another run.

Denny's anger flared, and her eyes welled with tears again as she remembered Geoff's yelp. She wouldn't let his bravery go to waste. She primed her shotgun, which was still in her right hand.

"Come on, you bastard!" she yelled. "What did you do to Geoff!"

The bear hit the door again, and it gave way. It skidded several feet into the building, its claws dragging on the cement floor. It looked up at Denny, teeth bared, and she needed no better opening. She lifted her gun and pulled the trigger.

The shotgun's bang hit her ears like a punch from both sides at once, bouncing off the cement walls with an echoing ring. At the same time, the bear's face disappeared behind a curtain of red spray. It gave a last yelp, a deeper version of Geoff's final call, then its knees buckled and it fell to the floor. Denny couldn't look at what was left of the animal. Her heart was pounding, and the spreading pool of blood on the floor wasn't helping the feeling that she was watching all of this from the end of a long tunnel. Wayne came, quietly, and put an arm around her, and turned her away from the wreck of the beast. The air was thick and mildewy and smelled like sweat and cement and dirty fur and it was hard to breathe, it was catching in her throat. And then she was crying, leaning on Wayne's shoulder, crying harder than she had since the first night she'd found Geoff without Dad. Everything hurt…her ears, her shoulders, her lungs, her legs…everything. Wayne trembled beneath her, even as he supported her. When he spoke, she realized that he was crying, too.

"Thank you, Denny," he repeated, over and over. "Thank you."

The top floor of the bunkhouse was unlocked as well. Denny and Wayne shuffled into it as night fell, to find the same scene as downstairs, minus the bear.

"I wonder what they'll think in ten years if someone comes along and finds the bones of that bear," Denny said as she unrolled her sleeping bag on the floor. "They'll have no idea what happened here, or why the bear tried to break in. It seems strange that so much can go on in a place, and when it's done, it all goes silent again, except for memories."

"Do you think the Screamers are just memories, then?" Wayne asked.

Denny thought for a moment.

"No, because there are so many of them…all of them can't still be remembered by someone. Some of them have to be from the far past, as well."

Wayne remained silent for a moment, watching the glow fade from the windows. The light played on his face, causing ripples to move across his skin. He looked as though he might transform at any moment, confident to coward, funny ha-ha to funny peculiar, and back again.

"I don't know how I'm going to handle tonight," he said. "Please don't judge me. I…I don't like people to see me cry."

Denny raised an eyebrow, a smirk on her face.

"I saw you nearly shit your pants back there. What's a little crying?"

TUNNELS IN THE ROCK

A howl sank into Denny's ears, rising in the night air and reverberating in her head like the boom of heavy bass. Closer to home, a whimper crept into the noise. Wayne huddled in the corner, heedless of the rotting mattress at his feet or the cobwebs growing there. He shook all over. Although he hid his face, a drop of water darkened the dusty floor at his feet.

"I don't want to see them... Denny, don't let them near me," he said.

Denny pushed herself to her feet, her hands catching a thin layer of dust from the cement floor. Her stomach ached, her legs ached...her head pounded, not with a headache, but with the steady drumbeat of her pulse. Every limb felt as heavy as the cement floor. And yet, as she listened, the howling morphed into the vibrato trill of an opera singer and then heightened into the silvery voice of a young girl. The melody she sang soared around Denny, like dove's flight put to music.

Denny concentrated harder, trying to hear the words, but she still floated in a sea of half-meanings, words that she knew meant something, somewhere, but that buzzed past her ears without landing. Then something deep in the centre of her being pulled like a rope tied around her core. She gasped, feeling a tug just beneath her ribs.

If she could get closer, she thought, she could hear those words. The little girl's voice was talking to *her*. The other Screamers they had heard since Suzie had just screamed away into the night, with no effect on Denny or her emotions. But this one wanted her. She could tell. She stood for a moment, swaying slightly, then moved toward the door, her knees and hips howling at her as loud as the voice.

She reached the door.

"No, please don't leave me," Wayne said.

Denny held out a hand.

"Don't worry, Wayne. There's nobody in here. Can you tell what they're saying?"

"No..."

"Then they don't want you," Denny replied, trying to make her voice as soothing as possible.

"How do you know?" Wayne said, voice shaking.

Denny gave an apologetic half-smile. "Because they want me. They're calling me."

Wayne's eyes, previously walled off with fear and tears, widened, an electricity flowing through them that she hadn't seen before. His spine went rigid. He got up, paced, pulled at his hair.

"No! Are you crazy? They'll kill you!"

Denny closed her eyes a moment. She listened to the voice, listened to the small voice inside of her.

"I don't think so," she said, slipping out of the door and into the night. "Not this time."

The moon was bright and full outside of the bunkhouse, casting a frosted light on the exposed planes of the buildings. The whole place looked like an art deco poster she had seen once of a futuristic city, all hard-edged patches of colour. A small cloud rolled across the moon, causing the poster colours to crawl over the elevator tower.

Denny listened. The voice was coming from that direction, as well. She descended the steps, heading across the laneway and through the tall grass. Beside the decaying tower was a long, low shed, the door of which hung open. Denny crept toward the black square of night inside the doorway. The voice bubbled up through this place from somewhere to her left.

A bright, almost blinding point of light jabbed out of the doorway. A bare, dirty bulb on the wall, screwed into a rusty box, buzzed out a yellow glow. Denny felt her pulse race, but she continued on inside. Whoever was calling her, it sounded like a little girl. Denny couldn't just leave her here if she could release her, like she had Suzie.

Inside the shed, Denny passed a double row of lockers, some with doors hanging askew. A scored helmet sat on top of one, its brim pointing the way to an open steel door. This door had visible pry marks on it, as though someone had forced it open with a crowbar.

Denny nudged the door open to find a cement stairwell beyond, tunnelling its way down through the Shield rock. She came to the end of the light, at the top of the stairs and wondered what lay beyond the beam. No Screamer glow had shown up yet, so the little girl, she concluded, must be further on. As if in answer to her stream of thought, another row of lights buzzed on, one by one, in a line down the stairs. Denny took one step down, then another, feeling the hairs rise on the back of her neck. The lights followed her down and down, lighting up before her and burning out after her. Her whole body broke out in goosebumps. Perhaps Wayne had been right about not coming down here...whatever was calling her had her right where it wanted her.

But it was a little girl. And she sounded lonely.

After enough landings, turns, and flights of stairs to make her dizzy, the lights led Denny to a small room carved out of the rock. Ahead of her, the floor dropped away and a cool breeze rose from below. A pair of cables and a whole bunch of pipes and struts descended into the pit. A control box hung off the wall by its wires. Something had made a nest in behind, and paper insulation and animal droppings spilled out.

The Screamer's song, which had held steady for a long while, swelled. Denny drifted away from herself for a moment, and in that moment, she felt only curiosity. What was down the elevator shaft? Was there still something in there? Did monsters live down there, under the earth? She crept to the edge and peeped over into the darkness.

"What the hell are you doing?" Wayne's voice delivered a jolt, which shook her out of her reverie, "get back from there!"

Denny stepped, almost stumbled back. What *had* she been doing? More importantly, who had she been while doing it?

"I just felt like I had to, all of a sudden…" she said.

"*We…*" Wayne yelled, then, his eyes darting around him, switched to a much lower register. "We're getting out of here, right now. Who knows why they closed this place? This tunnel could cave in any minute! There could be chemical spills or poison gas or who the hell knows what else!"

Gears squealed, machinery hummed, and the elevator cables slowly began to move of their own accord. They accelerated, faster and faster, until all of a sudden, with a crash and a bang, a cage-like elevator arrived at the terminus, billowing clouds of dust over the floor like graveyard mist. Denny looked back at Wayne. Wayne was stunned speechless, his mouth hanging slack.

Her knees shook, and her mouth went as dry as the dust billowing around them. Denny shook her head. No way. No. Way. Wayne was right. Who knew what was down that mine shaft, and…

One word, that she understood, echoed up the shaft. That one word grabbed her heart, squeezed, and wrung it dry.

Daddy...

Denny extended a foot and tested the floor of the elevator. It didn't sway or give way under the pressure. She walked into the elevator and turned around. The grate slid shut in front of her. Wayne ran to it.

"Denny!" he was almost on the verge of another sobbing fit.

Denny reached a hand up to the grate. Sweat broke out on her skin. For a moment, she wished the barrier between them would open again. Then the elevator dropped.

It happened all at once: the cage hurtled down into the black, as fast as it could possibly go without Denny flying up into the air. Her stomach flipped. Her hair blew around her shoulders as the elevator passed unseen shafts hidden in the darkness. She gritted her teeth. What would happen when this elevator reached the bottom? Already she felt weightless.

Brakes screamed, and sparks flew from the sides of the shaft. Slowly, slowly, the elevator came to a stop, dangling down into a large cavern lit with a soft, pink light. Denny, who had crouched down during the stop, fearing that she would be crushed on jagged rocks or thrown out as the elevator disintegrated, removed her arms from her head and assessed her surroundings. In the squeal of the brakes, everything had gone quiet; no Screamers, no rushing air, no nothing. The elevator dangled two or three feet above the floor of the cavern.

Someone stared at her. Ten feet away, a girl, no, more a smudge of pink light, like an upside-down exclamation point with a girl-shape in the centre, floated above a small, flat skeleton. She looked to be about seven years old, clad in jeans, a vest, and a long-sleeved shirt in a style that might have come from around the end of the last century. Her long, dark hair hung over her shoulder in a side ponytail. Her head tilted, and her eyes, two lamps in the darkness, widened as she sang,

Hello, hello,
It's so lonely down here,
You're not my daddy,
Is he there?

Daddy came exploring,
Wanted stuff to sell,
Wanted me to help,
Then I fell.

I know you can hear me,
Why is that?
Can I give you my locket,
To take back?

Please don't tell Mommy

Or she'll put Dad away,
She never let me ride my bike,
Or go out to play.

Denny, immersed in the song now, floated on its humming cadences. Energy flowed through her, connected her to the music of the little girl's soul. She opened her mouth, and it was almost as if the thoughts that had been collecting deep inside of her were sucked out, and she sang them as they left her.

I followed your voice
All the way down here
I don't know how to leave,
And I'm kind of scared.

I'll take your locket home for you,
If I can,
But others count on me for help,
A dog, and a man.

Help me keep them safe and sound,
By sending me back home,
My own daddy needs me,
My daddy died alone.

He suffers every night and screams,
Just like you,
I need to go back
So I can help him too.

The content of the message flowed from her as instantly and effortlessly as exhaling, but when it was gone, and she realized what she had said, she felt vulnerable, and a little stupid. Why had she admitted to being scared? Why did she tell a strange spirit about her dad? Sure, it was pertinent…but it just wasn't something she really wanted to talk about. It had just sort of…popped out there.

She locked eyes with the spirit as it hovered there, wave after wave of pulsating light beaming from it. A moment, what felt like an hour, of silence, and only the earth around them breathed, sending drafts up from far below.

Then, as smoothly and silently as a cloud rolling over the sun, a small object rose between them on a chain: the locket. Denny felt the shadow of it climb up and over her body, then her face. She reached out a hand, and it fell into her palm, the chain tickling as it settled almost weightlessly between her fingers.

The elevator behind her whirred to life again, a few flakes of corroded paint falling off of it onto the chipped rock. Denny climbed back into it, rust scraping onto her jeans as she did. She stood, one hand gripping the mesh wall of the car, and looked back at the little girl. She did not disintegrate into peaceful rest as Suzie had, but stood there much as she always had, a slip of light buried far beneath the earth, lonely and confused.

Something inside Denny ached at leaving her here like this. Something else inside her felt like it would stay forever, like she had already lived in this hole herself. Her only consolation lay in the locket: if she could deliver it, the little girl would be free.

One more wave of song washed over her.

"My name is Jessica," it said.

The elevator door slammed closed, and it shot up through the shaft like a rocket, gluing Denny's stomach to the floor. Everything spun. The car rattled into the terminal, leaned over and spat her out, causing her to stumble and fall to her hands and knees on the floor. Wayne was still there, although his skin had gone much greyer and his hair was matted down with sweat, and he crept toward her. Denny held out a hand. Her work wasn't done on the floor yet. She coughed, gagged, and then puked.

"Feels worse coming up than it does going down," she said when the spasms had passed.

Wayne offered an elbow when they attempted the stairs together, and for once, Denny took it. By the time they reached the top, both of them had to stop for several minutes to catch their breath. It was there that Wayne grabbed Denny's arm.

"Do you hear that?" he said.

Denny did hear it. Outside, somewhere out in the street, a single dog was howling.

Art by Robin McLean.

227

A CREDIT
TO HIS BREED

In the end, they found him huddled by the corner of the bunkhouse, beside an old drainpipe. From the moment Denny got close enough to see him as more than a silhouette in the shadows, she knew why he had been howling.

Geoff hung his head, looking up at them with huge, full-moon eyes, as if ashamed to appear before them in his sorry state, even after all that he had done. He shivered and gave a small whimper as Denny kneeled down and caressed his face, one of the only places on his body that she could tell for sure wasn't injured.

His front right leg was soaked in blood. Denny saw, on closer inspection, that he bled from a deep gash over his shoulder. Perhaps that was the reason for his slouch, if it had done damage to his neck muscles, too. His belly was intact, save for a few scratches, thank God, and his legs themselves didn't seem to be in any immediate danger from wounds. The other unpleasant area on Geoff was his tail. It was bent at an awful angle, totally broken, and bleeding from a deep furrow out of which Denny caught a glimpse of white bone.

Denny imagined that Geoff had beaten a hasty retreat when the bear swung at him, and a border collie could retreat most hastily indeed. The yelp she had heard had not been Geoff's death cry, as she had thought, but his cry of surprise as the bear's claw caught him in the shoulder as he ran off. The angry bear must have tried to grab Geoff's tail then, slowing him momentarily, but not nearly enough for the bear to catch up. Then, Geoff must have found someplace to hide until he was sure the bear was gone. *Smart boy...same strategy as the rest of us*, she thought. After that, he would only have had to follow their scent.

Both wounds had bound themselves up a little with matted hair and dried blood, but Denny was sure that they couldn't stay that way or infection would set in too soon for them to get him help...that is, if they still had any veterinarians at Hunting Bear, or ever did. Panic welled up in her at the thought of the miles ahead, and many miles behind, neither of them leading to any definite help for Geoff.

Geoff sensed her distress and tried to thump his tail. He let out another surprised yelp and only managed to twitch the stump a little. Denny closed her eyes and steadied herself for his sake. What was a dog without a wag? And for their sakes, he had given it up.

"Wayne, we need to get him upstairs. Can you lift him?" she said.

"I don't want to hurt him, but I'll try."

Wayne approached Geoff slowly, arms out in front, saying soft, comforting things. Geoff let Wayne wrap his arms around his midsection and gradually, carefully lift him an inch off the ground.

He thrashed a little, yelping. Wayne adjusted his grip and tried again. This time, Geoff kicked his back legs, but his body stayed still. Denny moved in to support Wayne. If Geoff decided to flip around again and he lost his grip, maybe she could minimize the damage.

They took the stairs one slow step at a time, the sound of their feet on the grating echoing in a way that still made Denny very nervous after the events of the day. Despite the bear carcass sprawled out on the floor below, Denny wondered about ghosts. Could bears become Screamers? She had never been near enough to one to find out.

Finally, they reached the landing, clanged over to the door, and entered the mildewy darkness of the bunkhouse.

Wayne set Geoff down slowly, gently onto the extra blanket. Holding Geoff, he didn't tremble, didn't jitter on his way to the floor. His eyes and his face were steady and stern as a cried-out funeral mourner.

"You're going to be okay, buddy. We'll get you out of here," he said in a whisper.

Denny grabbed the camel pack with the last of the clean water in it. She also dug into her first aid kit and brought out some antiseptic wipes and tweezers.

Geoff tried to get up, and Wayne pushed him back down with a firm hand.

"That's good. Keep him still," Denny said. She crouched down beside Geoff and stroked him a couple of times on his good side. She tried to stay as calm as possible…Geoff would pick up her fear and add it to his own. Already he panted, wanting to get away but obviously spent.

Denny wet the matted hair over Geoff's shoulder wound with a little of the water, then slowly, carefully pulled at a piece with the tweezers. Geoff thrashed and whined, but Wayne held him steady, and Denny released a breath as the fur pulled loose.

"I'm sorry, boy. It'll be over soon," she said, picking up a disinfectant cloth.

An excruciating hour later, it was done. Denny had cleaned the wounds to the best of her ability, and then bandaged them with strips of sweatshirt. Geoff stopped struggling about halfway through, resigning himself to the occasional whine and lift of the head. When they were done, all three lay down on the floor, barely summoning the energy to crawl to a blanket. Denny lay her head down on her arm, and remembered no more.

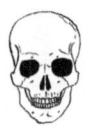

She awoke to the clicking of a camera shutter. The late morning light drifted in through the empty window sockets, and at the windows, nose to the wind, Geoff sat, like a statue gathering pigeons. Crouching a few feet away, Wayne framed him up for another shot and pressed the button.

He said without looking back, "He should be remembered. No matter what happens."

"Don't talk like that. We'll get him there."

Wayne stayed silent. Denny left the issue there. His silence begged the question: how *were* they going to get Geoff there? He wouldn't be able to walk long distances for at least a few days. They would need to make a travois, and even then it would probably slow them down, possibly even stall them out.

Well, now they'd really done it. Fleeing the power station had been one thing. She'd had enough supplies and equipment left to get *somewhere* safe, and the question had only been where to go. Now, a week out, with double the food and water gone that she had bargained for because of Wayne's presence on the expedition, they had to get somewhere that had food and fast. They had exactly the amount of time left that Wayne had estimated, and if they went beyond that, they'd either have to get really good at hunting or figure out how to get emergency phone reception from pine trees.

For a fleeting moment, Denny pictured what it might be like to leave Geoff behind, and the sickness that washed over the deepest part of her, the raw stab of conscience, told her that she could never do such a thing. Yeah, most people would say she was stupid for giving the life of a dog the same weight as her own, but those people had only known dogs as lounging house pets and ornamental playthings for their kids. Geoff was a member of their party. Had been since the beginning. He'd scouted out the trail with them, kept them warm, warned them of danger, and even saved their lives at his own expense. The three of them were a team, a unit, and all of them had sacrificed something to get this far. They would reach Hunting Bear together, or not at all.

Denny remembered yesterday, the way she had taken down the bear when backed into a corner. When the chips were down, she had done what she needed to do. She still had a shotgun. She still had ammo. If she could take down a bear, she could take down an elk or a deer. Now, for that travois...

"I'm going to go search for something to carry him on," she said, heading for the door. "We need to get a move on if our supplies are going to last."

Wayne, who had been crouching by Geoff, twisted himself around to face her.

"Don't run off on me again," he said, "we're responsible for him now."

Denny stumbled over her words as she closed the door to the stairwell. "Don't...don't worry about it... I'll be fine..."

It struck Denny then, as she descended the stairs into the yard, that Wayne believed that last night was his fault. That she secretly hated him so much that she was willing to run off and leave him for a Screamer. She still didn't entirely trust him the way that someone who *hadn't* fucked up big-time in the sexual harassment department would have earned her trust by now, but they had been through so much in the past few days...the fact that he still thought she itched to leave him betrayed something else in him. Suddenly, a whole bunch of puzzle pieces clicked together in her mind: his total distress after meeting Suzie's Screamer, his resignation to the life of a corporate shill, his surety that, even after sharing a tent with her and looking after Geoff and chasing her into that God-forsaken pit, he was sure that she would leave at the first chance, that she would let the next Screamer carry her off to who-knows-where and never come back. Denny knew, from years of seeing it on her father's face and in his actions, that this was guilt...guilt and shame and unworthiness. Colluding with Foster Towers Media probably accounted for some of it, but there was more, too, possibly a lifetime's worth of it, seething beneath his off-hand comments and easy grin.

She had seen it start to slip away the night he came into her tent to get away from the Screamers, and since then, the wilderness and the fear had been scraping away at his good-time guy act like sandpaper on a layer of sun-hardened paint. Denny wondered what the guy looked like underneath, and she hoped that after "party" Wayne had suffocated him all these years, that "real" Wayne would be strong enough to survive the journey. Because, like it or not, she needed him. Perhaps she hadn't realized it at first, because her store of provisions and her dog and her gun had made her over-confident. That was before she staved off the vengeful wraith of a murdered woman and plunged headlong into an abandoned mineshaft because of some strange, involuntary connection to the Screamers.

If the Screamers continued to call her, she would have to answer, and she would need someone to hold her back, to try and mitigate whatever damage they caused her. The dark place in the back of her mind also told her that if something were to happen to her, someone would need to be there to take care of Geoff. As fragile as Wayne had become in the last few days, she knew that he would do right by the dog if he possibly could. Nobody walking around with that much guilt would ignore a life debt they could so easily repay.

As she pondered all of these things, Denny wandered in and out of buildings, searching their cobwebbed corners and along their outer walls for something, anything, that could be used to build a travois. She found some PVC piping, but nothing they had, and nothing she found, would patch it together tightly enough to hold Geoff up. Outside of one of the locked buildings, she found some wooden skids, but when she put weight on them they crumbled into piles of rotted splinters boiling with pill bugs.

As the sun climbed higher in the sky, she shouldered open the door to a long, low hall at the opposite end of the compound. Inside, a couple of water-damaged plyboard tables sat against the wall. A long pass-through at the end of the single room led into a kitchen the likes of which Denny had seen at a million Lions' halls and summer fairgrounds. A cafeteria. There weren't any chairs lying around in the main room, but two doors led to the back, flanking the pass-through, and she bet that one of them was a storage cupboard.

She tried the one on the left, yanking the screaming handle around and wrestling the door open. The bitter smell of mould assaulted her nostrils, as old air wafted out of the room beyond. When the dust in the air had cleared a bit, Denny could see, via a shaft of light where the ceiling had been eaten away, that it was, indeed, an old storage cupboard. A stack of folding chairs leaned against the back wall amid mops whose heads looked made of moss and stacked plastic tubs of lard and beans that expired thirty years before. These would be perfect. With a pull handle on the top, a little bit of cushioning on the seat and back, and solid steel legs, they would provide just enough surface area to keep Geoff off the ground. Denny threw the top one away. That one had a rotted-out seat full of black mould and enough rust to give tetanus to a tree branch. The next one had several loose screws poking out, but the third one down was perfect: just rusty enough to not come unfolded easily, but not damaged enough to give Geoff an infection or drop him halfway through a hike. One of them could pull him by the handle on the chair back, or they could both carry it as a team, with one taking the handle and the other the legs. Just a few twine ties to keep the parts from moving, and they were in business.

Now, to find something to bundle him up in…it was getting colder at night and they couldn't afford to rip up any more blankets. She emerged from the dining hall and looked around. Something caught her eye from over at the edge of the property, in the tall grass. An old black tarp flapped in the breeze, half-tethered to a pile of steel spars. Not bad…not bad at all.

After a quick meal from the cans, Denny and Wayne set to work on the travois. They secured the legs and seat by wrapping them with twine, then placed the chair flat on the floor.

Geoff proved to be less challenging to get into the travois than Denny found entirely encouraging. When he didn't want to step over the chair willingly, Denny compelled him with a gentle shove of the bum. When he wouldn't stay lying down, he acquiesced almost immediately to gentle pressure. He panted a lot and wagged his tail very little. Denny felt his nose, and to her relief it was still cold and wet, however tired Geoff acted. Within an hour, they had Geoff wrapped up in the tarp, papoose-style, and the tarp secured to the travois with more judicious twine use. Although his panting indicated that he was less than satisfied with the arrangement, he still had a rather smiley look on his face as he peeped out of the top of his wrappings, as if to say, "I don't like this, but I trust you." Denny patted his head and offered him a last drink of water before they set off. He lapped it up, and then licked her hand. Yup, still a dog, even without a tail.

THE LONG HAUL

When the mine had faded behind them into a line of man-made wilderness on the horizon, and the sun began sinking down behind the trees, Denny drifted back there, to the corpse of the bear, the metallic, smoky smell of the shotgun blast, and the rivulet of blood that ran from its muzzle. As the darkness closed in around her, she bathed in it, felt as though she could fly away in it, so that when it crept away with the morning light, so too would there be nothing left of her but a vague memory. She said a prayer to that darkness, asking it to close in around the bear and take whatever awareness it had left away with the morning light, so that its murder would not join the many that wandered the wilderness. As she pulled more night air into her lungs, its cool, clear touch focused her thoughts and drifted her back to the night before, to Jessica, and her light shining in the eternal darkness of the bowels of the earth. The locket pressed against her leg from her jeans pocket, where it would stay until she found Jessica's daddy and delivered it home. She imagined Jessica's tiny, ethereal hands over hers, adding her strength to hers…or did she really imagine it?

The beam from Wayne's flashlight shone in her eyes.

"Geez, what are you doing that for, dude? You're blinding me."

"I've been trying to get your attention, and going 'hey' didn't work, and touching your arm didn't work, so I was a little concerned, okay? You were walking really smoothly over all the rocks and not looking at the ground…your flashlight wasn't even pointing the right direction. You haven't said anything for like an hour, and your eyes looked sort of glazed over," Wayne said, adjusting his weight so he could grab Geoff's travois with both hands again.

Denny shook her head out, and the light, floating feeling that she had been bathing in over the past hour left her head like water droplets leaving Geoff's fur when he shook.

"I'm fine," she said, "just tired."

Wayne held the flashlight up to his chin so she could see him raise his eyebrow.

"I know it's been a long couple of days, but stay with me, okay?"

Denny stopped. They had been walking down a rocky slope for the past couple of hours, toward a dark line of pine trees. The slope had mostly evened out where they were, and the rocks now appeared only about every ten or fifteen feet.

"Want to make camp, then? A good night's sleep will probably cure what ails me," she said, unslinging her backpack.

Wayne set down the travois and began picking at Geoff's ties.

"I hope so," he said. "A human settlement is one thing, but I don't know what I'll be able to do if you go running off into the woods without me tonight."

At this, Denny flashed back to herself, on the cinder block steps by the driveway, watching a car, with her dad riding passenger, pull out of the driveway. Her stomach turned sour in an instant, and she wanted to retch. She took a pull on the water they'd purified before leaving, but the stale taste of bush water just made it worse. She choked it down all the same. Mustn't waste water. She coughed and spat.

How could you love someone so much and still be this horrified when you realized that you were turning into them? She had lost time, trances, nocturnal manic episodes... She was going crazy, or something close enough to it that it made no difference to the others around her. She had fought doctors all her life, trying to convince them that she was different from him. Once, she had sought counselling after a particularly hard parting with her father. She hadn't been able to stop crying at night and wanted to run away. The questions had started, hard and fast. What happened to your parents' marriage? Does your dad have a job? Why not? Tell me more about his mental condition. Well, in this instance, given your family history, I'm going to say that you've got a serious case of depression here. I'm going to recommend that you take some medication for a while...

No! I'm a sad little girl, but I'm not depressed! Justifiable sadness and loneliness are an illness now? Are there no emotions I can have, other than ecstatic happiness or indifference, that are normal? I'd say a girl missing her daddy is pretty damned normal!

But this…this wasn't normal. She could talk to Screamers. She felt sympathy for the things that made every normal person run away in terror. Some people even ran off cliffs to get away from them. She ran down mine shafts to get *to* them. It all felt so normal as she was doing it: the trances, the songs, the pulls on her core telling her where to go, but she had heard that when you really go over the edge, everything you do makes perfect sense to you, but not to anybody else. You'd just start raving and swiping at invisible things, and then came the needles and hospital visits and the stints on disability while you came back around to reality.

As if on an ever-rotating wheel of varied shames, she realized that the people she despised, the thing she wanted to avoid more than anything in the world, was the father she loved most in the world. And if she couldn't get a hold on things, no one would ever find him, or care what happened to him. Not even her own mother. This was supposed to be about Dad. This was supposed to be about her love for Dad. Not about her turning into him. Not about her hating him.

A doggy kiss crept slowly up the tips of her fingers to her knuckles. Geoff had gotten out of the travois and limped over to her. He sat down on the side of his hip, so as to keep his tail stub from bumping anything, looked up at her, and gave her that tongue lolling, doggy smile. He whined a little, wanting her full attention. Denny crouched down and looked into his shiny brown eyes. He still looked tired, but also full of love and gratitude. Somehow, she knew he understood the sacrifice that they'd made for him, that they could have left him, probably should have, logically speaking, but they'd refused. She sat down beside him.

"Hey boy," she said, voice wavering. "Things are sure getting weird, huh?"

Geoff flopped over onto her lap, his head resting on her knee. He put his full weight on her and panted. That gesture of trust, when she felt so unstable inside, tipped her over and filled her eyes with tears. She cried, loudly and without a care for what the hell Wayne thought of her.

He let her go for a while without saying anything. She heard him spreading out tarps and hammering in pegs behind her. She eventually smelled smoke as he started a fire. She kept her back to it all for a while, snivelling and stroking Geoff's head, looking off into the horizon and counting the distant stars. All the pictures of families you saw in books and magazines looked so clean...but it really wasn't like that at all. Families were impure at their very core, and the ties of the heart, the ties of blood and bone and gene, carried both strength and sickness, eternal hope and desperate hopelessness at once. Her family wasn't Bob Cratchit sitting around the fire with his perfect, nobly poor brood, it was Maggie and Tom Tulliver of *The Mill on the Floss*, simultaneously loving and hating, dismissing and meddling with one another, and ultimately dying the same way they had lived, at the mercy of their bloodline and the land they lived on.

"Hey," Wayne said from behind her, "was it something I said?"

Denny summoned up all of her gumption to say, "Sort of. Not really. I would have figured it out sooner or later anyway."

Wayne came out and crouched down beside her, following her gaze and seeming confused at the view. He waited for her to continue, and eventually she did.

"I'm going crazy like my father," she said.

Wayne frowned a little. He had bags under his eyes now, and his curly hair stirred a little bit in the night breeze. He sighed.

"I'm not going to lie. You've put me through a lot in the past few days, and I haven't exactly loved you for some of it. I'm still not quite over the mine shaft, or Suzie, or any of it, really. I haven't felt this scared and vulnerable since I was a little kid. But you...you've faced all of it and come out the other side able to deal with whatever we've had to do next. You faced down Georgie's boys. You talked down two Screamers. You killed a rampaging bear that was two feet away from ripping our heads off. You're as sane as anyone I've ever met, and I'd be willing to bet that your dad wasn't as bad as everybody said he was, either. And hey, if you've got a little crazy in there, who's to say that it's such a bad thing to be a little crazy out here? Maybe that's why he liked it, why he had to get away so much. Maybe it wasn't so much that he had to get away from the memories as he wanted to make new ones, away from all the posturing, and the suits, and the urban grunge, and the constant rush-rush-rush to nowhere. And to me, that's starting to make more and more sense."

"Thanks," Denny said. The damaging heat within her began to cool, like a nasty sunburn slathered with Solarcaine.

"No, thank you," Wayne replied.

"For what?"

"For letting me cry. For letting me be afraid. I don't know what I would have done if you'd screamed and clung to me and forced me to be the man...I think we'd probably be dead right now."

"Oh," she said.

For a while they just sat there, both staring out at nothing, relishing the emptiness and the silence. Denny's tears cooled and dried on her face.

"I'm afraid, too," she said. "I don't want to run off on you and get lost. What happens if one of them is lonely and wants to keep me? How about if I can't convince it not to kill me and it's out for blood? What if I fall and break my neck in one of those trances? I don't want to lose control anymore."

"That's the thing about losing control. If you wanted to lose control, you wouldn't really be losing control...just kind of giving it up," Wayne said. Somewhere off in the distance, a frog started singing a steady, chirping note, then another.

"Is that supposed to help?" Denny asked.

Wayne shrugged apologetically.

"I don't know, but that's all I've got. This is all pretty new to me too."

Denny moved a touch, to let Geoff know that he needed to get up. She unfolded herself and headed for the campfire.

She said, "I guess we just have to go to sleep and hope for the best."

After a quick meal of trail stew and a refreshing break for Geoff out in the woods, Denny and Wayne retired to Denny's tent for the night. They both agreed that Wayne would need to be aware if Denny ran off again in the middle of the night. Their shared accommodations only further drove home to Denny that in some ways, her mind was not her own anymore. As she shimmied down into her sleeping bag, the shakes came back, and she felt cold despite the relatively comfortable temperature of the evening. She laid on her face and tried to clear her mind, but without much effort, the weariness in her arms, legs and back stilled her tremors and pulled her down into slumber.

She awoke in the darkest part of the night, damp with sweat and with a stab emanating from her stomach. The crisp, still air chilled her skin and magnified every noise around the campsite a hundred times. Beside her, Wayne slept in a big man-pile, tangled up in his covers with his curly mop resembling its namesake more than ever. Geoff lay at her feet. They had replaced his old

246

bandages with fabric strips and her sanitary pads, which made him look like a three-year-old who had put them on thinking they were mommy's shoulder pads. When he felt her move, he raised his head off his paws, then lowered it again. Nothing to see here.

Outside, grass rustled in the breeze. A stronger gust of wind sent a few pine cones falling to the soft earth with a series of muffled thumps. An owl hooted, somewhere far away.

So this is what it was like, she thought, before the Screamers. Just the cool darkness and tree sounds and birds. She loved this silence and the tiny, delicate sounds that skirted its edge, the undefined openness and quiet of it all. Finally, they'd stumbled upon a small patch of land that humans hadn't managed to ruin with their murders and their politics and their pollution, and she could rest, if only for tonight. Her shoulders relaxed, and her breathing grew deeper. At least they would have one, beautiful night in the eye of the storm.

The next morning, Geoff bounced around a bit and barked at a couple of squirrels climbing a nearby tree. It was harder to get him to hold still to go on the travois, although they both agreed that he still needed it. His tail had clotted up a bit, and looked as good as could be expected, given the circumstances, but his shoulder wound was too deep and wouldn't heal until they found somebody who could suture it properly. Until then, they would just have to keep him still and make sure he didn't damage it more. It wasn't bleeding anymore, and if they could keep him still, perhaps it wouldn't.

They set off again, into the woods, following a damp stream bed. Denny and Wayne started out carrying Geoff as a team, then they each did a shift and so on, in that order until nightfall. As they travelled, the land cut into a deep V shape, becoming a wide river valley flanked by thick forest. Once, they saw another bear, far downstream, and hid, shotgun at the ready, until they were sure it had left for the other side of the stream. The slope of the land allowed them to see much and keep themselves hidden, and so they avoided any more encounters with local wildlife the next day. That night, they were careful to bury any of their used food supplies in the soft riverbank.

The next morning, after breakfast, they sat on the riverbank and looked at the map.

"According to this," Wayne said, "we've got about another week's walk from here. This is a long, deep valley and it runs to twin lakes. At the end of the second lake, we'll find Hunting Bear."

Denny placed a hand on the cool, damp stones beneath her. A week was too much. Far too much.

"Geoff seems fine right now, but who knows how long his leg will last with part of the circulation possibly cut off. We don't know what that bear damaged, Wayne…"

Wayne looked back to where Geoff wandered about the camp, and Denny did too. Right now, he had a pine cone in his jaws and he was flipping it up into the air and catching it as if it were a small rodent. Every time he put weight on his right leg, he immediately withdrew it.

"All we can do is keep pushing on," Wayne said.

"*Surgite*," Denny said quietly.

"Yeah, that."

"At least the nights have been quiet," she said. "I guess there haven't been that many people down here, or at least not that many dying nasty deaths."

Push onward they did, down the river valley, as the damp stream bed became a shallow stream, then a placid body of water about fifty feet wide pulling itself slowly downhill. A large red-tail hawk soared overhead, and a couple of vultures. A thin layer of cloud covered the sky, keeping the day bright but cool. In the late afternoon, they encountered a large spar of granite jutting out into the stream. Denny and Wayne struggled up over it, fearing for their grip on Geoff's travois, and their balance, the whole time.

Aching and extremely sweaty, they continued on, until at dusk they encountered a limestone fall reaching into the centre of the river.

"A few more of these and I'm all for wading around and screw our shoes," Denny said as they picked their way from boulder to sharp boulder.

Finally, as dark set in, they reached the end of the fall. Denny leaned on the tent posts as much as the tent did, and when bedtime rolled around, she collapsed. Wayne did the same. They both smelled terrible, and the tent smelled terrible.

Over the next few days, the temperature rose and rose, until they laboured under the full heat of an unexpected Indian summer. The rocks sent up waves of heat, and even the shallow river felt as warm as a bath. Geoff writhed and shook in his bindings, knocking them off-balance several times each. Denny accumulated gashes on her shins and deep scrapes on her elbows, as well as an assortment of sunburns in various states of healing and peeling. Everyone was irritable, dreading the next rockfall, hummock, or spar, of which there were many. Geoff panted hard, and the black tarp did him no favours with regard to dehydration, but all they could do was try to give him enough water. They let him down a few times, but after a half hour or so, he simply couldn't keep up. He grew dirty-looking and tired again. Three days into the heatwave, Denny checked his tail wound and noticed that it had gotten darker and more discoloured inside. She broke down again that night and woke determined to fight all the harder.

The next day, they crested the brow of a long hill, and the valley flattened out, revealing a pair of long, narrow lakes in the distance. Denny gave a whoop that startled a flock of birds out of the trees on their right.

"Those are the lakes, aren't they? We've got a chance! Thank God, we've got a chance!"

Wayne nodded and smiled.

"I think I have more good news," he said, pointing up ahead, where a real, honest-to-goodness trail, about two feet wide, cut through the brush along the river's edge.

In the flash of complete joyful abandon that ensued, Denny hugged him.

THE GREEN QUEEN LIVE

Geoff staggered back out of the woods, his expression faded to the tolerant smile of the arthritic old-timer rather than the take-on-the-world, tongue-exposing grin he had sported when they pulled out of the bus station in St. Catharines. Denny had suggested letting him down for a drink and a pee, hoping to see a refreshment of his spirits, but he just looked tired and haggard, like he could fall over at any moment. Denny had caught pneumonia as a child, and he reminded her of what she saw in the mirror during those long months of recovery when she was perpetually sweaty, pale, and thin.

Denny picked him up by the midsection, wound outward. He whined a little but stayed still. She felt heat radiating off of him, bleeding through her shirt. Together, she and Wayne manoeuvered him into the travois, where he lay, panting as though he had just run three laps of the dog park. A wave of frustrated energy ran through her as she longed to take him and just run, as long and as fast as she could. She chafed against the restrictions of time and distance and begged him silently to hold on for just another day and a half...

But then again, who was to say that there would even be any vets up on the reserve, or that they would have the equipment needed to help him after all this time? Denny strapped her backpack on and banished the dark thoughts from her mind. Nothing mattered but the fact that, no matter what happened in the end, they could all look back and say they had done their level best for Geoff, as he had for them. That was the only thing that could make the thought of his death bearable.

The path that Wayne had found had led them about twenty feet up the valley slope, to a flat spot that snaked between the trees. Below them, the river continued on its downhill course, its reflections glinting in their eyes and playing off the deciduous tree, leaves flipping and flopping in the breeze. The smell of fresh water permeated this part of the valley, along with the funky aroma of weedy rocks baking in the sun. Denny imagined, with a pang, what it would have been like to walk with Geoff along here when he was in good health, with him prancing ahead and sticking his nose under piles of leaves, or finding a good mud pit and trying to have a roll before Denny or Wayne could yank him out of there.

Denny stayed lost in thought for a while, soaked in nostalgia and hypnotized by the rhythm of her steps until Wayne said, "Well, that's weird."

Denny looked up, and smack in front of her, painted on a tree in bright green spray paint, was an odd symbol. Like a "T", but with the two topmost arms pointed slightly upward, it resembled a crucified body without a head. Not just any body, however…two spray paint blobs, one on the chest, and one on the hips, made it a woman. In the place where the head should be, someone had made a large, ragged cigarette burn in the tree's bark. A shock ran through her at the sight of this...this tree-woman-thing...perhaps because it was the first sign of other humans they had seen in nearly a week, and perhaps because it was the closest thing they had seen to an actual human being (other than each other) in more than two. And yet, it seemed to have an unnerving quality about it unconnected to those two factors...something repellent, like a gang sign etched on a community centre window.

"I don't like it here. Let's go," she said, stepping ahead of Wayne with definitive steps that made the leaves underfoot crunch and crackle.

"What?" Wayne said from behind her. "I thought you'd be relieved that we'd finally hit Hunting Bear territory. Maybe it's a Native ritual symbol or something."

Denny replied, "No, I don't think so. It reminds me more of something terrible I saw in a movie once."

One of the things about being friends with Jordan was that he never just hung out on breaks, or drank coffee in silence. Most of the time, he wanted to share his obscure old movies and television shows, and any break in the schedule was a perfect opportunity for Jordan to vent his obsession *du jour* on unsuspecting friends. Luckily, Denny was the sort who could stomach the old horror movies, as long as they weren't just pure pointless torture and had some sort of a meaningful plot. In some ways, being a literature major brought your life closer to fiction, and in others, it allowed you to see just how far away fiction and reality really were from each other. Granted, the Screamers had made the fiction/reality distinction even more confusing for some people of late, but it was still hard to take some of the old slasher flicks seriously when everybody knew the biographies of the actors and the crude special effects made it very obvious how they were made.

At any rate, Jordan had assailed her one afternoon on her long break with an old-time, low-budget concoction called *The Blair Witch Project*, which apparently had been fairly popular for its time and helped to revive horror movies from their box office slump in the early nineteen-nineties. *Thanks, Jordan*, she thought with a sarcastic chuckle, *for putting this stuff in my head when I could have been cramming survivalist lore.*

The Blair Witch Project had mostly consisted of a lot of shaky camera, weird sound effects, and creepy innuendo, but the one really striking image in the film had been a weird human symbol made of sticks that kept showing up in the forest, chasing the characters down and scaring them senseless every time they found it. The roughness of that symbol, and the quiet aggression it conveyed, jumped out to her from that tree along the path. She wanted to believe that the uncertainty she now felt was a result of her extreme emotional and physical fatigue, and her worry for Geoff, but deep down, the symbol itself unnerved her.

"Wherever we are," she said, "I don't think we can call it human territory just yet."

The second tree-woman-thing appeared on a small, round rock stuck into the ground at the side of the road. Wayne glanced at it but said nothing. Denny tried to ignore it. It had the same body shape and the same cigarette burn head.

Then, a half hour later, they rounded a sharp corner that skirted the edge of a rock fall, and on the other side, three tree-woman-things faced them in a semicircle from a triad of three large birch trees. Denny stopped. Wayne kept going, and they almost dropped the travois hoisted between them.

"Maybe we shouldn't be going this way," she said. "Maybe we should go back down by the river."

Wayne tossed his head and rolled his eyes.

"No way. There are too many obstacles down there. I'm not delaying Geoff's medical care another day because some creepy tree graffiti is making you uncomfortable."

"It's not just making me uncomfortable... I know how stupid it sounds, but I think these things might be evil."

Wayne expelled air out of his nose, and Denny could practically hear him counting down from ten in his mind. He spoke to her as one might speak to a child that one absolutely cannot verbally abuse, no matter how frustrating it is that they covered your brand new white carpet in purple pen ink.

"I know Geoff's sickness is getting to you, but you have to hang in there! Be brave for him, okay?" he said, giving the travois a tug.

Denny followed him, giving the tree-woman-things as wide a berth as possible. Although she understood that Wayne's intentions were good, she seethed at his lack of ability to feel the unsettling atmosphere that surrounded those things on the trees and rocks. It felt like anger and hatred, long buried in the ground here, and turned to loam and feeding through the trees and the lichen and the plants on the forest floor. It felt like the rot of things long rotten, past the point of redemption or even identification. Even though they had passed the three tree-woman-things, this time the feeling followed them, growing with every passing moment. They walked for hours through air thick with malice, and Denny stared at the back of Wayne's head and pictured her eyes making cigarette burns on his scalp. How could he not feel this? It was so strong it was almost like a smell, sinking even into their clothes and belongings. After all that she had seen, and all that she had done, how could he not believe her? Betrayal, that's what it was...

Denny passed a long, excruciating time with these thoughts passing through her head like pork through a meat grinder, until, as the sun began to set, she was pulled out of her raw thoughts by the sound of rushing water. Soon, the path opened up, coming out of the trees, and onto the river bank. Up ahead, the river flowed over a sharp edge. Mist rose up beyond that edge and Denny could feel some of it on her cheeks.

"That's it, isn't it? That's the waterfall that leads to the first lake in the chain! We're almost there!" she said.

Wayne nodded.

"If all goes well, we'll be there by tomorrow afternoon."

Denny felt a burst of renewed energy.

"Come on, I see a divot in the hill over there without any trees. Let's make camp."

The place that she pointed to was about a five-minute walk away, nestled in a small crook in the hill. From a distance, it looked like an exposed limestone face that had eroded over the years from spring streams dribbling down it, but, at the end of summer, it would be bone dry. They could set up camp on the mossy area under the rock fall and be quite comfortable for the night, away from the wind. Denny felt some of her earlier anger fade as she strode toward the area. Perhaps it *had* been a non-issue. Perhaps it *had* just been their isolation, and her stress over Geoff, playing tricks on her. Sure, Wayne had seemed a little insensitive earlier on in more ways than one, but considering all they had been through, she could let it go.

During that small stretch of the walk, she really felt like the downhill slope of the ground was coming to her aid, as if she were walking the last, easy few feet toward total success. She got up ahead of Wayne, whose turn it was on the travois, and positively jogged around the corner to the clearing.

As she approached, Denny noticed that the packed dirt of the path got wider as it entered the clearing. Odd that there would be a maintained clearing all the way out here, but perhaps still lucky on their part. For all they knew, this place could be part of a hunting trail for the reserve. As she turned the corner, she noticed that there were logs at the entrance—chainsaw cut logs. Six of them ran around the edge of a very neat, clean packed-earth campsite, complete with fire pit. For a moment, Denny couldn't believe their luck. What were the chances of finding a real campsite out here in the wilderness?

The wind stirred the boughs of some short, stubby trees back near the rock fall, causing a flicker of movement that caught Denny's eye. Her smile faded as quickly as it had appeared. On the rock fall, a face easily fifty feet high, someone had scrawled a huge tree-woman-thing with a smeared, exclamation-point head of fireplace ash in bright green spray paint. Underneath, a phrase dripped to the earth: *THE GREEN QUEEN LIVES.*

Denny stepped backward, back across the path and into the grass on the other side. She intended to keep moving that way, but a pair of strong hands caught her behind her back.

"Whoa, watch out there! You're headed for the edge!" Wayne said.

Denny looked behind her and saw that she was one step away from heading over a ten-foot embankment to the river. She gave a little yelp and moved inland, her heart beating hard.

"Holy crap! I completely forgot where I was for a second. I just wanted to get away from that thing on the rock fall!"

Wayne picked up Geoff's travois again. Geoff had begun to squirm, as he didn't like being horizontal in the travois. Wayne moved into the clearing.

"The Green Queen, eh? Now I get it. There's nothing to worry about, Denny. Look more closely at the symbol. Doesn't it kind of look like a doob being pinched between two fingers? And the ash is the lit end. Get it? The 'Green' Queen? Mary Jane? We just found a stoners' hang out, that's all."

Although that nasty, rotted-vegetable-juice-on-your-flesh feeling had crept back over her at the sight of the painting, Denny shook it off. All the pieces of Wayne's argument seemed to fit—the isolated clearing, the logs, the symbol that served as both a trail marker and a semi-threatening ward for adults or cops—it had all of the signs of a hangout for teenage bad-asses. She had been scared because a bunch of unruly kids had been trying to spook her with the quasi-devil-worship bullshit that most rebellious teens used to ward off adults. Geez, she hadn't thought she was getting that old already.

After a moment of scrutiny, she said, "Okay, you got me. Let's make camp here. It's not like we can march all night anyway."

They got the tent up and the fire going by the time the sky turned red and the night frogs began their peeping on the other side of the river. Denny pulled out some tinned hot dogs, and, in a fit of nostalgia for a summer camp she never really attended, she scouted out a clean stick and stuck three of them on the end. When they were done, she picked one off the stick, but despite the gnawing feeling in her gut, and the aching in her joints, she hesitated before taking a bite. She still felt...not right. Wayne's argument had mostly convinced her that she must be externalizing her emotions over Geoff and everything else that had gone on, but still, she couldn't shake the feeling that something in the world had become a little skewed, or a tad unglued. Oh boy, back to feeling crazy, she thought, and this time, Wayne wasn't feeling supportive.

She forced herself to chew and swallow a bite of hot dog. It felt as dry as sand, and she had a hard time swallowing it without three gulps of water. Geoff padded over to her, favouring his injured leg in a fashion both heartbreaking and endearing, and Denny gave him the rest of it.

She looked across the fire pit to Wayne, who struggled with a shepherd's pie in much the same fashion.

"You know," Denny said to him, "I accept your argument, but I still find it creepy here."

Wayne took another bite, then set the shepherd's pie aside and didn't look at it again.

"Now that it's getting dark out here, so do I," he said.

"Want to get inside, then? We should make an early morning of it anyway."

Wayne put the rest of his food on the ground for Geoff, who limped over after finishing his hot dog.

"Yeah, let's turn in. I want to get out of the way of whatever might come around tonight."

Denny, who sat closest to the tent, unzipped the flap and stepped inside, carrying her last two hot dogs with her. If she kept trying, she could probably finish them soon. "With any luck," she said, "it will only be raccoons."

For a few moments, Denny teleported, in her dreams, from a fight with her mother about not having enough flavours of jam in the pantry to a high-contrast, black and neon concert venue, filled with humanoid insects wearing dishevelled plaid shirts and khakis and little black dresses with real, wilting flowers sewn onto them haphazardly.

She awoke, confused for a moment as to where she was. Green lights, half flame, half water reflection danced over the sides of the tent, lighting it like noonday. That had been the neon lights, but then there was the music. The most hellish, unearthly din pounded against her ears, a limping, staggering heavy metal melody with nothing but screams, guitar squeals, and hard pounds on the drums. It barely held a rhythm, and the voice behind everything was more like the pulsing of a flame in a guttering candle than anything resembling a melody. In fact, the flame-like reflections on the tent moved with the screeching.

Denny swivelled in place, looking for Wayne and Geoff. They cowered in the corner, Geoff in Wayne's arms.

"I...I thought the fire got out of control. I went out with the extinguisher, and then I saw it...this must be some kind of Satanic worship site!"

The left-hand flap of the tent swung open, revealing a crease of bright, lime-green light that consumed all else like a camera flash.

As her eyes made contact with that light, Denny sensed the Screamer, and the Screamer sensed her. She forced herself to breathe deeply. She had handled two of these things now, and that's all that would happen this time. This one might be close and overwhelming, but she knew now that it was still just the spirit of a human, nothing more.

A wave of anger, from outside of her, washed over her and left her aching. She shook her head at Wayne to reassure him that this wasn't a demon, then stepped outside the tent.

Outside, the skunky, cloying smell of pot smoke permeated everything. The air had acquired a thick, smoky tinge as well, obscuring everything around. All of the normal sounds of the forest—the frogs, the gurgle of the river, the loons down on the lakes—had disappeared, and all that remained was this terrible, wounded metal concert playing in her ears. She could only imagine what it must sound like to Wayne...probably like the world was ending.

Denny lifted her hands to her ears without even thinking about it. She could see tons of smoke and light, turning and intertwining around each other like the inside of a basket, but no Screamer.

She heard a hard crumbling sound erupt from the direction of the rock fall. Out of a small pile of slag at the base, one green-glowing hand clawed its way to the surface, and then another. The thing gave a mighty shove, and a set of decayed arms, a rotted torso, and a fragment of hip bone drifted up out of the earth. The rest of the Green Queen (as Denny was sure now that this was she of the tree-woman-thing drawings) filled itself in with ashy darkness, like the centre of a cigarette burn. She had no face, only a void which formed an oval head, and long, tattered tendrils of waist-length black hair. The thing reached down to the ground and picked up one last piece of itself, a lower jaw bone, and snapped it into place on the blackness that was once its face.

Denny stayed in place, wondering what the Green Queen would do next. The amount of anger this thing carried inside of it had fermented over the years, becoming more and more powerful...but how?

DISTANT EARLY WARNING

The Green Queen glided forward, void-head first, and stopped an inch from Denny's face. The stench of decay around it was sickening in a way that she didn't remember from any of the others, a putrefaction of the body and the soul. It screamed, and when it did, Denny's head emptied of all thought.

Where is he?
He's mine,
And you're out of time,
You nasty piece of trash

He's handsome,
He's smart,
And I have his heart
And soon you will be smashed

So what if he hit me?
Sometimes I deserved it,
But you took me up here,
and knocked me down the falls

What's the problem?
You look unnerved, bitch!
We'll see who's his bottom bitch
After you fall...

For all his beatings,
For all his lies
The Green Queen lives,
And you die.

Denny, thrown back, stumbling, tried to formulate a response through a spinning head and rubber legs. What followed was a devilish counterpoint, between her and the monster.

I didn't…

NO!!!!

I couldn't have…

LIES!

Please…

DIE!

I can…heeeeeelp!

Denny screamed as two sets of arms—human arms—grabbed her shoulders, and another swept her feet out from under her. Denny struggled, but they only clamped down harder. These people were young and strong, by the feel of it. She also felt warmth and a pulse, but why would living, breathing humans collaborate with a Screamer? Another waft of pot-infused air passed by her. The Green Queen hovered overhead, her ashy face spiralling, mocking Denny.

Boys will do anything
When they're high,
The Green Queen lives,
And you die...

Denny's captors, still just foggy figures in all the smoke, carried her back toward the waterfall. Her stomach lurched as she realized what the Green Queen was going to make them do to her...

The loud bang of her shotgun cut through the Green Queen's screeching for a moment, and Denny felt her captors go stiff, stopping in their tracks for the split second that the bang lasted. The Green Queen screamed all the louder in response, but Wayne was determined to be heard.

"Stop right there or I'll shoot! I mean it!" he yelled at the top of his lungs. Somewhere behind him, Geoff barked.

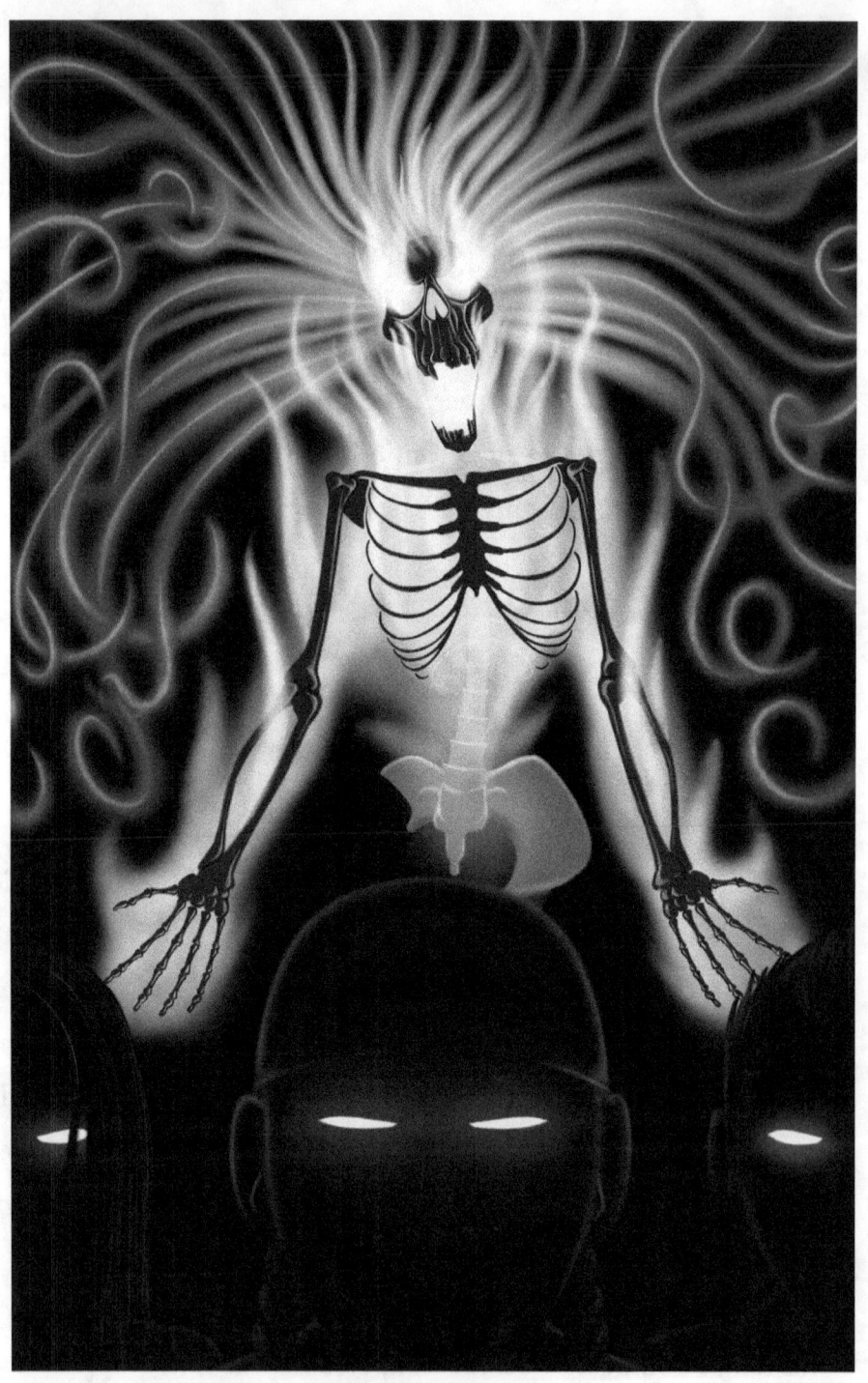

Art by Robin McLean.

Denny knew immediately that it was a bluff. Whether her captors did too, or whether the Green Queen just had them too far under, they just kept moving. Wayne couldn't shoot them with the shotgun without hurting Denny, too. They cleared the smoke and emerged onto the path, ten or twenty feet in front of the waterfall. Out in the open, Denny checked their faces, to see if they looked conscious. They were barely more than fifteen, any of them, solidly built and with the black hair and prominent cheekbones of Native people. A swirling, lime green haze filled their eyes, and lime green smoke drifted out of their noses and slack jaws like wisps of dry ice from one of those Halloween cauldron decorations. The Green Queen had scooped out their heads like jack-o-lanterns the minute they got high.

Denny yelled at the top of her lungs, hoping Wayne would hear her.

"Stay there and keep Geoff safe. I've got a plan!"

Denny focused her mind, bringing herself back onto the plane where she could sing. She looked at the boys, trying to imagine what their life must be like. She got a lonely picture of life in isolation from everyone but your own community, cold lake and a long field of dead grass studded with wooden crosses. Frustration at the ignorance of many of the others around you, but no way to become less ignorant yourself. School rebellion. Drinking, then drugs. A small group of friends that meant everything, but also controlled everything. Adults who wanted to lay down rules rather than talk.

Denny breathed this all in, and when she breathed out, she sang,

I know what it's like to be lonely,
My mom left me long time ago,
It's not something killing you only,
There are others that suffer and know.

One of the boys shook his head, as if in a sudden dizzy spell. The Green Queen sang louder, but so did Denny, pushing with all of her spiritual strength into her voice.

The adults around you don't listen,
When you tell them you're going through hell,
They're all too wrapped up in their problems,
To care if you're really that well.

No! She'll tell on you!

I know that you feel like you're trapped here,
And the pot you found helps you feel free,
But the Green Queen gives gifts to control you,
The drugs strengthen her tyranny.

270

We're...friends...

The boys reached the edge of the waterfall. Denny could see down the cliff now, to the tiny trees and fallen rocks below. The smoke coming from the boys' noses and mouths had slowed down, and their expressions had begun to turn back to normal, but the Green Queen was now screaming at a fever pitch, like a giant engine without any lubrication or brakes. Denny put everything she had into one, last verse.

Please put me down and stop walking,
Please, I'm not who she says,
We can go back home together,
And I'll help you find another way...

One of the boys, the one on her right, closed his mouth and his eyes. He let that side of Denny go, and she found herself dangling precariously by her feet and her left side like a half-pitched tent. She balanced herself on the ground with one elbow and looked up at him. He pinched the bridge of his nose like he had a migraine coming on.

"Hey, what the hell...? Guys, what the shit?" he said, shaking the other two, who stirred as if waking up from a deep sleep and dropped Denny as well. She scrambled back to a safe distance, in case the Green Queen possessed them again, and watched. The Queen herself slunk back a bit, too, pulling her heavy metal opera into a repetitive holding rhythm. Denny turned around and stared her right in the cigarette-burn face.

Go back to your grave, Slave!
Back to the ether, Creature!

Your anger destroys you,
Your hate feeds your flames,
Leave us alone,
Or I'll show you true pain.

The flames and the smoke and what was left of the Green Queen slunk down, back under the shale, and were still.

Denny ran to Wayne. He and Geoff, thankfully, had been unharmed and largely unnoticed by the creature. Wayne placed a shaking hand on her shoulder for support. Her knees shook as well…hopefully, they both wouldn't go down.

The three boys by the waterfall crept toward them. In the dying embers of their evening fire (which had somehow survived all the Green Queen's theatrics) their faces looked lined and creased with worry beyond their years. The one that had let her go first, a heavy-set boy with a ponytail and plaid shirt, stepped forward, hands out.

272

"Lady, I didn't know what I was doing…I just woke up and you were there and I was about to…I don't know… Oh man, what the hell?"

Denny kept her expression neutral with great effort, as the residual fear from the incident threatened to cause a scowl that she didn't mean to aim at these boys.

"I think everything's going to be okay now. I've got the Green Queen on the run, and it doesn't feel like she's coming back, at least not tonight," she said. Wayne started to step forward, but she held him back with an outstretched arm. The tension in his body through that touch telegraphed that he had moved from fear to anger. Healthy, but not helpful.

"What the hell were you doing raising that thing? You think you're cool? Huh? You almost killed my friend," he said.

The teen on the left stepped forward. He had short, buzzed hair with long bangs and a grey sweatshirt.

"We didn't *raise* anything, man. Joab's telling the truth. We saw your tent, we sat down over there for a toke," he said, raising an arm to the half of the log circle furthest from their tent, "and then the next thing we knew, we were holding her up by the waterfall and we dropped her. I bet you're journalists, aren't you? You're here to start a war with us, and this is just another fake story to get the feds to attack us."

The third boy, well-muscled and angry-looking, stepped forward as if to protect the other two.

273

"The Elders warned us that terrorists might try to bring chemical weapons onto our land. They probably sprayed us with something and put us over there by the falls! I say we take 'em in to Verity and have 'em thrown in the pit!"

Denny gritted her teeth. She pushed Wayne back, with a dirty look, then stepped forward to meet the third boy.

"We did no such thing," she said, her voice growing louder, but not returning the boy's anger. "You were under the power of a Screamer called the Green Queen, the nastiest thing I've met yet over the hundred-plus miles I've walked, yes walked, to get here, and if it hadn't been for my ability to sing her down, we could have *all* gone over the falls."

The boy stopped moving forward, but he tossed his head and rolled his eyes.

"The Green Queen? That's all you got? That's just a stupid story our parents used to try to scare us away from drugs and going too far from the rez. We came here on purpose, 'cause that's where they said she died, and *we* put up all this stuff around the woods to scare adults away. They find out we smoke weed, and we'll be living 'the life of our ancestors,' you get me? Out here for good with no place to go."

This time, Denny rolled her eyes. "I assumed *you* put up the graffiti. It doesn't change the fact that she was using you the whole time, letting you get high and then making you do anything she wanted you to do, including making the paintings. Did you not see the green fire and smoke thing hovering over there? The thing with an ash smudge for a head?"

The boys all looked a bit sick at her description.

"Yeah, that's what I thought. Funny thing about drug hallucinations is that nobody *ever* sees the same thing. But I'm sure you knew that."

The first one to have spoken, Joab, coughed a couple of times in a rather portentous way, then threw up into a nearby bush. The boy with the buzz cut went to him and bent over him.

"My mouth tastes like the bottom of a campfire..." Joab moaned.

The third boy screwed up his face. She could tell he was trying to find another answer but not succeeding.

"Are we going to be okay?" he asked. "People used to say that she'll follow you home and kill all your sisters."

Denny shook her head. "I don't think she can leave this place. But even if she can, I'll deal with her. If I've sung her down once, I can do it again. As for your friend over there, he's just experiencing a common side effect of Screamer possession. It'll pass."

"Dude, I'm never doing pot again..." Joab chimed in.

Denny couldn't help but smile, just a little. "That's totally up to you, but I'm not sure that's what caused the problem. I'm no expert, but from what I've experienced out here, Screamers can only talk to you if you can help them in some way or if you identify with them. If it makes any sense, it's probably not the fact that you were doing drugs that made you vulnerable so much as the fact that she was a drug dealer's girlfriend that caused her to identify with you."

Joab just moaned.

"Sorry, but nothing makes enough sense right now," said the boy helping Joab.

The boy in front tossed his head back toward the others.

"That's Tim and his brother, Joab. I'm Four-by, as in four-by-four," he said.

"His real name's Leonard," said Tim, snickering.

"No, my *real* name is Four-by. My birth name is Leonard."

"Denny. This is Wayne and Geoff," she replied, holding out a hand.

Four-by crossed his arms. "Consider your hand shaken."

Denny shrugged. "Can you sit down?" she asked, gesturing to the logs.

"I think we need to get out of here," said Tim. "We stay away much longer, and we won't get back before people start getting up. They'll know we left, and we'll get in shit."

Denny looked back at Wayne and Geoff. The dog leaned against Wayne, as if his last efforts had been spent barking at the Green Queen. He had brown marks running down from his eyes and his fur was more matted than ever.

"So…you've got vehicles?" she asked.

"They don't call me Four-by for nothin'," he said.

"Then take us with you. Please. My dog is injured. We've been carrying him most of the way. He fought off a bear for us and he needs a vet."

"If my dad finds out I was sneaking out to go smoke pot, I'm going to need a vet," quipped Tim. "And you know they aren't likely to look too kindly on you when you get there, right?"

Wayne stepped forward, with pursed lips, looking as guilty as he did that first night after meeting Suzie's Screamer.

"They can hate us all they want. They probably should. But your Elders are going to want to hear what I have to say. I have documents detailing the Foster Towers Media Corporation's plans to spark an attack on Hunting Bear. I stole them and I escaped here, on foot, to warn them."

"And her?" said Four-by, looking at Denny.

"I'm looking for my father," she replied, "Sean Dennigan?"

The three boys looked at each other. Four-by tilted his head as if to say, "why not?" Joab still looked wretched but he nodded, then wiped his mouth with the back of his hand. Tim studied Denny, Wayne, and Geoff for a moment with his intense, dark eyes, then said, "Okay, we'll take you to back to rez. But if anybody asks, we were out joyriding along the lake edge. Got it?"

Relief washed over Denny like the discovery of a nearby toilet after being stuck in a traffic jam for hours. Finally, Geoff would get some help, Wayne could atone for his mistakes, and she could get some answers.

"Okay guys, you've got a deal," she said, smiling. "We'll have our stuff packed within the hour."

HUNTING BEAR

Denny's hair whipped out behind her, the cold night air buffeting her face like a cloud of frost-coated blush sponges. She felt the blood rush to her cheeks in response to both the assault of the wind and the close proximity to Four-by's well-muscled chest. Sure, she was way too old for this guy, but she could still enjoy, seeing as he invited her.

When they had gotten on the ATVs, Denny had looked around for a seatbelt—none. The seat itself was made from that slippery nylon stuff that they used on tacky car seats, just a backrest and a flat place for her bottom. Four-by had a sort of padded straddling cushion but no real seat. He would have to lean over to drive.

"Now, normally you two would have helmets," they had begun, solidifying Denny's apprehensions, "and we're going to be going over some bumpy trail, but we kind of pinched these in a hurry and didn't have a lot of time for safety, so…"

The "so…" they were referring to was Denny, no heavy coat, no helmet, no riding suit, rocketing down a half-overgrown track by some power lines with a slippery flat seat beneath her and nothing to stay her fall on either side except for her tenuous grip on a bouncing teenager. Her teeth chattered from the cold, then smacked together as they went over a series of bumps. She glanced over at Wayne, who had Geoff strapped to his back, in addition to all the other difficulties of the ride, and he looked back at her with an expression that clearly said: "Maybe walking was preferable."

On they went, however, under the vibrant light of the full moon, racing along the edge of the first lake, then down through a valley where the wind shushed about them like the hems of a Victorian skirt. Then they roared up into a section of thick forest, dark and still, which seemed to echo the howls of the ATV engines back at them a hundredfold. This added yet another element to Denny's ride that made it feel like she would imminently lose her balance. Finally, they crested the rise of a hill, and Denny saw, over Four-by's shoulder, the track snaking away like a living thing below them and, at the end, curving around the far end of the second lake, a cluster of houses and low-slung buildings, sending twinkles of light out into the darkness. She held on as they barrelled down the slope, willing herself not to look at the ground flashing by beneath them.

I've been pulled down into an abandoned mine and chased by a rampaging bear, she thought, *but this is by far the worst travel option for dizziness and general instability.*

Finally, as they reached the grassy clearing surrounding the reservation for a couple of kilometres on all sides, the boys slowed down their ATVs and made the engines as quiet as possible. They swung around to what Denny assumed was a back gate, given that they had crossed a far better-used dirt track leading to a large gatehouse on the other side of the complex, and unlocked the padlock on the frost fencing with a well-worn key.

"We've got to roll in with the engines off from here," said Four-by. "You guys will have to walk."

As delighted as Denny was at that statement, her legs didn't seem to want to walk properly anymore. Her knees, having been locked into a strenuous crouching position for the better part of three hours, decided that they would only hold her weight for a maximum of half a second before dropping her where they may, which led to her clomping along with a half-baked gait like that of a newborn foal. Her back, having been holding the considerable weight of her boobs up for that whole time, decided that her lumbar vertebrae had the muscular equivalent of sunburn, and so every expansion and contraction of her lower back fought her and burned like the sun. The rest of her, right down to the hair resting on her neck, was chilly...very, very chilly. At this point, she actually felt thankful for the mud splattered all over her calves as a form of insulation. With her arms folded, she followed the boys down a sparsely lit dirt street concentrating on the catch-fall, catch-fall of her gait rather than any of the other less pleasant sensations of the evening.

All around, bungalows rose out of the night, brick squares of a cozy red colour, the kind of prefab farmhouse you'd see lining any rural route with little whirligigs on the lawn and maybe a toy bridge over a bathtub full of flowers. There were a couple of two-story houses along the street as well, cape cods with plastic siding and bicycles leaning against the porch. All looked well worn by weather and time, but nonetheless well-maintained and home-like. If she had seen a picture of this place without knowing that they lived in the epicentre of Screamer territory, she wouldn't have thought anything was out of the ordinary. In fact, it looked nothing like the stereotype of a reservation, either. She saw one portable trailer, over in the far corner of a large lot, with a sign indicating that it was a police station, and that was about it. There were certainly no beat-up car parts or other junk around, at least not more than you'd see back home on George Street. Up here, what use would they have for cars anyway? It would be ATVs and Ski-Doos all the way, if they left at all.

In the globular fairy light of the street lamps, the whole place had kind of an eerie quality about it, as if someone had just taken a normal little town and teleported it into a larger-than-life wilderness. The street lamps fought with the immense darkness of the untamed lands all around, creating a Van Gogh-like war of layered oranges and blues. This place felt like an oasis, one small island in a sea of troubles. She knew, from the moment she crossed the threshold, that there were no more Screamers here. Someone here, possibly all of them, had seen to that, and she would have to find out who. No wonder the boys had been so incredulous. Their Elders had been shielding them all this time, and they had to run away to see what the rest of the land around them was going through.

Tim motioned them onward, with an urgent wave of his hand.

"Come on, we have to hurry. The night raiders are going to get back soon, and you don't want to have to answer to them first, especially not with these stolen ATVs."

Despite her aching back and troubled knees, Denny leaned over to help Joab push his ATV faster. They passed between two houses, and behind them stood a long, low hall, not unlike the dining hall at the mine, with a parking lot full of ATVs. Most of them were different makes and models, some beaten up, some almost brand new. Denny noticed with an inward chuckle that the boys had selected the flashiest and most well-equipped vehicles for themselves...the only three that boasted two seats and a trunk.

"Who do these all belong to?" Denny whispered to Joab.

"We all share them," he replied. "Our raiders bring them back from the abandoned towns, along with gas, food, and lots of other stuff. We're just not supposed to take them out at night."

As they finished the slight downgrade to the parking lot with the ATVs, Denny heard a quick hiss from behind her, like the sneaky form of a wolf whistle. Wayne lagged behind the rest of them, waiting for a limping Geoff to follow along with him. He hadn't been able to walk with the sling and, unfortunately, their travois had been too bulky to bring in the tiny ATV trunks. Geoff whimpered a little, his nose pointed pleadingly toward Denny.

"Denny," Wayne whispered, "he's fading fast. We have to get him to the vet."

Denny's heart clenched up, and her face crumpled. Poor Geoff…they'd made it, but still, they weren't at the vet, and he looked so weak and helpless.

Joab's face filled with compassion when he saw Geoff struggling along, favouring his injured leg. He wheeled his ATV into the nearest parking space, then said, "The vet is that-away, man, up the hill and over to the end of Algonquin street. You guys can…"

At that moment, a light snapped on over the parking lot. Joab, Tim and Four-by half-crouched, squinting into the light and holding their arms up to shield themselves.

A middle-aged man with a potbelly, trucker hat and a long braid pushed open a side door in the meeting hall and stepped out into the parking lot.

"Hold it right there, boys."

"Dad?" said Tim.

"That's right," said the man. "I knew somebody was stealing ATVs from the gas gauges. Thought you were so smart, but you didn't think to refill the buggers, huh? Just proves why we don't let you boys drive at night. Four-by, I don't think Janna's going to be very pleased to hear about this, either. She's put up with a lot from you lately."

"Dad, you can't turn us in to the Watch...we didn't hurt nothing!" said Tim, with his characteristic emphasis.

The older man squinted into the darkness at Denny and Wayne. He didn't seem to regard Geoff much at all. He frowned, and this caused creases in his round chin.

"Well, maybe I should turn you in. Who the hell did you bring in here, boys? Couldn't get enough thrills out of grand theft auto, you gotta be towing journalists back in with you? We gotta get these white folks out the back gate before we all get ourselves in a load of shit."

"They're not journalists, Mr. Dore, and their dog is hurt. He could die if we don't get him to the vet soon. Take a look at him. We didn't make it up this time," said Four-by.

Mr. Dore peered over Tim's shoulder at Geoff, really seeing him for the first time.

His frown softened somewhat. He pursed his lips and blew out a hard breath through his nose.

As they all looked at Geoff, he slumped down onto the ground, as if the weight of their gazes were too much for him. Denny ran the few steps to where he lay and touched his head.

"Geoff, come on boy. Get up. We're almost there."

Geoff raised himself on one leg, then fell down again.

"Geoff, oh my God..." Denny said, then, turning tearful eyes toward Mr. Dore—who avoided her gaze, pursing his lips. "Please, have mercy on us, for his sake, at least. He's hurt. He needs help! We've come over a hundred kilometres on foot...just get Geoff to the vet, and you can deal with us however you like."

Mr. Dore stared out at them for a long moment, the way a mother of three toddlers regards her third broken vase of the day. Finally, he turned slowly and re-opened the door to the meeting hall, saying, "You pick him up, I'll take you over there and wake up the doc. Can't guarantee he'll do anything for you, though. That dog looks pretty far gone."

They waited, in the harsh floodlight of the clinic yard, holding Geoff and their breath. Finally, Mr. Dore came down the walk with an old man, hair stark white and crew-cut, wearing jeans and a dress shirt that he smoothed every few seconds or so.

"George..." he said when he caught sight of them, "who are these people? Are you getting me into another one of your capers?"

George shook his head.

"The dog...please. Just look at him. He needs help. I'll sort out the rest in the morning."

"I'm an old man, George, I don't have time for this anymore."

Nevertheless, when the old man reached the floodlight, he stopped and regarded Denny the way a parent regards a child who has strayed too far from home. He leaned forward and, with a gentle hand, spread apart the dried fur over Geoff's shoulder wound. Geoff twitched and moved his head toward the man's hand but didn't make a sound.

"What the hell did this? It looks like bear claw marks," he said, the wrinkles on his forehead and cheeks growing deeper. "What have you been putting this dog through?"

"He saved our lives," Denny said, eyes welling. "I called and called to him, but he wouldn't come."

"Get him inside," said the old man, turning away from them. His voice had taken on a roughness that hadn't been there before.

The inside of the vet's office was worn all over like a beloved old shoe. An examination table stood in the centre of the room, its linoleum worn colourless at the corners. The cupboards were similar, all fading mint green paint and stickers from thirty years ago worn down to not much more than paper backing. A faded poster promoted vaccinations with alarming pictures of heartworms and their ilk.

The metal and glass instruments and containers, however, shone bright, cleaned, sanitized, and well cared for. The Doc looked well cared for, too, despite his age. He fit with this place.

Denny, Wayne and Mr. Dore sat in a row of orange plastic scoop chairs along the wall behind the door and watched as Geoff floated out of their hands and into the unknown. The Doc lifted the dog, placed him gently on the examination table, and began his work. Geoff held still through the thermometer, the probing of his shoulder, the lights in his eyes, but when the Doc touched his tail, he howled and struggled to get away, with a shocking amount of energy that Denny hadn't seen from him in days.

Abject fear played across Geoff's face, his paws scrabbling on the linoleum. Denny put one hand to her forehead. One more second of that scream and she would be screaming too.

"It's going to be touch and go for a while, and he's going to need a lot of antibiotics. He's also going to lose his tail, if he pulls through," said the Doc. Denny struggled to listen. After that howl, his words had all the impact of a washed-out radio signal.

"What do you need from us in return?" Denny asked. She'd find the money or whatever he wanted, somehow, if he was willing to treat Geoff.

"I don't want anything in return," said the Doc, his voice gruff again.

A soul-deep fear coursed through Denny. Of course. It was too risky, and maybe he didn't have the proper medicine up here after all this time...and then, like turning a corner into the path of the sun, the old man's face emerged into the light. His cheeks were wet with tears.

"I had a dog like this one once... The Watch can go to hell. The dog stays with me and so do you."

Mr. Dore stood up, his stance tentative.

"You sure, Doc? You can treat the dog, but let me take the heat for you. They already hate me."

"No way, George. You've got those boys to think about. I've done some pro bono work around here...in fact, I seem to remember a young lady named Verity who came to me, back in the bad old days, when her cat used up one of its nine lives getting its paw caught in a steel door. No, my name can take a little mud, George, don't you worry."

"In that case, I'd better get home," said Mr. Dore. "You tell them boys where to run in a fire, and they get themselves burned up instead. Guess it was too much to hope for them to learn by example, eh?"

"They should have named Joab 'Apple Doesn't Fall Far From The Tree,' George."

Mr. Dore gave a final nod to the Doc, then exited the building with a little tinkle of the bell over the door.

After George's departure, the Doc grabbed some swabs soaked in solution from the other side of the room and a syringe from the fridge.

"This is going to be a while, kids," he said without looking up. "You might want to bed down in my office for the night."

"I want to stay with him," Denny said.

The Doc shook his head.

"There are some things you shouldn't see happen to your best friend. You head on in there. You'll need your strength when the

Watch finds out you're here, and it's only a matter of hours. You can't drop a pin eight miles out of town without somebody calling you butterfingers when you get back," he replied.

"All right," Denny said with a sigh, "I'll do my best."

"You do that. It's the only door on the left."

When Denny slouched into the room, an exhausted and wind-blown Wayne close behind, she wondered if the Doc had hosted these sorts of parties before. The office was a tiny square room lined with plyboard bookshelves on two sides. A ceremonial drum decorated with a medicine wheel sat on one shelf, alongside the textbooks and records. On the other wall sat a very well-worn brown couch with a couple of embroidered throw pillows.

There was also a very worn and creased photo in a frame, the paper rubbed away to the white in places, of a young Native boy, long-legged with a goofy grin on his face, and one arm slung around a scruffy terrier mix with a partially bitten-off ear. The dog smiled as much and as goofily as the boy. Denny paused at the picture. She missed her dad and it ached. Tired, lonely, worn out…all these feelings piled on her as she slowed down like wolves on a wounded deer.

Wayne's voice brought her out of it a little.

"You want the couch or the chair?"

"I could sleep on a pile of broken bricks right now. I'll take the chair."

He had carried Geoff after all. It was only fair. Denny settled into the armchair, and as her head drifted down to her shoulder, she smelled the woodsmoke permeating her clothes.

"Denny?" Wayne whispered after turning out the lights.

"Yeah?"

"No matter what happens to me tomorrow, promise me you'll stay with me to the end of it."

"I promise," she said, and yet, she wondered how possible that promise would be to keep when revenge and guns came into play. Still...he had carried Geoff. She would always remember that morning, when Wayne took his photograph in the abandoned bunkhouse. They both loved Geoff, and somehow, against all odds, it bonded them together.

With uneasy thoughts drifting slowly through her head, Denny took long, slow breaths of the smoke-scented air by her shoulder, until it pulled her down into a hazy world filled with softly calling voices and orange street lamps dotted across a vast, indifferent wilderness.

THE WATCH

Four-by's aunt dropped their bags on the floor. Wayne cringed visibly as his equipment box clattered onto the lino.

Mr. Dore stood in the corner, his shoulders hunched and a conciliatory smile on his face. The Watch had brought the four of them (Denny, Wayne, Mr. Dore, and the Doc) back to the meeting hall, where they waited in a foyer plastered with old community notices and brochures for help centres that probably weren't so helpful anymore. The walls were yellow-painted brick, the trim a clashing shade of walnut. It reminded Denny of every community centre ever, except for the weapons locker stashed in one corner and the huge plastic water cubes stacked up in the coat closet.

Four-by's aunt, Janna McKay, a round-faced, stout woman with a no-nonsense set to her lips, opened the door to the main chamber.

"Get your stuff and get in there. Verity just has to see you before we decide to kick you out."

Denny picked up her bag and slung it on her back. She noticed a weight shift. They had been rummaging, and she wouldn't be surprised if her knife and axe were gone. She hadn't received her shotgun back, either.

And, she thought, *what will happen to Geoff if we get kicked out of here? Best case scenario, we never see him again, but he stays with the Doc.*

She pressed her lips together at the thought of losing the last piece of Dad she had left to her. If she got sent away now, all she would have left would be a battered book of poetry and the memory of garbled screams and dead eyes on a flickering TV screen.

Well, they wouldn't derail her life that easily. One way or another, she would get her answers and continue on for her dad, and for herself.

She passed into the next room, into the yellow light of the overhead fluorescents. Berber carpet, a backsplash, and ceiling of warm oak. A board of careworn men and women behind a row of folding tables met her as she entered. In the centre of the group was a thin, older woman with a lined face and a short-cropped, masculine haircut. Although she couldn't have been any taller than five-four, she sat straight, shoulders pulled back, and exuded confidence, both in herself and in the obedience of those around her. One tip of her chin, Denny thought, and they'd be out with the Screamers, and not as spectators this time.

Denny looked back at Wayne and the others. Far from being the confident jokester that she had left the Upper Duck with, Wayne ducked his head almost between his shoulders, reminding her of those old cartoons where someone would get bonked so hard that their head would disappear into their chest for a moment. His hands shook at his sides, although she could see him going stiff to try to hide it.

Denny felt a surge of compassion for him. There was good in him, despite all of his mistakes, and she knew what it was like to wake up every day hoping that today…today would be the day when everything would start setting itself right, when that window would open and out you'd fly, on your way to finally fixing all of the things that hurt you. And truly, this was the moment of truth for both of them. Rejection here, she knew, would be as good as destruction. But she also knew then, even if she never intended to say it, that they had already been through too much together to give up. Somehow, some way, she would journey on with him until they got to where they were going. Because redemption was a place…all they had to do was find the right co-ordinates.

Verity let them stand there, in silence, with all the board studying them, for an uncomfortably long time.

Fine, Denny thought, stare at me like a monkey in a zoo. I've got nothing to hide and nothing to be ashamed of.

Wayne, on the other hand, turned an awful shade of warm grey. Denny willed him internally to hold on, to fight through it— it would hurt for him to face up to everything that he did, but he needed that pain like the pop of a dislocated shoulder being put back in the socket.

When Verity spoke, her voice struck like the first syllable of someone talking into a loudspeaker.

"Doctor Goodrow," she began, "as an Elder of this tribe, I expected you to know better."

"As an Elder of this tribe, I expected you to respect my decision," he said, eyebrows raised. "I guess I expected too much."

Verity wrinkled her nose. Denny noticed that her nose was covered in a thick layer of freckles, forming strange patterns and overlapping.

"I understand your compassion for animals, Doctor. We all do. But…"

"But you just can't extend that compassion to human beings," finished Goodrow.

Verity flushed.

"Don't interrupt me when I'm talking! This is a council of equals, a time for sharing our grievances, not for talking over one another like children on a playground."

Goodrow folded his hands. His face and posture grew as calm and quiet as the eye of a hurricane.

"Very well then, Miss Twoflower," he said, causing another scrunch of Verity's face. "If this is a council of equals, then hear them out before you expel them from the reservation. I suggest you start with the young man before he faints."

Verity narrowed her eyes and went silent for a moment. She then addressed Wayne quietly, with the eyes of a sadistic executioner.

"I know you, boy. I saw you up at Rabbit Lake, and don't tell me I didn't. You journalists have big balls, I'll give you that. Let's skip the chat about kicking you off-property and cut right to the topic of why I shouldn't kill you. After all," she gave an icy smile, "your bosses have already made us into criminals. I wonder if we'll even get a trial, or if they'll just ship us off to a secret prison somewhere hot."

Wayne shot a furtive glance at Denny. She nodded, firmly. *Go for it, Wayne*, she thought, *or you'll never have another chance.*

"I split from Foster Towers a few weeks ago," he said, straightening up and squaring his shoulders. "I didn't want to go along with them from the start, but I'm poor, and they held my paycheck. I had nowhere else to go. I know it wasn't an excuse then, and it isn't now, but I thought you should know."

"Uh-huh," said Verity. "Until you get a publishing deal from them for a tell-all book. I can see it now: Life Among Savages: How I survived Canada's most vicious terrorist cell since the FLQ. Brilliant! I'll buy a copy right now." She gave him another sour, shrunken-up little smile.

"I'm done with that part of my life now. You don't have to believe me, but please accept what I'm bringing you as a token of apology for all the trouble I've caused. However you choose to deal with me, I have information that could exonerate you and bring the Foster Towers Media Corp to its knees."

"And I suppose you want to trade it for immunity, do you?"

"No. It's a gift. Take it. Use it. Look in the camera case you confiscated from me, behind the lining. I've got documents, signatures, videos that no one is supposed to see...some that I shot. I'll testify for you...but I can't testify if I'm dead."

They pulled out Wayne's camera case, yanked out the lining, and produced two notebooks, a folder full of photos and legal documents, and an envelope which they dumped out. Three storage disks clattered to the table.

"You're either very brave or very stupid," Verity said. "My money's on both. We don't need your testimony. We've got plenty of our own. However, it would be unwise of us to let you leave. You'll stay here, under guard, until our conflict with Foster Towers is resolved. If the conflict is resolved, we'll let you go."

"And if not?"

"You said you were on our side. If that's true, you should have no problem sharing our fate. Our land needs us, and we would rather die than abandon it when it's screaming out for help..."

Denny's skin tingled. This woman knew...she could hear the Screamers too. That must have been why they voted her leader, and why the reservation was so quiet at night...she had put them to rest.

Denny said, "I can hear them too...I can hear them singing."

Verity's face mingled indignation and surprise.

Verity pulled back in her chair, gripping the edge of the desk like she'd had a sudden dizzy spell. "Who told you about that? Who sent you?"

"No one told me about the singing. I can hear it. I can sometimes even sing them back down. In fact, on my way here, I ran into a particularly nasty Screamer called the Green Queen. I saved the Dore boys, and I think they were possessed."

Verity's hawk eyes flickered to Mr. Dore.

"George?"

"Yeah, they did it. Thought they could go up there and smoke weed. Don't ask me how they got in the contraband shed."

"We'll discuss this later," she said, then, back to Denny, "What's your name?"

"Felicia Dennigan," she said. "I'm not a journalist, I'm a teacher. I came up here to find out what happened to my father. He became a Screamer, and I saw him on TV. I couldn't leave him suffering."

Verity's face softened. She looked at her hands. Without her mouth set in a straight line and her eyebrows knit together, she became somebody that Denny had met before. A nurse who had worked long years coming back to school for a second career, or a veteran police officer warning people about stranger danger even when she was supposed to be fishing at the lake. Caring, out of her depth. Holding the darkness at bay with a beaten-up birthday candle.

"Sean's girl," she said, more to herself than anyone else.

"Excuse me?" Denny said. "How do you know him? Please, tell me."

Another long silence from Verity. She looked to the side, at the floor, anywhere but at Denny.

"Mr. Sarafian, I'm sending you home with Janna. You'll be living with her and her nephew until the end of the conflict. George, I would beg you one more time to stay out of trouble, lest someone take lawmaking into their own hands, but I'm beginning to believe that trouble finds you. Or, perhaps, the boys are now reeling trouble in for you. Either way, there's no real remedy that I can prescribe for being an accident waiting to happen. And Doctor Goodrow, since I can't convince you to end your involvement in this matter, the Watch will allow you to continue treating Geoff."

"How did you know his name?" Denny blurted out, and a line of angry faces focused on her. George elbowed her.

"Don't interrupt when it's not your turn. That's not how we do things here."

Denny stuck her chin out at him.

"She knew his name, and no one told her. Dr. Goodrow has been in his clinic all night! He couldn't have told her. What's going on? You know where he went, don't you? You all know."

She paused, and her eyes filled up with tears. "You knew Geoff. You knew his name, and you were still willing to turn him out into the wilderness to die. How could you?"

Janna and two others stood up. "You're lucky you're alive, white girl, and the dog, too. Do you know how many ways they've tried to get to us? Go back to the suburbs where you belong. You won't last five minutes once the real fighting starts," she said.

"There's not going to be any fighting," Verity said, voice raised. She stood up with her hands pressed against the table. "There is every chance that we can use this new information to counter the news men. Everyone get back to your business. This meeting is adjourned. And if I find out one club was swung or one gun fired before we all agree—unanimously—that it's the last viable plan…I will use every ounce of my training to hunt the culprit down and expel them from Hunting Bear. And I know I'm not the only one who feels that way. Now go, all of you, and *play nice.*"

The Doc left first, his hand on George's shoulder. Denny heard him offer George a cup of coffee on the way out the door. Janna strode across the floor next, and she, too, placed an arm around Wayne, but in the manner of a bailiff, her hand a subtle warning that he'd better not try anything funny. Wayne looked back at her on the way out, and she longed to follow after weeks of staying together, but she'd gotten the distinct impression that she wasn't welcome in de facto prison.

Come to think of it, where *did* she go now? She shuffled her feet and tried to catch someone's eye for some indication of what came next. As the other Watch members drifted out of the building, Verity stood behind the tables, her arms crossed, studying her. Soon, they were alone, the only sound between them the buzzing of the electric lights.

"Come closer. Let me get a good look at you," Verity said at last.

Denny crossed what seemed like an echoing mile, feeling the familiar awkwardness enter her step that she got from being studied too closely. After all, you could always walk until you wanted to show someone.

Now, across the table from one another, Verity looked into her eyes. The woman who, minutes ago, had been a battle-hardened old soldier, now trembled, her mouth quivering and her eyes sad.

"I didn't expect you to look so much like my mother," she said.

THE TRUTH ABOUT MONSTERS

Denny's hands trembled, and the harder she pressed them to the coffee mug, the harder it jittered. She thumped the thing, with its orange-brown floral pattern, onto the table and shifted in her seat.

"So...Dad was your half-brother?"

Verity sat across from her at an aged linoleum kitchen table with chrome edging. She said this was her house, but this was not what Denny had pictured a famed militant radical's house looking like, to say the least. No stockpiles, no bunkers, no weapon safes. She wasn't even sure there'd been a lock on the door when they came in. It seemed that Verity enjoyed floral prints...a lot. And, judging from the row of copper pots on the wall, she was pretty serious about cooking, too.

"My mom had me when she was a teenager," Verity replied. "Dad stuck around, but they were young and they couldn't make it work. She remarried when I was eight, to a white guy."

"Grampy Joe," Denny said.

"That's not what I called him."

"Oh..."

"He took us off-rez. He made out like he was saving us, pulling us up to a better life. I missed my life here, my dad and my friends. He wouldn't even let me write to them. Worse yet, he started putting Mom down all the time. When Sean was born, Joe was determined that he would never become a 'no-good, drunken Indian.' He played up to Sean, while bullying my mother and I. For a while, Sean listened to him, and there are still things between us that we'll never really reconcile from that time of our lives. He started living like a white man, telling people he was Irish...and I ran away. Hitched back to the reserve to be with Dad. Then, when I was old enough, I joined the army."

Denny took a long swig of her tea. Inside her, a million happy memories with Grampy Joe developed permanent burn marks. Sunny days in the kiddie pool in his backyard greyed. The taste of the strawberry candies he kept in a dish by the front door faded to the taste of boxed mashed potatoes in a corporate cafeteria. What would she have said to him if she had known that the colour of her skin was a pre-requisite to loving her?

"So when did you come back here? How did you make up with Dad?" Denny asked.

"Honestly, I never thought I'd see him again," Verity replied. "He had his big, southern city life with the white folks, and I had the forest and the fight to make things better and bring our dignity back from within. I wish I'd kept some of the articles they printed before the Rising...we were held up as the beginning of a

303

movement to make things better for Native people everywhere. I guess Sean had been following the coverage, and when he had his breakdown, he came back here, looking for some pieces of himself that remained undamaged.

"He stumbled in here one night just as the sun was setting, a grey shadow of himself with barely enough strength to stand. He called me Very...he hadn't called me that in years. Not since he'd gotten sick of tacking nasty adjectives to the end of it," she said with a chuckle. "I knew something was different about him as the weeks went on. He woke up screaming in the middle of the night. He took long walks and never said where he was going. I'd seen it before, in the war. And yet, there seemed to be parts of him that were better for the change. Walls couldn't hold him anymore. Success, as he had defined it, held no more charm for him. He grew closer to accepting his true identity, and he seemed to exist in an ever-ready state of listening, drinking everything in even when it hurt him."

Verity's words socked Denny in the mouth. She felt her jaw and realized that while Verity had been talking, she had clenched her teeth.

"So all this time, he had been coming here? Living in a house? He lied to me...all those years, I thought he was a drifter, when he really just had another life without me in it. I guess I see the point now."

All this way, all this danger and sorrow, only to discover that he had wilfully abandoned her? Maybe her mother had been right. Maybe he had just been a selfish man who made bad choices and didn't really love her the way he should have. The tiny dock she had been standing on in a sea of troubles washed away under her feet, and she plunged down, down into cold confusion.

She lifted the cup of tea to her lips again, stared at it, contemplated hiding behind it before realizing that it was only a few scant inches wide and she was huge, taking up space, the only other human being in the place. Plus, Verity's eyes were locked on her. Her hand trembled. She put down the cup, her stomach souring. She took in a couple of deep breaths, and after the third, the sobs escaped on their own. They came howling out of her like demons from Pandora's box, and Verity let them. She simply watched as Denny laid her head down on the table, not caring at the chrome edging dug into the sides of her arms. After a while, she got up and dumped out the cold tea sitting in the pot on the counter.

"I won't try to tell you it's okay," Verity said, her back turned. She turned on the tap and squeezed some dish soap into the stream. "My mom stayed with that bastard she married until she died. My decision to leave ended up severing our bond. We barely talked, even as she was dying of liver cancer. I was lucky he even let me in the hospital room. I had a corner all to myself at the funeral. I guess I should feel good that he left me alone, but I never will."

"What's wrong with me?" Denny croaked. "Everybody leaves."

Verity turned around, leaning on the counter with her hands behind her back.

"What I wouldn't give for a God-cam right now. Except for the haircut, you and I could have been twins. At least on the inside. But in the intervening years, I've learned a few secrets. The first one is this: everyone hasn't abandoned you. One person abandoned you. The rest of them, you abandoned yourself."

Denny stood up. Her feelings switched gears with a palpable stomach flip, from sorrow to anger. "You're implying that I caused this?"

"I'm saying it. Let me guess…this is the first time you've cried in front of someone in a long time, and every time you do, when you can't help yourself, you feel humiliated for a week. I'm also guessing that you didn't tell people about your dad much. Is that true?"

"I wasn't ashamed of him!"

"Weren't you? You jumped to that conclusion, not me."

Flip. Gear change, this time without any lubrication on the gears. Rusty muscles ground together as she sobbed anew, layers of revelation tearing at one another and her. She shook her head at Verity. Why would she do this? Why would she reach inside her and tell the truth? The truth was poison, one that she had drunk a long time ago and held inside, that rotted inside her bones, poisoned the marrow until she was too sick to remember. She sobbed out of control, unable to respond. The table below her wavered with tears, making the faux marble wiggle like sound waves on a screen.

"Until you can talk about your life...all of your life, you'll be doomed to Sean's mistakes and his loneliness, too."

Denny looked up. Loneliness? Dad had always seemed so self-contained, even in his illness.

"It surprises you that he was lonely? Well he was. Desperately, wretchedly lonely. For you, for the approval of his dead, bastard father, for the wife and the family that he lost. He loved you. I know he did. He wanted to tell you. But he feared for your safety, and when you're addicted to keeping secrets, when you live for the approval of others, it becomes impossible to let people in. Sure, they can't share the secrets that terrify you...but after a while, you also lock them out of joy, love, friendship...and before you know it, you're in Hell."

The sobs quieted to trails of tears coursing down Denny's face, but the turmoil inside her persisted.

"I don't know what to do now," she said. "I came up here to try to fix things. I gave up everything I had to come and find out what happened. Now that I know, I'm not sure what the right answer is. I don't even feel like the same person anymore."

Verity's hand, lean and firm, squeezed her shoulder.

"There's more you need to know but not now. I'll show you to your room, and then you can go wherever you want. I'd suggest a good long walk out to the lake. I'd also suggest a walkie-talkie. I'll keep mine on in case of trouble."

"What kind of trouble? Do you think I'm in danger here?"

Verity's expression darkened.

"No. Just bears, that's all."

THE DEPARTURE

Around four in the afternoon, at that time of day when the light fades an almost imperceptible degree, beginning the transition to evening, Denny crept out of Verity's door and down the wooden stairs. She wound her way downhill, through a part of the reservation she hadn't been to before. She passed a bungalow with plastic pinwheels on the lawn and a trailer home turned convenience store turned darkened stockpile for non-perishable food.

Halfway down the slope to the lake, she stopped in front of a two-storey white Cape Cod with a small side porch. This had to be the one. Verity had insisted that Wayne stay in solitary confinement, but she had also not-so-subtly mentioned Janna's address a few minutes later, as Denny was heading out the door, under the guise of providing helpful landmarks for her walking route.

One of the windows on the second floor had bars on it. There was a light on in a corner of the dormer, casting a warm yellow light on the ceiling and part of a wall. After standing there for the better part of a minute, she began wondering what she had expected to see and how long it would take for someone inside to notice she was there.

Someone stumbled to the window. Some of the light left the upstairs room as a door slammed behind them. It was Wayne, and he saw her. He placed a hand to the windowpane, then the other, his face full of longing. Denny held up her hand, her heart feeling like it had walked a thousand miles that day and still more to go. She spread her fingers, and in her mind, they linked hands. As soon as that mental picture flowed through her mind, she felt him, flowing down to her through a link made of light the yellow of black-eyed daisy petals. She felt loneliness, deep and abiding, a sense of being marooned by his life, and a terrible fear that he would die here before having a chance to live with any kind of happiness. Wayne's eyes went wide and he pulled back from the window, staring at his glowing hands, but the connection held. No one else would be able to see this. She knew inherently that this was something only they could share.

Her heart raced, and her head swam. What the hell was she doing? She was no mind reader... The connection faltered, fading down to a few twists of golden light. And then, through the fading conduits, a surge of *something* washed over her, warm, strong, and as strengthening as a hot cup of tea on a bitterly cold day. Wayne smiled, and then she knew. He was sending her love.

Denny opened up the place where she sang, the place where the light shone through, and the purest white shot through their connection.

Stay strong, she poured into every fibre of her being, *I won't abandon you.*

With the message sent, the connection fizzled like the remains of a Victoria Day firework. Wayne pressed the top of his forehead to the window, his thick, serious brows seeming almost soft and friendly for once.

Go, he mouthed to her.

She went, shaken like someone who has just pulled out of a dead faint. She stumbled down to the lakeshore, where she found a large outcrop of Shield rock amid the pin-straight pine trees. There, she collapsed, allowing herself to get lost in the slow lapping of the water against the shore. She lay there until the pine needles left impressions on her skin and longer. She lay there as the night chill set in. She heard the siren announcing the closing of the reservation gates for the night and felt nothing but numb. Let them shut her out. Going back would only imply that she had a direction, and directions eluded her. Dad had made another life without her. Out of the blue, she had just made some sort of weird link with Wayne, and he had sent her love. Love. From the guy who had doctored news footage and grabbed her tits the first time they met. And the screwiest thing about it all was that, if her impressions were correct, they could have switched hearts and not known the difference.

By the time Denny sat up and looked around her, stars dotted the sky and the old pines swayed in a gentle night breeze. She shivered. The chill from the rocks had seeped right through her as she lay there, adding itself to the wind and the night dew. She hugged herself and rubbed her shoulders. Her feet felt like cold stones strapped onto her legs.

Up above the lake, the crescent moon shone bright, unobscured by the clouds that had hung over the landscape the last couple of days. Denny bathed in the clear, white light, drank in the silence. Despite the deep chill entering her body, she was drunk on the peace of this place, the total mental quiet she felt while here, grounding herself in the stability of ancient rock. Were she to die here, right now, she knew she would rest.

Denny heard an ATV engine approaching from the direction of the reservation and stop about thirty metres away, where the soft ground around the lake ended.

"Denny?" called a familiar voice. "Where are you?"

"Over here, Verity," she said, sliding down off of the rock face.

Verity strode out of the darkness like a grey deer. She locked eyes with Denny and didn't let go.

"Why didn't you come back by lockdown?" she asked. "I asked around to everyone on the rez, and they said you'd come down here and had not come back. I thought…"

"Thought what? That one of your own people might kill me or drive me away? I can see that the balance of power here is shaky at best. I thought it might be easier for everyone if I just did a fade. To where, I don't know. I don't feel like I know a lot anymore.

There really are people here that want to have a war though, aren't there?"

"They've lost their faith in humanity. When I came up here and made all the reforms, I gave them power, and then the Screamers rose, and the people down south wanted to blame them and take it away again...the only self-respect some of them have had for generations. Janna comes from a line of alcoholics and abusers, starting from the days of residential schools, but she bucked that legacy and became somebody who builds things up rather than tearing them down. She's not the only one to have overcome a difficult past for the greater good."

"So what happened? How did Hunting Bear go from model society to Canada's Most Wanted?"

Verity frowned, as though she had just tasted something very bitter.

"When I came back from the war, I was ready to give back. You don't see the things I saw without needing, deep down, to make your home better and make the people around you feel more human. I got involved in our government, and I started building on my old friendships. Some of my friends were in a bad state...George was probably the worst of them, a drug dealer always on the run from somebody. He kept the knack for mischief but gave up the crime. Or as far as we know, he did." She chuckled at that. "He was always that kid throwing crabapples at the mailman anyway."

Denny smiled too, and nodded for her to go on.

"The first thing we did was get them educated," Verity said. "Remotely from the rez, because the hardest thing to overcome for a lot of them was to leave and go down south, to a place where they didn't know how to live, without their family around them. I got computers to do it, and I kept them under tight lock and key, military style. We organized support groups and put pressure on the addicts to deal with their issues. We also founded the Watch to keep an eye on the troublemakers. It wasn't strictly legal, but a lot of stuff up here isn't," she said with a wicked grin. "At least our little quasi-legal endeavours were helping people to be safe and happy. Once a few of us had degrees, we trained to be home school teachers and started a co-operative. We each took one day a week teaching the kids, and the rest of us worked on our own business. Once the junkies had lost their stranglehold on the place and we'd won a lot of them to our side, businesses started cropping up. People weren't afraid to start things anymore. The media got wind of the improvements we'd made, and soon we had become an example for Indigenous communities all over the world. There were some rumblings in the government and the media about vigilantism and militancy even then, but it was mostly just ignored as the racist clap-trap it was. For the most part, the government was just happy we were making the country look good and that we wouldn't be requiring as much aid money.

"We continued on for about ten years like that. We still had problems, but they were smaller, and we had systems to deal with them now. Then, almost overnight, we started hearing reports from the far North about screams in the dark, rampant suicides, murders in cold blood, and glowing devils grinning over it all. To be honest with you, I suspected a poisoned water supply or a gas leak somewhere in the rock. But then, it spread. We had a sizable stash of emergency supplies and good security measures in place by this time—a necessary precaution when you live so far away from help—and so we locked down. But it didn't keep them out. All the murders we'd never solved, all the bodies we'd never found, every suicide with unfinished business rose, and screamed. We were going to flee like the rest of them, but the Green Queen blocked our main avenue of escape. She bewitched nine of my men with her screams, and they tried to kill us. Stuck with my back against a rock wall, with a gun trained on me, I learned to sing. I didn't realize that none of the rest of them could hear the words...until I sang back, and she faltered. I sang long and loud then, a fierce battle chant from my youth, and she shrunk back into the earth to fester."

"So why did you stay after all?"

"I can't leave something that I know I can fix. It's an obsession with me. It dawned on me after the fight with the Green Queen that if I could subdue that monster, I could probably put the smaller ones to rest altogether. There were also the others...many

315

of them had never left the rez. We didn't fight all those long years to heal our home just to leave it at the first sign of trouble. We came back, I sang the Screamers down, and we continued on."

"So, how did Foster Towers get involved?"

"They sent a couple of producers up here in a plane when it first started. They had heard that it was a quiet zone and they wanted to establish a base camp here. That wasn't all they wanted, though. The Fosters had been doing some homework on us before they arrived. They suspected that I had the ability to quiet Screamers, and they forced my hand one night when we were out, supposedly scouting. Threw an intern to a particularly nasty customer about a kilometre out from the rez. It was either save him or watch him dig out his own eyes. After they had confirmation of what I could do, they were all promises and privileges and money. They wanted me to work for them. They wanted me to go behind the government's back and take down as many Screamers as I could."

"But why? What would a media company want to do with any of this?"

"Ahahaha," Verity said, holding up a finger, "you assume that this is just about media. But the Foster family reaches much farther than that. You forget that Daniel Foster, CEO of Foster Towers, has a cousin, Terence Foster, who develops land. He specializes in clean-up jobs. Buying up slums and converting them into trendy condos, building old folks' homes on partially poisoned factory land...that kind of thing. It's the biggest business of its kind in the country. Since the flooding down south, the North has become very attractive to affluent types wanting to escape the damp and the crowding. The Fosters wanted to secretly clean up the land, buy it off of the owners at a tiny fraction of its value, and then declare the epidemic over and sell it back at an exponent of the buy price. And I was the tool they wanted to use to do it. I told them I wouldn't. I threatened to go to the government, and the next day there was an exposé about me on the news using footage they'd secretly gathered while visiting us, of us looting nearby towns for food. And that's how I became a terrorist. When the footage they had got boring, they ramped things up a notch. They kidnapped a child from the rez, lured us out with threats to kill him, and then taped the ensuing fight. Now they're claiming we're attacking refugees passing through our land, hoping the army will come in and silence us for them."

"Oh my God. Did the boy survive, at least?"

Verity shook her head. "Joe got killed by a stray bullet during the fight. Your dad died trying to get him away from the newsmen. They're all still up there...it was all we could do to get away once the place was blanketed in fresh Screamers. You think the ones you've seen so far are bad? Try the ones that just died. They have more power for the first few months, and they can scream in the daytime. We lost eleven people in the fight, and

Gary Benoit went crazy in the aftermath. He's been drugged senseless at his brother's house since it happened."

Denny paused for a moment. So Dad had died defending a child. Had he seen little Kendall, the child he loved and lost, in the face of the boy he died for before the darkness closed in?

She also thought of Wayne, of the loneliness and sorrow in his heart, and the way he cowered from the Screamers like a man-sized Pavlov's dog. If he had seen all that Verity claimed, he had been through Hell and been forced to smile about it. Maybe Hell was just as bad for the demons as it was for the sinners.

One thing occurred to her, though, a flaw in Verity's logic.

"Why didn't you tell anyone what you can do? If there are more people like us out there, we could help. We could get that government reward money and live like royalty," Denny said.

"I don't think they'll ever disappear completely. The ones I put to rest, I helped because I identified with them. In some cases, I knew their families and their stories. It's empathy that puts them back down...empathy and the satisfaction of their reason for rising. Many of the Screamers will be from times long gone and families long dead. The odds that we can deal with all of them are slim. And then there are toxic entities like the Green Queen, who rise because they were insatiable in life. Their hunger will never let them rest," she said, sighing. "No, there's something bigger at play here. I'm not terribly religious, but I think the wrong that caused the Screamers to rise is bigger than any individual. It's a spiritual malaise, and it will take more than you and I to stop it."

"But you said it yourself—you're a fixer."

"Yes, and I believe there is one aspect of this situation that we can fix. But it will be a huge risk, and I'll need your help."

Denny cocked her head to one side. Verity continued.

"I've been looking through the documents that your dubious friend brought with him. They give us proof that the whole fight was staged and then re-edited. They also tell us that the fools left something behind while they were fleeing the scene. One of the downed men had a data disc with information on it concerning the search for more singers and what they planned to do with them. He died, and they had no choice but to leave them. Get the disc and then we would not only have proof that they murdered people to advance their shady dealings, but also what those shady dealings were, in detail, and I'm sure the government won't be too pleased that they were keeping people like us a secret, either. I need to go up there, get the data disc, and put as many of the Screamers back in the ground as possible. The cops are going to need to get into that clearing sometime, and the easier we can make it for them, the better for our case," she said. "If I'm not mistaken, you came up here to give Sean some rest. This could be your last, best chance."

At the sound of her father's name, Denny ached again. But then she thought of him standing in front of that little boy and taking a bullet for him, so eager to make amends for what he saw as the greatest mistake of his life, and she knew she had to do it. Sean Dennigan may not have been the father she needed, he may not have been a great man, but he had been a good one, and his torture had to end now. Also…she liked Verity. For all she had done, and however nasty her entrance had been, she seemed to genuinely want to do what was best, and least violent, for everyone in her care. Although Denny wondered if Verity would ever submit to the term, she realized then that she was, for all intents and purposes, her aunt. And that meant that many of the people on the reserve were probably her cousins. Bigger things were in play now than whether she liked her father or not, and Wayne's life was one of them.

"I'll do it," she said, "but what will happen to Wayne? And if your friends are as desperate as you say, how will you prevent them from moving on and attacking government forces without you?"

"I don't know the answer to either of those questions. I think, in both cases, we are going to have to trust our friends to take care of themselves, and then do what we need to do. There are no good decisions to be made anymore, only choosing from the best options as we see them. And I think our best option is to head for Rabbit Lake."

"Won't they try to stop you?"

"The people who could stop me already know. As for who will take care of business in my absence, I left the Doc in charge. We may have had our differences, but I trust him to use his words, not his weapons. Now come on. My ATV is waiting. I took the liberty of packing anything from your bags I thought we'd need."

Verity turned and headed back the way she had come. Denny paused a few seconds before following her, thinking.

"Did you know I was going to say yes, or did I not really have a choice in the matter?" she said, half amused.

Verity's voice drifted back through the darkness.

"The supplies could be returned to their bags if you said no. I never leave unprepared when time is of the essence. Sure, it wasn't very polite of me, but politeness doesn't serve in situations like these. The less time we take, the less time everyone has to get fighting. And based on the way things are going, we don't have more than three days. We might not even have that," she replied.

When Denny reached the ATV, Verity already had it revved up. She tossed Denny a helmet and a leather jacket.

"Gloves are in the right pocket. Suit up and get on. If you get tired, eat the energy bar in the left pocket. It's caffeinated."

Denny slid onto the back of the ATV, where she zipped up the jacket and put her bug shield down.

"I don't do well with caffeine," she said, "makes me super grumpy."

"Well, your choice is eat the bar or fall off the back when you pass out asleep. Cause I ain't stoppin' till midday tomorrow. Think of it as a character-building exercise."

Denny rolled her eyes.

"If fatigue and moodiness build character, then I should be the Dalai Lama by now," she said.

Verity let out a laugh, then with a loud whoop, she punched the gas and sent them rocketing off into the night.

"And I must be Saint fucking Francis," she hollered over the roar of the engines. "Let's give 'em a dose of enlightenment they won't soon forget!"

FIRST, DO NO HARM

Wayne reached through the bars of the stainless steel stacked cage and wiggled his fingers through Geoff's fur. Geoff lifted his head and gave him a weak little lick, his tongue sand-papery and too warm.

Geoff's tail was gone and all that was left in its place was a bandaged stump. He wiggled the stump twice, then stopped. His wounds had been cleaned and bandaged, but bacteria still coursed through his system, causing his nose to be too hot and his eyes to glaze over. Although Wayne knew better, Geoff looked like he had just finished a good long cry.

He reached into a nearby jar of dog treats and passed one through the bars. Geoff licked it up, chewed it for a very long time, then swallowed it with a few laboured smacks of his tongue.

"Good doggy," Wayne said. "Keep eating for me, buddy."

On the other side of the room, Janna shot him a dirty look, as though his low-voiced encouragement to Geoff was making it impossible to hold her very loud conversation. She was fighting with the Doc again. They had been at it all day, first on the phone and now in person.

"She abandons us as everything is falling apart, and you expect us to just sit here and do nothing? It's time for us to take action, before they can."

"The army may not take any action until they see what's really going on," said the Doc. "We just don't know, and until we have a chance to talk things out and tell our side of the story, we can't just go around waving our guns and expect them to treat us like anything but militant criminals, which is what we become by using violence to solve our problems."

"Verity wanted to use violence to solve our problems, if we were trapped."

"If and *when* we are trapped, we will re-open this discussion. Until then, I am the one in charge, and I say, we wait to negotiate," said the Doc, in his usual calm manner.

He may not have trained to be a people doctor, thought Wayne, *but I think in some ways he still is. I'd hire him at the loony bin in a heartbeat. He has a great bedside manner with psychos.*

Janna's cheeks turned red and Wayne could see the muscles in the back of her jaw clench. He could tell from her posture that she was almost jumping up and down in frustration, like a spoiled little girl denied her third cupcake.

"You really think they're going to listen to us? Hundreds of years of ignoring us, arresting us, and making us the butt of their jokes, and they're just going to sit down for a cup of tea and ask us for an informed reason that we killed a bunch of white journalists on camera? No! They're going to come in here and they're going to smash us to pieces and then pretend like we never existed. Because that's what they *do*."

The Doc tried to put a hand on Janna's shoulder. She pulled away, then stormed out the door, calling, "Send out the fucking journalist when you're finished with him. Or just finish him for all I care. Nice dose of ketamine and we're all a lot happier."

The Doc pinched the bridge of his nose. He looked up at the lights and shook his head.

"Remind me to thank Verity for re-discovering her faith in me, would you please?" he said.

"What's wrong with her?" Wayne asked, unconsciously scratching Geoff through the bars as he did so. He had been scratching Geoff through the whole conversation and not even noticed.

"Ever since she cleaned up and got her diploma, she's been really mad at *them*, but I'm not sure even she knows who *they* are. White people, the government, her parents...most likely some strange mixture of all three that she's wrapped around her brain over the years. There are many things to be angry about in this world, and many of them apply to us Natives, but she's always used anger as a way to explain away her own vulnerabilities. She just wants so badly to have a place in the world...and she always idolized Verity. Now that both are in peril, I'm afraid of what she might do."

Wayne thought of his "breakfast" this morning, a half bowl of plain porridge that would be chintzy for an eleven-year-old. He had stared at it until it was cold and congealed, wondering if there were drugs in it, and then he had been too hungry and unsure of his next meal to care. Based on the way Janna had treated him thus far, he was sure that the only thing keeping her from drugging his food was the fact that most drugs had been cut off from the reservation a long time ago.

"But you're in charge now…can't you at least do something for me?"

"I'm about to," said the Doc, taking the treat jar and placing it back on its shelf. "You're going to move to my house. If you hear a scuffle, I need you to come out and help me."

The Doc went to the door, back straight as a fire poker. Wayne admired his calm gait under the circumstances, still as smooth and deliberate as if he were rolling on a rail. His memories of Verity still made him very uncomfortable, but for a moment, he respected her and her decision to leave the Doc in charge. Clearly, they had their differences, if the meeting was any indication, but she had had the wisdom to pick someone who, by trade and by nature, was cool under pressure.

Based on the things he had heard at Janna's, the Doc would have to be made of ice pretty soon. Verity's lieutenants were mad. He could hear them arguing all day yesterday in a secret meeting at Janna's house. A few of them wanted to ride out and attack the nearest RCMP outpost. All of them believed that the army was on its way and would be at Hunting Bear in a matter of a few days.

The Doc stepped out of the door with a tinkle of the bell. Wayne stopped scratching Geoff. In the silence, he wrapped his fingers around the bars of the cage. Like a gentle rain building to a thunderstorm, it began with lowered voices, building and building, until they were screaming at each other or, more accurately, Janna screamed at the Doc, and the Doc talked to her with his voice raised, trying to get her to speak more rationally. Wayne contemplated going out there, but he heard no physical scuffle.

Through the bars, he felt the vibration of Geoff scratching around and a brush of fur over his knuckles. He looked back for a moment, afraid to take his eyes off the door but needing to make sure Geoff was okay. Geoff stood up on his front legs, his hind end still flopped down where he had been playing. He dragged his front end up to the bars, stuck his nose through, sniffed the air, and let out a high, thin whine.

With a final clap of verbal thunder, the conversation outside receded into silence once more. The Doc came back up the stairs, visibly drained and messy-haired. Geoff whined again when he saw him, giving a tiny little bark to get his attention. He came over to the cage and held out his hand. Geoff licked it a few times, then lay back down.

327

The Doc gave a great sigh. Up close, Wayne could see beads of sweat standing out on his forehead. He looked at Geoff, then at Wayne.

"Did you know that border collies are sometimes born without tails, Wayne?" he said.

Wayne gave a low smile.

"That's pretty good," he said. "I was worried about him ever getting a date again."

TWILIGHT IN THE VALLEY OF THE DEAD

Denny wiped the sweat from her brow, her hair following her hand in soaked strings. Two hours of lifting, hauling, hammering, and knotting, and finally, the tent roof held up and the fire pit was dug and filled with wood. Off in the distance, she heard another howl, followed by a chorus of screams. The ghastly melange of dissonant sound echoed through the air.

She had lived by the highway in St. Catharines for much of her life, just a few blocks away, and on certain nights, when the wind was right, the sound of the transport trucks hurtling down the highway, the air screaming through their squared bodies permeated the house, even with the windows closed and the doors locked. Lying in bed as a young teen, she would hide under the covers, soaking in the eeriness of the sound and feeling strangely comforted by the all-surrounding howl of girders and bearings and rubber tires.

Down below them now, a highway of spirits rushed past them and all around, constant, surrounding, and inescapable. If Denny hadn't heard it with her ears, she would have heard it with her heart, feeling the vibrations shaking it like the constant hum of a truck motor. She fought to keep her mind on her work, to keep her attention on Verity's face, to listen and stay alert, but that howl, that seductive highway of sound, threatened at all times to pull her in like a whirlpool.

"I don't think I'll be sleeping while we're here," Denny said, loudly. "I don't know if I can."

Verity gave a stretched, stressed smile. "The tent is here in case it rains or snows. You may find time gets away from you when you're dealing with new Screamers, but we can't get unhooked from time entirely. We have to get back to the rez soon. More importantly, we have to remember to eat and drink."

Another barrage of sound rumbled through her lizard brain. She jerked in the direction of the sound, twitched in an almost orgasmic manner, then pulled away hard, putting her head in her hands. She looked at Verity, wide-eyed, feeling like her aunt had just walked in on her at a very intimate, and possibly kinky, moment. Verity was rooting through the small cooler they had brought.

"They want you to come to them. I feel it too. Don't be ashamed," she said. She tossed Denny a ham sandwich.

"I don't know if I can," Denny said, feeling a roiling in her stomach and a lump in her throat after that literal mind-fucking.

Verity sat down on the ATV seat. "We stay until it's done. Here's some water to wash it down. Drink all of that too."

Denny opened up the plastic wrap and took a bite. Under other circumstances, her rational mind told her that this bread would be quite fresh and moist…by all accounts, easy to eat. This time, it tasted like swallowing sawdust. The rough mustard that Verity had put on it burned on her soft palate and travelled up her nose, where it ached in her sinuses for a while. The ham was like a slimy dog tongue.

She took a bite and washed it down with a third of a bottle of water. She took another, and it wasn't so bad. Then on the third one, her throat seized up, and she gagged. Everything ached, and the world was slightly blurry. The energy that normally coursed through her body dimmed to a brown-out.

"I feel like I'm dying with them," she said.

"We will, in a way," said Verity. "Fresh Screamers want to pull you into their state of being, and for a few months, they have the power left to do it. They don't know they're dead."

Verity patted Denny on the back and took another bite of her own sandwich with a forced smile. "Yum, pickled skunk anus," she said.

Denny broke up laughing in spite of herself, and after that, swallowing the food and water was a bit easier. Verity had picked the right profession. It took a very special person to make you snarf ham sandwich in a war zone.

When they finished the sandwiches and water, they sat there, on the back of the ATV, both feeling the pull at their core, knowing the other felt it, and yet not moving...not yet. Denny didn't know what Verity was comparing this to, but in her own mind, she was Dante facing the gates of Hell, an impression only deepened by the darkening sky and the sickly yellow-green glowing working its way through the interwoven boughs of the trees. Dante had relied on the poet Virgil to guide him through the abyss...Denny would have to find her own Virgil, be her own Virgil, or it was *abandon all hope, ye who enter here.*

"How do we make it out?" Denny asked.

"We won't know that until we make it in," said Verity.

"If we make it out alive, can we be family?"

"I thought we already were. And Denny?"

"Yeah?"

"Call me Aunt Very."

They had made camp on a short, rolling slope leading down to a band of forest in between two other hills made of Shield rock. In the twilight, even without the glow of the Screamer colony, the place mimicked the quasi-abstract daubs of a Thom Thomson painting, with tall pines leaning out in strange formations and tangles of trunks playing games with the light. With the glow and the screams and the strange, shambling movements behind the trees, it became a Group of Seven opium nightmare. Amid the surreality of it all, Denny half-expected to see strange cracks of rust-orange primer peeking out from behind the birch bark.

Toward this scene they now travelled, as light on their feet as spirits, half in the other world already.

When they reached the trees, Verity said, "You look for Sean, but don't get in over your head. I'm going for the data disc. If either of us gets swarmed, we hit the highest high C we've got. If that happens, come in with your voice blazing louder than it's ever been."

She heard Verity's voice, but were her lips moving? In the wavering shadows of the trees, she couldn't tell. She nodded. Inside, however, she wondered if Verity would be okay by herself, if either of them would be.

"Some answers just have to work themselves out, kid. We do what we have to, and the bones fall where they will."

Okay, Verity was speaking inside of her head. How long had she been able to pull that one off? And yet, Denny didn't think she'd been able to do it before. Something about the energy of this place, and the freshly dead Screamers, was amplifying their abilities. Were they dying already? She felt panic grip her ribcage in a vice, scared for a moment to go any further. Then, etched in light on the backs of her eyes, there but not really there, she saw:

Let the bones fall where they will.

Denny took in a deep breath, squared her shoulders, and ran at the light dancing beyond the trees. She could see rotting figures stumbling toward her, eyes glowing, moving to encircle her. Let the bones fall where they will. She was more than bone.

A wall of cloying warmth greeted her, smelling of mould, old attics, and rotting meat, all at the same time. It sucked the moisture from her skin and pulled and pulled, until she began to forget her name, struggled to remember it, Felicia, no, Denny, no, what was she remembering? It was so hard to breathe here, let alone sing, but she had sung once, in times like these…yes…no…singing? Screaming. Screaming… *Screaming*…

From somewhere far off in the distance, she heard a voice, cutting through the fog in her mind. Singing! A high, clear war chant warbled to her over the radio static in her mind. Denny! That was her name. Wayne, Geoff, Verity, all people she needed to protect, to live for. The voice off in the distance…that was Verity. She was singing, strong and proud, beating them back, putting them to rest. Denny had a voice, but how to use it? What power could she wield to remember, to stay connected to the world of the living?

Let the bones fall where they will…for I am more than bone.

The words flowed from her lips like the soft song of a robin in spring. She felt the truth of them, and they lodged in the living light in her heart. She sang again, with all the power of her soul.

Let the bones fall where they will…for I am more than bone!

It soared from her, rising and falling in peace and tranquility like a Gregorian chant straight from the throne of Heaven. The shapes around her dropped back, their light weakening. She walked between them, a white-robed figure with a candle brighter than any she had ever known before, her line of truth flowing into a song.

Let the bones fall where they will,
For I am more than bone!
I may be ever lonely,
But I'll never be alone.

The cacophony of screams around her softened into a symphony, the chorus in her harsh, heavy metal opera. Flames licked at her feet, adorning them. Figures danced to her left and right in heavy, thrashing motions.

Let the bones fall where they will,
For I am made of light,
I need no other candle
To take me through the night.

This had never happened before. Perhaps it had never happened before in the history of the world and never would again. Here, in this place, she witnessed the savage beauty of death, of memory, of loss playing out around her like a brutal cosmic ballet. Still, one dancer was missing. His name had been Sean, and he had been her father once. It was time to call him to the stage.

Let the bones fall where they will,
For I was made to see.
All the flames that Hell can burn
Will make no mark on me.

In my flesh I hold the truth,
In my bones I hold the past,
In my mind I hold the other things
That were too good to last.

Father… Father… where are you Father?

If the preceding cacophony had turned to an opera, the voice that sailed to her now, over the waves of noise, was the voice of a child singing on a sunny day.

Denny…

She stilled, and the flames and the screams and the thrashing stilled with her. She lowered her hands, and they fell, like the demons in the old cartoon about the Night on Bald Mountain. In their place, a low flicker of green light in a halo of mist and smoke, tall and straight like a road flare, floated at the base of a lump of shield rock covered in scrub. The mist slowly rolled away, and underneath, she saw her father, not as he had looked on that newscast, wretched and mangled, but as he looked when she was a little child, when he had been plump, and happy, and his skin had shone like polished leather. So this was what it was like to meet someone whose message was meant for you…

Denny went running to him, tears standing in her eyes. When they touched, they were in a different place, a bright, pink-white place with no floor and no ceiling. He swept her up in his arms, and he danced with her. They twirled in a slow waltz, and he sang, but nothing with any words…it was filled with sadness and regret and an overwhelming love that she would feel until the end of her days. So this is what filled other people's hearts…and it had filled Dad's, as well. They danced and danced, until they drifted too close to the place where she wouldn't be able to return. She saw it shining there, a portal of brightest white, and would have gone running into it then with him, feeling his love for the first time, but he stopped.

"This is where we stop, and this is where we say goodbye," he said.

Denny hung her head.

"We were always saying goodbye. You were all that I wanted, and I was never good enough for you. I was never good enough for anyone."

"Oh, baby, that's not true...I came up here trying to be a man good enough to be your father. One day, I had this epiphany...I had to deal with my own childhood before I could be a good enough dad to my kids. There was only one link to my past left, and let me tell you, she didn't want me around. I stayed, though, and I rekindled my friendship with Very, and I tried to learn how to be myself again...how to love something more than the idea of a family that didn't exist. That was what came crashing down for me when Kendall died. My perfect family and my idea that I was a perfect father, who had outrun his past and his heritage."

Denny laughed, though her heart bled.

"I guess no one can outrun their past and their heritage. I tried that too, and I just had to realize that I'm my daddy's daughter, no matter what people think. You have to inhabit your role before you can defy it, otherwise..."

"You're nothing," Dad said, nodding.

"I heard you died trying to save a kid," Denny said. "I don't think I've ever been this proud of you."

"And I was so proud of you…but I was trapped, sugar beet," he said, and she nodded through her tears. "I trapped myself. And then when I wanted to love again, I couldn't undo what I had done my whole life. I'm so sorry."

Denny put her head on his shoulder.

"I forgive you. I loved you all along."

"You loved me. You will always love me, but you have other people to love now. And yes, dogs are people too. I need you to take care of Geoff for me. Do you know what broke my heart most about you, sugar beet?" he said, his eyes turning from brown to white light, and his edges blurring.

"No…"

"I saw you becoming just like me. Not being able to let people in. Trapped in your own head all the time. It was my fault, and I'm sorry. But you need to reach out. Let people know you. I wanted so desperately to know you, too, but I lost my chance. Give that chance to others. That's what I want from you. If they don't like the real you, let them leave. I learned it all too late, but better late than never. You may be lonely, but you'll never be alone. You get me? Just like your song."

"I will, Daddy. It's going to be hard, but I'll be brave. For you."

"That's my girl," he said, and then, fading to a translucent man shape covered in interference like a sound wave, he turned his head toward the light.

"Kendall? Is that you, baby?"

339

And with that, he disappeared.

MEMORY BEACH

Denny felt a strange sensation, like a flip-flopping of her centre of gravity. For a few moments, she spun, unable to decide if she were standing or laying or on a hill…then the ground solidified at her back. She flexed her fingers, eyes closed, and drew in a handful of what felt like slick, wet pebbles and pine needles. There was glue on her eyelids, but she pulled them apart anyway. Another wave of dizziness spun her around as she stared into a high blue ceiling of infinite distance.

She coughed. Trails of spit flew from her lips, but it felt good. Both to breathe and to have her lips moistened felt wonderful. She breathed in, slowly, and out again. She still had a body. She could feel its weight pressing into the ground, the soft pulse running through her ears and her chest and the tips of her toes.

A finger of cold seeped through her skin, which rapidly became a crowd of twenty hands crawling all over her. Her clothes were wet. There had been a dew.

She had never felt gravity, truly felt it, until she sat up that morning. The ground felt like home…why would she want to leave her home and go up and up where her head spun? She put a hand to her head, then felt her face. Her skin was damp and dead cold.

In front of her sat a small, still lake, guarded by those same oddly-shaped pine trees that they had run into the night before. The night before...the night before...a single tear trickled down her cheek as she remembered going swimming in the sea of memory. Now, washed up on the beach, her heart ached, fuller and more full of longing than it had ever been.

A small sniffle drew Denny's attention to the shore over to her right. Verity crouched there, her military clothing scuffed and burned. In her hands, she held a small, round data disk. She stared at it, her lips taut, shaking her head. Her shoulders trembled with repressed sobs. She looked up at the sky, asking why.

"Aunt Very," Denny called. "Aunt Very, I'm alive!"

Verity fell backward off her heels onto her butt. She shuffled back a half step in the sand.

"No, no, you weren't. You were dead or at least in a very deep coma."

Denny held up her arms and smiled, half a shrug and half an invitation to a hug. She shook her head. Verity sat there for a moment, eyes wide and breathing hard, then scrambled over to her on all fours, scooping her up in a big, hard embrace. Denny smiled and laughed. So did Verity.

"What the hell, girl? Where did you come from?"

"I was with Dad. I almost followed him through the white door...but he held me back," Denny replied.

Verity sprouted a huge grin. She began spouting like an excited thirteen-year-old at a party. "I never thought I'd get to talk to you about your song! I've never seen anything like that. One minute, I was singing them down, the next, we were both part of something...a big cosmic singing... I could hear the drums of a thousand generations of my ancestors, beating at the heart of the world... I think together...I think because of you, we reversed the negative energy. We changed it from screams into a symphony! They're all gone, kiddo! We did it! And we can keep doing it... That's our calling, I think."

"We really are fixers, aren't we?"

"We're healers...we put the land at peace," said Verity. She paused, and her joy faded to a look of concern. She put a hand to the ground and closed her eyes. "But we still have a lot more to do. We were fighting those things for an entire day and didn't even know it. You were out all night, and I waited. We're late, Denny. We have to get going."

Denny struggled to her feet, her knees knocking together.

"Help me to the ATV," she said, "I'll eat on the way. Christ, I feel like a deflated balloon."

HERE COMES THE RAIN

Wayne stood at the window to the Doc's clinic, a wide, square pane of glass that looked out over the plains to the east. The hills of Shield rock rolled away from them for about ten miles or so, cow-splotched with dark green stands of forest. After that point, it met with two sets of dark grey clouds. The first set of clouds sat in the sky, darkening the landscape and roiling around in rotten-cotton-candy clumps, threatening the storm of the century—a superstorm that would rip up trees and demolish trailer homes. The second cloud had flown in with carriers full of troops and tanks strapped to the bottom of helicopters. Wayne watched them set up and spread out, a line of storm far more deadly than any wind or lightning.

The first few drops of rain tapped against the window, then disappeared as quickly as they had come. Still, Wayne saw the evidence of their presence in the few drops left rolling down the glass. A horrible, fleeting thought entered his mind. He saw blood rolling down the glass instead of water. He left the window and concentrated on de-tangling his stomach.

Say one thing for the Doc, he left his door open right to the end. They'd gotten Geoff out of his cage just that morning. He'd tottered over to them, struggling on the tile floor, and they'd petted him like it was the end of the world, and then he'd gone and laid down on a doggy bed set up in the corner. Then, they'd waited.

Last night, Janna's people had ransacked the Doc's house. They had shown up at three in the morning, throwing bricks through the windows and piling in. He and the Doc had escaped via the back door, but it wasn't them they wanted anyway. It was the ketamine and all the other drugs he kept for the vet clinic. They wanted his weapons. They wanted his authority, the rest of him could be damned.

When they had arrived at the clinic, Wayne had begged the Doc to lock the door, but he wouldn't hear of it.

"I believe in dialogue, son," he had said. "It's my culture, my philosophy and my truest conviction. If I don't leave myself open for it now, even in the greatest peril of my life, it won't mean anything. You can run if you want to. I'll give you what I can, and you can go to the army. I'll even let you take the dog with you if we can find something to carry him. He's well enough to travel now if you're careful and you remember his medicine."

Wayne had thought about it. Truth be told, he was still thinking about it. It turned itself over in his mind every once in a while like a rotten hot dog on a warming tray, but by God, he wasn't going to eat it, no matter how tempting the smell.

"No," he'd said. "Verity was right. I'm staying here and seeing this through to the end. It was cowardice that got me here, but cowardice sure isn't going to get me out of it. At least not in any condition I'd want to be in. Sorry Doc, but you're stuck with me. You're *all* stuck with me."

Since then, he had been thinking of escape plans for the two of them, all of which ended in them getting shot. They could steal an ATV and then…nope, George would have let them get away with it, but he was tied up in the community centre. He'd told them that Joab and Tim weren't fighting, and that was the last straw for the Watch. He'd always been a troublemaker anyway. They could go on foot, but by the time they met the army, the others would be on their way, guns blazing. Everything had just toppled, all at once, like that old game, Jenga, when somebody, shaking and painfully slow, finally took out the piece that broke the tower.

Wayne came to the examination table and put his elbows down on it. The Doc squatted down by Geoff, slowly stroking his head as he slept.

The dog's head raised suddenly, their only warning as five of them barrelled in through the door. Three of them Wayne had met before. Joab, Tim, and Four-by stood there, AK-47s in their hands and terror on their faces.

The Doc raised his hands and stood up slowly.

"Now boys, there's no reason to point those weapons at us. We can talk about this like reasonable people." he said.

Joab's hands shook, but he held the gun steady.

"You need to come with us."

Wayne raised his hands and cleared his throat. Three barrels immediately jerked toward him, but he continued anyway.

"You escaped the Green Queen. It's all the same thing over again. You can escape this too. You don't have to do this."

"They're going to kill us!" barked Four-by. "We have to get out of here!"

Tim gulped, then spoke.

"Enough talking. You come with us, or we shoot," he said, voice cracking.

"All right," said the Doc, walking into the line of guns, "just leave the dog alone. He might be the only one that has a chance of getting out of this mess alive."

As they marched Wayne down the wooden stairs at gunpoint, he saw what they'd been doing all night. Out on the common, under the flagpole, a fleet of ATVs, pickup trucks, and jeeps sat, filled with weapons, some homemade, most plundered from the surrounding farms and hunting lodges. It was an impressive militia for regular people, especially Canadians, but they would last approximately three minutes in the face of army fire.

Unfortunately, Wayne didn't have a tank to protect him or a bullet-proof vest. The militia now gathered could probably blow him up about ten times over without batting a collective eye.

"Joab, Tim, Four-by," he said as they got closer, "remember we're friends. Friends don't do this to each other. No one has to do this."

He heard someone behind him sniffle. Four-by answered, and Wayne could tell he was crying.

"They're going to kill us. You saw what they're bringing. They're not going to listen to a bunch of thieving Natives. They want to believe we're bad 'cause it's easier."

When they reached the head of the vehicle fleet, Janna was waiting with other members of the Watch. Wayne and the Doc stumbled forward, shoved by gun barrels. Somewhere behind them, Four-by spoke again.

"I'm sorry, Wayne," he said.

Janna, now dressed in full camouflage, waved at the Doc.

"Take him away. Stow him in the back of Kenny's truck. He's no good to us anyway if he won't fight."

"You're making a mistake, Janna," said the Doc. "We need to surrender. We have to give them the documents."

"They'll destroy the documents and anything that doesn't fit their story!" she yelled, "just like this scum-sucking piece of shit tried to do. We can rot in some southern prison, or we can fight, and die, in the place we love."

The Doc lowered his head as if he finally understood something he'd been puzzling on for a long time. He said, quietly, "The whole world is not your father, Janna."

"*Get him out of here!*" she bellowed. Her followers dragged the Doc back through the lines of vehicles and out of sight.

348

Once the Doc was gone, Janna swooped down on Wayne. Two people grabbed him from behind, pinning his arms behind his back and pulling him onto his heels, off-balance.

Janna leaned uncomfortably close. She pursed her lips, then released them with an audible pop. "You should've run while you still had the chance, white boy," she said, "but, since you're still here, you can have the place of honour. We're going to put you right out front."

Wayne cried out as his arms were forced out and a vest slid onto his chest. There were wires and pockets...too many pockets. They buckled it on, first around his chest, then with a crotch harness like they had on climbing gear.

"We picked up some nitro a while back from an abandoned mine, while Verity wasn't looking. We thought it might come in handy eventually. Walk softly, and if we see you fucking around..." Janna held up her thumb and forefinger like a little gun, "Ka-pow, ka-boom, cracker on the rocks."

Wayne trembled.

Come on, Denny, where are you?

Although at this point, he wasn't sure what Denny could do...

Maybe I should be wishing for her to stay away until it's too late.

And yet, he had seen the glow in her eyes when she sang down the Green Queen and the quiet determination with which she had stepped down an ancient elevator shaft to speak to a forgotten little girl. He trembled, but deep inside, a candle stayed lit for Denny, and it would take a lot more than dynamite to blow it out.

HERE I COME ~~TO~~ SAVE THE DAY

"Ouch!" Denny slapped the side of her leg as they sped along twenty minutes out from the reservation. "We got bees this time of year?"

"Nope, bees're done," said Verity.

"Then what the hell is stinging my leg?" Denny said, shoving a hand in her right pocket. "Ow, ow! Hot!"

Something in her pocket burned like coal fresh from the fire. A lump of metal on a chain. Jessica's locket. She yanked it out of her pocket by the chain, and it immediately cooled down to the temperature of being pressed against her leg and not a cattle brand. It swung in the wind, twirling and flashing. Denny steadied it against Verity's back with one hand and paused to regain her balance.

With everything that had gone on in the last week, she had forgotten about Jessica almost entirely. Clearly she would not be forgotten so easily.

"What's going on?" she asked under her breath. She slipped her other arm out from around Verity's waist and leaned on her aunt's back.

"Whoa, watch it there. We can't stop now," said Verity.

"I know, just give me a second," she replied.

Denny held the locket in her left hand and flipped it open with her right. The ATV went over a bump as she did, knocking out a small dusting of filth lodged inside. The interior of the locket was pretty standard for the dime-store variety. On one side was an inscription, on the other, a plastic-coated picture. Both were covered with a thin layer of grime. Denny licked her right thumb and scrubbed away the dirt on the inscription side.

Love forever 2010, said the inscription. Definitely a cheaper model, sold in dollar stores at a certain time in the past. Denny always enjoyed the Chinese knock-off stationery there, sporting slogans like *You Heart My Heart Give Always Happiness Heart*. It was the kind of gift a child would give another child. Denny thumbed off the other side, and beneath, crinkled but largely undamaged, was a faded photo of a little Native girl with a familiar round face, determined chin and serious smile.

"Did Janna have a sister, by any chance?" Denny asked.

"Yeah. Went missing on a salvage trip with her dad when she was six. Her dad died in jail for her kidnap and murder. They said he got drunk and pushed her down a mine shaft, but they never found the body. He had been too drunk to give them proper details. What's going on, Denny? How'd you know that?"

They reached the downward slope toward the reservation and, as the land sloped away from them, Denny saw everything laid out before her. The small army standing on the commons and the huge, earth-trampling one sitting on the horizon.

"On my way here, I had an adventure at an abandoned mine and met a very lonely little girl. She wasn't murdered. She got too close to the edge and fell. I think Janna's sister wants to stop this just as much as we do," Denny said.She slipped the locket over one wrist and gripped it tight."Stay with me, Jessica. Maybe we can make this right together."

A small sliver of hope opened up, like a crack of light in the rainclouds overhead. Then the clouds themselves dashed that hope in one, fatal stroke. A huge bolt of lightning coursed down from the heavens, sending a flash of cold light across the land. It struck a patch of forest a few kilometres off. Flames appeared in its wake, like the vista had flipped to the other side of a coin. Tails. Tails all the way.

Verity jammed her foot on the accelerator and the ATV zoomed into high gear, flying over bumps and threatening to jolt them right out of their seats. Denny wrapped her arms around Aunt Very's waist and held on tight, her cheek pressed to the other woman's back. She squeezed her eyes closed, wishing with all her might that they would get there in time.

THEM

Denny and Verity sped through the open gates of the reservation, down the wide main avenue to the commons. There they stopped, but only for a moment. The tire tracks told them everything they needed to know.

"Wayne!" Denny called. "Wayne, are you here?"

No answer.

"They've taken him, and Lord only knows what they plan to do with him," said Verity. "We should have taken him with us."

Verity re-started the ATV and sped off down the slope, toward the rumble of engines and voices.

"Don't blame yourself, Aunt Very," Denny said. "He never would have survived the din at Rabbit Lake. Besides, how could you know if he was telling the truth?"

As they passed the Doc's office, Denny spied a black-and-white blur looking out of the glass door. She heard a faint, far-off bark, then two. She wrenched around in her seat. Her hair whipped her face and stung her eyes.

"Geoff? *Geoff!* Oh my God, he's back there, and the forest fire is coming," Denny cried.

"We can't stop, or everyone down there will die!" said Verity.

Denny uttered a wordless moan.

"Look! Up ahead!" Verity called. Denny peered over her shoulder to see a long line of vehicles at the bottom of the next hill, their passengers armed to the teeth, moving much slower than they were, and at their head, about forty feet ahead, a lone figure stumbled, arms tied back, and wearing a vest full of pockets.

"Oh my God...Wayne! They've got him wearing a bomb!"

Verity tossed her head in frustration.

"Denny, do you have a plan?"

"I think so..."

"Then we're going in. If it comes down to a firefight, I'll protect you as long as I can. If it comes to that, I want you to run as hard and as fast as you can. I want you to get your dog and go. No arguments."

"I won't desert you!"

"If you don't, I'll die for nothing. Promise me!"

"I promise...but why?"

"Because you know how to fix all this. And I'm the only one who has a chance to get you to the people you need to talk to. Sometimes, even the fixers have to rely on someone else. You're it, kid."

Denny's stomach flew up into the stratosphere and didn't come back as Verity plunged the ATV down the hill. They swung hard around the line of vehicles, dirt spraying from the tires. For a moment, Denny thought they would flip, but the tires made contact again and then, just like that, they had skidded to a stop in front of a heavily armed line of vehicles. Denny swivelled her head around, trying to get her bearings after that dizzying ride, and saw that Verity had steered them directly in between the line of vehicles and Wayne.

Denny dismounted the ATV, her legs rubber. Verity came with her, doing her best to shield Denny with her body.

"Denny!" Wayne cried. He started wiggle-walking toward them, but someone turned on a loudspeaker.

"Stay where you are, shitface, we've got snipers trained on you."

He stopped. His chest heaved in and out, and Denny could see that his forehead was slick with sweat. His hair, usually game show host perfect no matter what he did to it, stuck out at all angles in tangled clumps.

One ATV at the head of the pack sped up and out of formation. Two more followed. Janna pulled up first, then three of her male counterparts.

Janna strode up to Verity, who regarded her with a veneer of indifference, but Denny could feel Verity's fingers shaking where they brushed her arm. Janna tilted her head and narrowed her eyes.

"The vote is in, and you lost. The tribe wants to fight. So, the two of you have a choice. You can fight with us or you can ride along in the trunk. You get to decide if you're going to be breathing or not when that happens."

Denny looked back at Wayne. Wayne nodded, stuck out his chin. His eyes said it all.

It's now or never, baby.

Suddenly, a lava flow of anger rose up from her core and she spilled. She stepped out from behind Verity and spat her words directly at Janna.

"You fool...you utter moron. Clearly, you like living in this hell, running from Screamers and having the media treat you like a pawn in their epic wild west drama...how dare you threaten to *kill* the two people who are able to heal the land! You're not going to make things better like this. All you're going to do is start a war, make more Screamers, and burn your reservation down because you weren't there to fight the *forest fire* that's raging toward it as we speak. Step down, Janna. Tell the others what your real motivation is for all of this."

"You wanna talk about motivation? Huh?" she said, getting in Denny's face, pacing around her. "What the fuck do you know?"

Denny looked at the ground.

"I know your sister," she said quietly, "and she knows what's happening right now. She's begging you not to kill yourself. She loves you."

The punch hit her left cheek quick and hard, knocking her back. Pain blossomed through her cheek, aching her sinuses and travelling up into her eye socket. Her left eye watered so hard she couldn't see out of it. Denny heard the sounds of a scuffle peppered with swears as Verity struggled against Janna's bodyguards to come to her aid.

"Verity told you that, bitch! You made it up! The two of you make it all up." she yelled, voice catching.

A boot hit her square in the chest, knocking her to the ground. Her hand went limp, and the locket went flying away to Lord knew where. The back of her head hit the dirt and her teeth knocked together. She saw light and the world above her spun. Janna appeared over her, grimacing, pointing a shotgun at her head.

"You're going to tell the truth, if I have to…"

Crack.

Janna's boot cracked on something loud and she looked down. She picked up something gold from the dirt that flashed in the light…the locket. Its hinge was now broken, hanging off-centre, but Janna just stared and stared at the picture in the centre and the inscription. She breathed hard, just staring and staring.

A pink glow, like the one Jessica had made in the mine, crept out from the locket, down the chain and into Janna. Soon, she glowed too. Tears stood out in her eyes.

"He didn't do it," she said, in a whisper only Denny could hear below her. "Dad was innocent." She blinked hard and gulped, saying. "I know where you are now, Jessica. I'll come for you, I promise."

Denny rolled onto her side, everything aching, then stood up.

"You have to live to find her, Janna. You'll have to use dialogue and evidence if you want to clear your father's name. We can clear your father's name together. But we have to stop this madness. Defuse the bomb and put away the weapons. Give Verity back her command," she said.

"I knew he was innocent all along," she said, falling to her knees. "Goddammit, I knew he was innocent. Why would nobody listen to me? Why?"

"Tell your story until they listen, Janna. This time they will listen."

Janna raised her head and addressed her muscle men.

"Release the Doc. And apologize to him. Tell him we need him to help negotiate."

The men hesitated.

"*Do it or so help me God...*"

They ran back to one of the trucks to release the Doc. Another few people ran forward to release Wayne from the vest.

Janna looked up to Verity with abject humiliation playing across her face.

"Is it too late to fix things?"

Verity smiled.

"Not for a fixer," she said.

US

Wayne fell into her arms, trembling and weeping and smelling vaguely of woodsmoke.

"Denny," he said between deep breaths, "you came back for me. That's more...than I would have done...for me."

Denny adjusted his chin so she could look into his eyes.

"But not more than you would have done for me, I think."

A pause and a shudder.

"I would do anything for you," he said.

Denny felt her heart swell. The usual urge to clamp it down rose up within her. They couldn't...she couldn't...he had problems. But then again, after chasing her dead father over hundreds of miles of open wilderness, didn't she? She remembered her dad's final words to her. It was time to let someone in. Someone who knew her, good and bad. Someone who could know her in the future.

He had bowed his head again, eyelashes shading his big brown eyes. She pulled him up level with her, and their gazes connected. She leaned in and pressed her lips to his, and suddenly there was magic all around them, unseen but still there nonetheless. His arms slid around her and he held her, then tenderly, sweetly, he returned her kiss. His trembling subsided. When they parted,

Denny heard a crack, far off in the distance. A column of smoke rose on the horizon, dangerously close to the reservation.

They looked at each other.

"Geoff," said Wayne.

By this point, the convoy was moving on, Verity and the Doc running ahead to convey the tribe's peaceful intentions. They had left Denny and Wayne an ATV with a decent-sized open trailer. Denny hopped into the driver's seat and turned the ignition.

"Do you know how to drive one of these things?" Wayne asked.

"No and neither do you. City kids, right? Get on."

When they reached the Doc's clinic, they could hear barking and smell smoke. The trees just beyond the edge of the reservation blazed with bright orange flames and the air was hot like the back of an industrial kitchen. Soon, the fire would spread to the dry grass on the common, and it would sweep the plain faster than any of them could ride. They could only hope that the army had dug a break line between them and the travelling inferno.

Denny yanked the door to the vet clinic open, and Geoff jumped up on her in a doggy hug, whining and whining. Denny scooped him up under the butt and lifted him into the trailer. Wayne ran in while she was doing so and grabbed his medications.

"Alright, family's complete. Let's motor," she said.

And as they rode away, racing the fire, Wayne holding her from behind and Geoff on the back, she felt for the first time in a very long time like there was a net, a network of love, holding her up. Redemption *was* a place and the co-ordinates were inside of her, when she connected to those she loved.

I may be ever lonely, but I'll never be alone, she thought, as she tested the engine and they sped off into the unknown.

ACKNOWLEDGEMENTS

This book, for me, is primarily about Canada, and so much of the material for the book was pulled from my own life. However, we live in a large province with many different cultures and biomes represented within it, and so there was a lot of information that I had to get right.

First of all, I would like to thank the Oakville Public Library for supplying the books for my research on Northern Ontario, its climate, creatures, geography and ghost towns. Free information is a treasure that no one should take for granted.

Secondly, I would like to thank Leonard Doxtator, of the Onyota'a:ka Nation of the Thames, for being my consultant on First Nations culture. In this book, I wanted to create a story that everyone living in Canada could identify with, and you have helped me to go farther toward that goal than I ever could have gone alone. Thank you for helping me make my genre fiction more believable and inclusive. Thanks also for being a friend. If this book is still totally clueless, don't blame Leonard. He did his best.

Next, I would like to thank my publisher, Renaissance Press, and specifically Nathan Fréchette for his tireless advocacy for my work and his support of unique Canadian stories, and for the awesome new cover he designed. Big thanks also to the team of editors who helped make this edition of the book even better than before. Together, you've helped me fulfill a dream for this series. I would also like to thank my publicist, Beverly Bambury, who has helped tremendously with building relationships with my readers.

And finally, thanks to my amazing husband, Robin, for providing the original illustrations for this book. I'm glad that I was able to pull you out of the daily grind of drawing sexy ladies and facilitate your love of monster drawings. Not everyone would know how to handle a woman who bawls in front of her computer screen over something she made up.

Renaissance
Diverse Canadian Voices

Renaissance was founded in May 2013 by a group of friends who wanted to publish and market those stories which don't always fit neatly in a genre, or a niche, or a demographic. We weren't sure what we wanted to publish exactly, so like the happy panbibliophiles that we are, we opened our submissions, with no other personal guideline than finding a Canadian book we would fall in love with enough that we would want to publish and sell.

Five years later, this is still very true; however, we've also noticed an interesting trend in what we tended to publish. It turns out that we are naturally drawn to the voices of those who are members of a marginalized group (especially people with disabilities and LGBTQIAPP2+ people), and these are the voices we want to continue to uplift.

To us, Renaissance isn't just a business; it's a family. Being authors and artists ourselves, we are always careful to center the experience of the author above all else.

pressesrenaissancepress.ca

pressesrenaissancepress@gmail.com

The Face
in the Marsh
Elizabeth Hirst

Kenzie is twenty-five, with two degrees and no job prospects. When her parents offer her a job curating their museum, Ettenby's Log Palace, she accepts out of desperation, despite their history of family conflict. She arrives praying that her secrets will stay buried, and her hard-won mental health won't relapse. Once at the Log Palace, Kenzie is fascinated by an unsettling collection of junk dolls found on the property. As she follows the thread left by the collection, she discovers a history of poltergeist activity, witchcraft and death on the small island housing the museum.

pressesrenaissancepress.ca

BLOOD STATE

RALUCA BALASA

Three generations ago, the Modernist Mission arrived on the ice planet Tählti to find it already inhabited by the Firsts, humanoids who have evolved an antifreeze glycoprotein in their blood. With the next ice age nipping at everyone's heels, the Modernist government will do anything to get the protein – even experimenting on the Firsts in secret.

Despite Modernist general Lucian Devereaux's best efforts, what began as a medical research facility to ensure his people's survival becomes a concentration camp. When an exiled vigilante learns this secret, he threatens to tell the world and spark a war between Modernist and First – a war neither can afford before the ice age. Surrounded by enemies, Lucian must figure out whom to trust, or neither subspecies will survive much longer.

Raluca Balasa has penned a dark, gripping tale of colonialist and indigene as the world around them begins to freeze. Blood State is a slick, twisty, chess game of a novel that sucked me in and held me until the last page. – Stephen Graham King, author of A Congress of Ships

pressesrenaissancepress.ca

The Cypher
Matti McLean

Penner had always considered his life ordinary-but when his lover Chess receives a divine revelation that can't be explained, he finds himself on the run from mysterious forces.

Upending their idyllic life in a small town, Chess propels them on a journey to find answers to deep questions that plague his thoughts and his sanity.

Partnering with Fred, a boisterous sky pirate with an enigmatic past, they head out to find the answers they need on her airship. But the closer they get to their mysterious destination, the more danger they find themselves in.

Facing betrayals, battles and a malevolent being that seems to be hunting them, soon they find themselves deep into conspiracies that threaten the very fabric of their reality.

With their wits, their ship and a spot of tea, their quest for answers will make them confront the forces that created the universe.

With only each other, will their love be enough to save them?

pressesrenaissancepress.ca

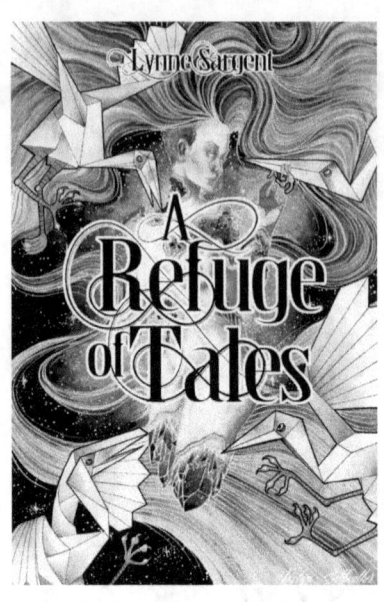

A Refuge of Tales

Lynne Sargent

What does it mean to make a home inside a story? Stories are safe, comfortable, familiar. Fairytales and myths, these stories we all know and grew up with are even moreso. *A Refuge of Tales* takes everyday tropes and asks: *safe for who?* This is a collection of poems for anyone who has ever felt outside of the myth. With language both sharp and lyrical, Lynne Sargent weaves a treatise on the power of stories, and how those who have been left behind can take up that power and use it to build a new, better world.

pressesrenaissancepress.ca

If you enjoyed this book, please consider

leaving a review where you bought it!

www.ingramcontent.com/pod-product-compliance
Lightning Source LLC
Chambersburg PA
CBHW072024020726
47501CB00006B/1946